THE
INCREDIBLE
CRIME

WITHDRAWN

THE
INCREDIBLE
CRIME

Lois Austen-Leigh

With an Introduction by
KIRSTEN T. SAXTON

This edition published 2017 by
The British Library
96 Euston Road
London
NW1 2DB

Originally published in 1931 by Herbert Jenkins

Cataloguing in Publication Data
A catalogue record for this publication is
available from the British Library

ISBN 978 0 7123 5602 2

Typeset by Tetragon, London
Printed and bound by
CPI Group (UK) Ltd, Croydon CR0 4YY

THE
INCREDIBLE
CRIME

INTRODUCTION

Kirsten T. Saxton

The Incredible Crime opens with a blisteringly funny scene. The main character, Prudence, tosses a crime novel across the room, mocking the improbable "bilge" that is "modern detective fiction": "When you go to stay in a country-house," she exclaims, "you do not step on corpses or meet blood trickling down the stairs." Her friend remonstrates, "but what with 'complexes', 'unconscious urges,' and 'compensations,' people in the country-house may be up to any devilment you like."

Lois Austen-Leigh's playful satire lets us know we are in the hands of a capable and confident writer. That *The Incredible Crime* is, in fact, a country-house mystery is delicious.

The granddaughter of Jane Austen's favourite nephew, Lois Austen-Leigh (1883–1968) purportedly wrote her novels on the very writing desk at which her famous relative penned her masterpieces and which was donated to the British Library by Joan Austen-Leigh, founder of the Jane Austen Society of North America and Lois's niece. Published in 1931, *The Incredible Crime* is the first of the four critically acclaimed novels Austen-Leigh published during the Golden Age, that period of crime fiction spanning the period between the two world wars.

Her novels are infused with the adroit plotting, cheeky humour, and modern sensibility that enliven the Golden Age. The plot of *The Incredible Crime* is as entertaining as its humour, with a narrative described by critics as: "very exciting… thrills and sensations go hand in hand" in "a most readable yarn." The thrills are accompanied by deft forays into the tradition of coastal smuggling, academic satire, the drug trade, government spies, the pleasures and dangers of country house life, modern policing, and the exigencies of romance for spirited young women who know their own minds.

Set both in a venerable Cambridge college and a stately manor, *The Incredible Crime* cleverly bridges the academic and the village mystery traditions, using and upending the conventions of each. Its Cambridge sections locate the novel solidly within the tradition of British university crime fiction. The novel leads us through hallowed college halls with their sometimes touching, sometimes amusing daily rituals, petty jealousies, and potentially deadly plots. As a professor, I can attest that the novel's good-natured send-up of Cambridge academics remains painfully pertinent (nobody gets promoted just for being a good teacher!).

As for the village, Wellende Hall, the "magnificent stately old" country house on the sea, evokes an ancient rural sea-swept England of smugglers, fox hunts, nobles, and loyal servants, a slow-paced counterpoint tied to the rhythms of the land in contrast to the bustle of the university. Austen-Leigh is at home in the almost feudal setting of the village, and her descriptions of Suffolk evoke her love of the coast's natural beauty, its "soft brown russets" and the "startling whites of the gulls."

Just as *The Incredible Crime* combines conventions from the traditions of village and college mysteries, it also offers a sparkling union of the Jane Austen novel of manners with the mystery genre. Like Austen, Austen-Leigh focuses on insular communities, and our pleasure derives in part from the affectionate, sometimes mocking, particularities of habit, locale, and ritual. Austen-Leigh also uses the particular to comment on the general. While we may not identify with Cambridge in the 1930s, we understand the peccadilloes of self-importance and the genuine power of radical intelligence. We might not "know" the country house world, but we recognize the shared emotional landscape of a closely connected community, the generosity wealth makes possible, and the envy and parochialism it instills.

Austen-Leigh's fiction is typical of the Golden Age in its descriptions of crimes set in a world that, while modern in sensibility, is also deeply nostalgic. In her novels, both the university and the village estate should rightly be ruled by kindness, wisdom, loyalty and merit. However, Austen-Leigh avoids simple stereotypes; when she employs stock characters—the faithful retainer, the oblivious professor, or the idealized patriarch—she does so to interesting ends. Ethical people cross legal lines, and crime can be morally murky. Although men are haunted by their combat experiences, these traumatic memories also create an appreciation of both the absurdity and the comfort of social niceties. Women drive fast cars, swear, and push against old-fashioned limits, but seek idealized romance with benevolent successful patriarchs-to-be.

Like her well-known relative, Austen-Leigh accomplishes this complexity through the use of a slightly ironic narrator whose distance from the characters allows a more knowing voice to shape our point of view. For example, to critique the detective's suspicions of local drug smuggling, the professor pulls out a "dirty looking book" and reads aloud a long quote about the improbability of holding such "dreadful suspicions" of evil occurring in "the country and age in which we live." The detective comments, that's "very good. Who wrote it?" The professor responds: "A parson's daughter—more than a hundred years ago."

If we recognize the source as Jane Austen's *Northanger Abbey*, we get the irony. Both Austen's novel and *The Incredible Crime* are genre novels that overtly take up the question of the value of genre. The quote also establishes the detective as a reader of Austen—fine praise indeed, and yet his interpretation signals his good-natured naiveté: as the agent knows, England *does* indeed include such evil. Both Austen-Leigh and Austen defend the homely English countryside, while locating danger as coming from within rather than without.

The Incredible Crime was hailed by critics as "the very essence of mystery" for its plot, well-drawn characters and "passages of unusual beauty... especially in her descriptions of Cambridge and the coast of Suffolk." The *Times Literary Supplement* praised the novel as "writing and analysis of character... of a much higher order," adding that, "Miss Austen-Leigh might consider a more serious vein of writing."

We who love crime fiction can be delighted that she did not.

LOIS AUSTEN-LEIGH (1883–1968)

Lois Austen-Leigh and her siblings grew up on stories of the genius of their famous Aunt Jane. Her father, Arthur Austen-Leigh, Austen's great nephew, was Rector at Winterbourne, Gloucester, where Lois was born and lived until they moved to Wargrave, Berkshire, where he served as Vicar until retiring in 1911.

Lois's diaries from Wargrave (1898–1906) offer a snapshot of an exuberant, comfortably situated English girl in the years before the War: swoony commentary on her brothers' Cambridge friends; dramatic accounts of the horrors of caring for chickens; and the various joys and travails of teachers, cancelled picnics, and new frocks. They also record her excellent ear for language and eye for detail and hint at the sparkling tone we see in her fiction decades later. As a young woman, she seems to have had the same flair for the unconventional that we see in her heroines; she reportedly carried out her parish good deeds by zipping about on her motorbike.

Few records remain of her daily life other than these early writings. We know she learned about the inner workings of Cambridge from her uncle, Augustus Austen-Leigh (1840–1905), Provost of King's College, and his wife Florence Lefroy Austen-Leigh. He was the first Provost under the new system whereby the college was open to the world beyond Eton, and Austen-Leigh's fiction demonstrates that heady atmosphere.

During World War One, between 1916 and 1918, Lois worked as a gardener for the Red Cross in Reading while her sister, Honor, worked as a nurse in Malta and then France. She was for many years the companion to her widowed aunt Florence; after Florence's death in 1926, Lois invited a top Cambridge architect to design and build Cob House for herself and Honor in Aldeburgh, on the rugged Suffolk coast that animates all of her fiction.

The sisters thrived as part of the Aldeburgh arts community: young local resident Benjamin Britten played the piano at their home, accompanied by Honor on viola; family friend M.R. James set his famous ghost story in the local inn down the road. Lois wrote her crime fiction in a room of her own with a view of the sea.

Austen-Leigh took her writing seriously. Her novels are carefully crafted, and she did not change them in the face of criticism. M.R. James, the author who succeeded her uncle as Provost of King's and was a close friend and mentor, wrote in a posthumously published letter that he refused Lois's request to review *The Incredible Crime* because "the heroine, who's the daughter of a retired Bishop, Master of a College, takes occasion to swear solidly for two whole minutes: the language isn't reported, but I can't imagine anyone being able to swear for 2 minutes without trespassing a good deal over the limits."

Lois Austen-Leigh stuck the course, and she was rewarded by critical success and a multi-book contract with the reputable publisher Herbert Jenkins. Her novels appeared in quick succession: *The Incredible Crime* was followed by *Haunted Farm* (1932), *Rude Justice* (1936), and her final novel *The Gobblecock Mystery* (1938).

Like many women writers, however, Austen-Leigh downplayed her literary ambition; claiming she wrote novels only to "keep herself in champagne." Her persistence, her novels' self-consciously literary frames, and the excellence of her work suggest the claim was, like Jane Austen's own description of her work as "the little bit (two inches wide) of ivory on which I work," a wry, self-deprecating cover.

World War Two brought an end to Austen-Leigh's writing career and to the Golden Age of detective fiction. Aldeburgh was a crucial defence site, and one can still see the marks at Cob House where the army set up defences to head off Germans approaching by sea. Lois and Honor drove an ambulance and worked in the fire brigade, and Lois's letters express the exhaustion they felt in the face of the constant threat of bombardment and uncertainty.

Despite her fine reviews and popularity in her lifetime, Lois Austen-Leigh seems to have fallen almost entirely out of memory. Robert Davies, editor of this series, comments that "even experts in the field have not heard of her." Until now, her books have been almost impossible to find; I read them in the Rare Books room at the British Library, close to where Austen's writing desk now sits. I am grateful to the Library and to Poisoned Pen Press for this chance to help bring them back into circulation.

ACKNOWLEDGEMENTS

I am grateful to the following people and organizations for their help on this project: Diana Birchall, for sharing her work on Lois Austen-Leigh; Tony and Debbie Bone, for welcoming me to Cob House; Damaris Brix and Freydis Welland (great-nieces of Lois Austen-Leigh) and Viola Jones and Valerie Peyman for kindly providing primary materials; Kristen Hanley Cardozo, for the initial find; the generous folks of Aldeburgh, Winterbourne, and Wargrave who shared their stories and time, and Lucy Cavendish College, Cambridge, Mills College, and the British Library for research support.

CHAPTER I

"SHE KICKED THE CORPSE FRETFULLY WITH HER DELICATELY-shod foot and, staggering dizzily against the bloody lintel of the door, looked fearfully over her shoulder. 'God!' she hissed, 'shall we ever clean our souls of this ghastly crime?' Her companion spoke not. Rage, pleading, lust, and pride, struggled for the mastery in his hot eyes!"…

"What im-possible… in-credible… unutterable bilge; and that," said Prudence Pinsent, pitching the book across the room, "is modern detective fiction!"

"There is nothing stranger in fiction than there is in real life," said a sententious voice.

"Rot! When you go to stay in a country-house, you don't step on corpses or meet blood trickling down the front stairs."

"No, but what with 'complexes,' 'unconscious urges,' and 'compensations,' the people in the country-house may be up to any devilment you like."

"Rot again."

"No, Prudence," said Mrs. Skipwith, "there really is something in it; the tricks heredity can play—and the fact that the lengths of self-deception are endless; it's always possible your friend may be an undiscovered lunatic or criminal."

"Rot again, but I wish you wouldn't all talk when we are playing bridge."

"Well, I *do* like that, and you began by reading aloud when you were dummy."

Four people were seated playing bridge in the comfortable house in Cambridge of Susan Skipwith, wife of the Dolbey Professor of

Entomology. They were four friends who met regularly once a week to play what they called bridge, but what others might have been tempted to describe as cards and chatter. The rubber concluded, they cut afresh for another.

"Yes," said Prudence, in her soft, refined voice, answering a question, "I love watching a good rugger match, but some blasted wife always gets between me and the realization of my desire."

"What do you mean?"

"Why, you know as well as I do that a member may only take one woman into the pavilion—and whenever I suggest to a friend that he should take me, why, his… wife wants to go!"

"Your father is not a member, I suppose?"

"No, and would not go to a rugger match if he were."

The chatter ceased for a short time, while a hand was played. Mrs. Skipwith, Mrs. Gordon whose husband had come up to Cambridge a few years earlier with a great reputation from some Scottish University, Mrs. Maryon, a smart young woman recently married to a young Fellow of Prince's College, and Prudence Pinsent, the only child of the Master of Prince's College, a retired bishop. The Pinsents had been connected with their college for some generations, and the present Master was a perfect specimen of that fast disappearing genus, the courtly divine. His daughter was singularly good-looking—she had a face that should have adorned, and would have been a valuable asset to, a saint in a stained-glass window, surmounted by a head of glorious red-brown hair, and when on duty in Cambridge she comported herself with the utmost dignity, though she reserved to herself the right to swear like a trooper when she chose.

Susan Skipwith, her great friend, attributed this weakness to the overpowering effect of the background of awful respectability which surrounded her. Prudence herself was more inclined to lay it at the door of a far-back buccaneering ancestor.

"I always think, Prue, you know," said Susan Skipwith, "that on the whole you are singularly untroubled with wives."

"How you can have the barefaced immorality to make a statement of that kind I cannot think," said Prudence, and in her indignation she laid her cards on the table; "you who know what my life is—Fellows' wives that are, and Fellows' wives to be, and the Lodge run like a private hotel for them all."

"Yes, yes," said Mrs. Gordon soothingly, "we all have our bit of that. Why, is it true—"

"Yes," interrupted Prudence, "but you haven't just been told by your best friend that you are untroubled by wives; why, d— it all, after the war even *undergraduates* had wives!"

"Prudence," said Susan firmly, "if you don't pick up your hand and go on with the game I shall—" Silence reigned for a short time, broken only by the assertion from Susan that the rest were hers; this was met with a unanimous denial on the part of her opponents; finally, when with the air of a maligned martyr she succeeded in making the rest, Mrs. Gordon pointed out to her that it was only done owing to a slip on the part of Marcella Maryon.

"As I was going to say before when Prudence interrupted me," said Mrs. Gordon, "is it true that there are some eminent foreigners coming to Cambridge specially to see your Thomas about some discovery of his?"

"Yes," said his wife. "Thomas, I would have you all know, says every fly carries some disease; they have long located special diseases to each fly, all except the old bluebottle, and though they all entertained the very darkest suspicions about the bluebottle, no one knew for certain what mischief it was he was promulgating. Now Thomas has discovered it, and I expect the other entomologists are coming up to say he's wrong! However, whatever they say, he is now set on getting some plutocrat to start a world crusade against all bluebottles and exterminate the lot."

"Oh, dear," said Mrs. Gordon, "I do hope not that. I love the buzz of a bluebottle fly, it's one of the sounds of summer, and think of how many of the associations of one's youth are connected with it!"

"Yes, my dear," said Prudence, "but the associations of your misdirected youth are all being weeded up in this enlightened spot. All the old hymn tunes are gone, and ones that are better for your educa-tion and not your sentiments substituted. Now the bluebottles are following suit. I met our Dean after chapel on Armistice Day," said she, laughing, "and I said, 'Mr. Dean, how is this, we have had the National Anthem to the original tune, it must have been an oversight!'"

"What did he say to that?"

"He went off growling that if he had his way we shouldn't ever have it at all in chapel."

The pretence of playing bridge finally came to an end, and Mrs. Gordon and Mrs. Maryon took their departure. The husband of the latter had only recently become a Fellow of Prince's College. He had spent a good many years in the East, was learned in Sanskrit, and was popularly supposed to speak seventeen Eastern dialects. His wife was rather flattered at being admitted to play bridge regularly with the three ladies, who were old friends. She entertained a great admiration for Miss Pinsent, which she began expressing as they left the house.

"Yes," said Mrs. Gordon, "she is beautiful as you say, and reli-able—and kind—yes, and clever—yes, I quite agree with you, she is not a snob as so many people say, she's very fastidious, and I love her, but I should never be quite surprised if one day she kicked over the traces altogether."

"But what do you mean by that, Mrs. Gordon... she's most conventional, except that perhaps she uses rather strong language sometimes."

"Yes, my dear, I know she appears to be conventional, indeed she *is*; but, I don't know, I have known Prudence for years, and I somehow have always felt I don't trust her."

"Don't trust her!" exclaimed Mrs. Maryon.

"I don't mean that, I only mean I don't trust her conventionalism. I would trust her with any secret. Why, you know there was a don up here once who posed as a bachelor for twenty years, and all the time he was married. Even his best friends had no idea of it, but Prudence got to know of it by an accident, and she never, never let slip that she knew it. I would trust that woman with anything after that."

"Then what do you mean?" pursued Mrs. Maryon in some distress; "do you mean you think she might suddenly go off with someone else's husband?"

"Yes, I think I do mean that sort of thing, though it will never take that actual form with Prudence, she is too independent now to want a man, or to marry; but at bottom she is completely indifferent to public opinion, and if she wanted to flout it, she would do so without hesitation."

"It's comparatively easy to be indifferent to public opinion when you have so assured a position as she has," remarked Mrs. Maryon shrewdly.

"Yes," said Mrs. Gordon with a laugh, "but with her it goes deeper than that. I tell you what I should have expected of her. I always thought she would have been a militant suffragette and gone to prison, and I don't understand now why she wasn't; perhaps she was too academic in her point of view."

"She was brought up with boys, wasn't she? some cousins—that might make her character more masculine."

"Yes," said Mrs. Gordon, "I believe she lived a good deal with some Temple cousins in Suffolk, relations of the great Professor Temple."

Meanwhile at the Skipwiths Prudence resettled herself into a comfortable chair. "I am not going yet, Sue," said she. "I am going to stop and see Thomas. When does he come in from the Labs.?"

"Oh, any time about now, indeed I fancy I hear him slamming the front door," and a moment later into the room came Professor Thomas Skipwith with an evening paper tucked under his arm. About the last thing in the world that Skipwith looked like was what he was, an eminent scientific professor. He was not only washed, he was even shaved.

At first glance you would have taken him for an amiable farmer, at second, for there was something distinctly arresting in his face, you would have put him down as a naval officer.

"Did you see in the morning paper that there had been another murder with arsenic?" said he, as he came and warmed himself by the fire.

"I simply cannot understand the crude stupidity of anyone using it now. Why, look at the amount written about it in fiction; you would have thought that alone would have prevented anyone using it seriously."

"I suppose it's the easiest of all to get hold of," said Prudence.

"It seems to me they always succeed in tracing whoever does get hold of it," retorted Susan.

"Ah, but you've no idea how many may get away with it successfully!"

"Don't be gruesome, Prue. Wasn't Professor Temple holding forth on poisons the other evening in the Combination Room—didn't you say, Thomas?"

"Yes, yes, he was," said Thomas slowly, as he rubbed his back appreciatively in the warmth of the fire. "By Jove, and he said some things, too, which I don't believe he would ever have let out if he hadn't been filled up with our best college port; he's a taciturn beggar as a rule"—here he paused—"let me see, he's not a cousin of yours, Prue, is he?"

"Yes, but a very distant one—I call him a kinsman; but go on with what you were saying."

"Well, he was holding forth on poisons generally; then he told us he had one himself, it is tasteless, and after swallowing, acts almost immediately. It just stops the heart beating, so that the victim dies of heart failure, and there is no trace whatever left in the body. You could never catch a fellow out using that," said Thomas with an amiable smile.

"How ghastly!" exclaimed Susan, "and the man is mad already, he ought never to have such stuff in his possession."

"His isn't the sort of madness that turns to murder," replied Thomas; "besides, he isn't mad, it's genius with him."

"Bosh, Thomas—he's mad all right, and you can never tell what madness will turn to."

"How does he get hold of this drug?" asked Prudence, "is it imported?"

"No, I understand that it is a vegetable poison and he makes it himself; more than that, mark you—he says if you take small doses at regular intervals, you become immune to the poison; so you see, Sue, he could give you a dose of it, then finish the tumblerful himself and say to the police, 'there couldn't be poison in the cup because I have drunk the rest!'"

"The idea of it seems to amuse you," said his wife frigidly.

"The most interesting part," said Thomas with a laugh at his wife, "was that I had the feeling that afterwards he wished he hadn't said so much, and tried to laugh it away."

"Really, Thomas," said Prudence, "you don't think Professor Temple wants to murder?"

"No, I don't, but he undoubtedly could if he did want, and would certainly never be found out." Thomas piled some more wood on the fire, then he said, "Temple had a queer guest, for him, up to the last College Feast—the young Duke of Banbury. I can't think what they had in common, because the Duke hasn't an idea beyond hunting, has he?"

"No," said Prudence, "it was an odd guest for Professor Temple to entertain, and no less odd that the Duke should come away just as the hunting is beginning."

"Is it the hunting season?"

"Now, Thomas, pull yourself together and answer that question yourself. It's November."

"Well, I should say it probably was, as I know hunting goes on through the winter, but 'pon my word, I wouldn't be certain."

"No," replied Prudence with some bitterness, "I can well believe you really don't know for certain—for sublime ignorance on general topics, ignorance that would shame a preparatory schoolboy—give me the expert."

Thomas shouted with laughter—"Never mind, Prue," he said, "when will you come for a run in my new car?" The Skipwiths had recently acquired a 6-cylinder Bentley. Susan considered this a piece of unnecessary extravagance for people in their position, but motoring was Thomas's greatest relaxation, and a lucky gamble on the Stock Exchange had made him feel extravagant, so he asserted, and he went a splash.

"Drive me down to Suffolk on the 8th," said Prudence. "I am going off for a bit of hunting till Christmas, and you can stay the night; it's a place well worth seeing, I can tell you."

"What day of the week would it be?"

"Tuesday."

"No, I can't. I am lecturing at twelve on Tuesday and Wednesday, but I should simply love to see your cousin's place. It's famous, isn't it?"

"Yes, and I mean Susan and you to come some time; you've just no notion what it is after the strenuous up-to-date life of Cambridge. Get into your car and drive a hundred miles east and you come to Wellende Old Hall, seven miles from a station, seven miles from a shop, seven miles from anywhere; the Temples have lived there for nearly eight hundred years, and Ben has managed to remain feudal— no, that doesn't quite describe it, there has been no 'management,' he just *is* feudal. The old butler once summed it up very well, when he said to me, 'as it was in the beginning, miss, is now—and h'always shall be, that's the motto for this 'ouse.'"

"It sounds simply entrancing," said Susan.

"Come out for a drive to-morrow after my lecture, Prue. I'll have the car at the Labs., and it's only a step for you along from Prince's." And so they settled it, and Prudence rose to depart.

"Wait a moment," said Thomas, "there's a story going its round about you, that someone stepped off the pavement just in front of your car, and you swore so lustily at him that the Vice-Chancellor, who was coming along and overheard you, nearly fainted, and said he wouldn't have you inside the precincts of St. Benedict's."

"It's one long lie," replied Prudence, "but it may have its origin in the fact that his wife stepped on my toe the other day and I dropped a mild oath, at which she said she shouldn't ask me to dinner to meet the Archbishop of Canterbury, I wasn't fit to meet him."

Thomas threw himself back in his chair and laughed.

"I really must go now," said Prue, and with that she was off. Thomas came back into the room after sending off Prue; as he gazed into the fire he said, "That cousin of Prue's she goes to so regularly for hunting is unmarried, isn't he?"

"Yes," said Susan.

"It's unusual for a man in his position, unless there's something wrong with him—do you suppose there was ever anything between them?"

"No," said Susan. "I am sure she never has been in love with him; she was brought up very largely with him and his brother, and I am sure all her affection for him is fraternal. I can't quite imagine Prudence in love with anyone, you know. I wouldn't criticize her to anyone but you, but there's something hard about her." Thomas assented.

"She's too independent for a woman," he said.

CHAPTER II

I T WAS A BRIGHT SUNNY MORNING AND IN A ROOM OVERLOOKING the great court of Prince's College the Master and his daughter were at breakfast. The sunlight lit up the old grey fountain in the middle of the court, and the splashes of colour made by the late autumn flowers in the bed surrounding it. Hurrying figures could be seen going in all directions; undergraduates in gowns and no caps, attending early lectures, with sheaves of papers and books under their arms, went round by the paths; while senior members of the College walked with dignified step across the grass. Tradesmen's boys occasionally appeared strolling along and above all a flight of glorious white pigeons against the blue sky—settling on the old grey chapel—cooing and chuckling. Prudence strolled towards the window.

"Aren't there many more pigeons than there used to be, father?"

"I am sure I am unable to say, my dear, I have not considered the matter—Drask"—(mentioning the Head Porter)—"would be the person to ask."

"Yes, I suppose so; he looks after them, doesn't he—there," said Prudence, peering round the corner of the window, "there is an undergraduate in his dressing-gown; I really do *not* think it ought to be allowed in the front court at nine-thirty."

"As long as there are so few baths in the College, my dear, it is impossible to circumvent it, unseemly as we may consider it."

Prudence turned her attention away from the window and transferred it to the breakfast-table. She gave her father his coffee, and proceeded to help herself to the hot dish. The Master sat at one end of the table surrounded by papers. A waste-paper basket by his side, into which he pitched a proportion of his correspondence, the rest he made a pile of on the table by his side.

"Have you many engagements to-day, father?"

"I've a meeting of the Council at twelve—another board meeting at three, and some young men coming to see me this evening."

"I am sorry for that," said his daughter. "I was going to suggest your coming for a drive this morning. Thomas Skipwith is going to take me out in his new car, after his lecture."

"Ah," said the Master, "I find driving with Skipwith a mixed pleasure, and so am able to regard my inability to accompany you with composure."

Prudence went about her household duties and then, wrapping herself in a warm fur coat, sallied forth. As daughter of the Master she walked across the grass to the College gate and Drask, the Head Porter, came out of his office to wish her good morning. The Head Porter of Prince's College was a magnificent person, tall and clean-shaven, with hair just beginning to grey; he looked like a middle-aged Apollo, with the manner of a beneficent bishop. Strangers frequently took him to be the Master of the College—and there were those, who should have known better, who had often been heard to regret that Drask could not be made permanent Vice-Chancellor. Prudence turned in at the gates of the Entomological Labs., where in a corner of the court stood Professor Skipwith's Bentley car. She got in and tucked herself up. Peace reigned for a short time, and then a door opened and a stream of young men issued forth. Prudence watched them idly at first, with her thoughts far away; then suddenly she became interested; they all came out looking as if a tornado had passed over them, the majority had a dazed look, almost bewildered, and their hair for the most part ruffled and standing on end; one or two looked merely very thoughtful. After a short interval out came the Professor; he always walked with a slight sea roll, and he had a happy smile on his round, cherubic face. Prudence burst out laughing at it all; someone had recently described Skipwith to her as "a live wire and a tremendous force in the University," and the result of one of his lectures as seen in the faces of the young men was distinctly amusing.

"One moment while I get rid of my gown," said Thomas, on coming up to her, "and then we'll have a good two hours to tool around."

He slid through the traffic of Cambridge, the narrow, over-crowded streets, motor-bicycles with four people up, push bicycles with two up, with the consummate ease of a practised driver. But when once out of the town, Thomas let her out, and they "tooled" to Huntingdon in a quarter of an hour. When at last Prudence could make herself heard and understood she protested vigorously.

"I suggested to father he should come out this morning with us, and he said he'd be d—d rather than drive with you, and I'm not sure he wasn't right."

"I know very well," laughed Thomas, "that the Master did not say that, though he may have declined your invitation. All right, all right, we'll go into the fens and go really slow." They turned into the flat fen country and drove at a reasonable pace. On a bridge over a broadish bit of water they pulled up for a moment.

"This is very fascinating," said Prudence; "is it a 'drain,' the Ouse, or the Cam, I wonder?"

"I think," said Thomas, "that this is what you might call a drain—it's the New Bedford Cut. It was made I don't know how long ago by some Duke of Bedford, and cuts off a long bend in the Ouse; we shall pass the depleted bit of river farther on."

"Is this how you get from Cambridge by water to the sea?"

"No, you do that by going down the Cam into the Ouse by Ely, by Denver Sluice into the Wash. I suppose that Huntingdon traffic, what there is of it, would come this way into the Wash; it's a pity the waterways aren't more in use, I am sure we should get our coal much cheaper if it was brought by water."

"You're a keen yachtsman," said Prudence, "have you ever been by water to the sea from home?"

"No, I keep my boat at Mersea; it would take too long to get her up to Cambridge, besides she's not the sort for canal work." He slid the gears in as he spoke and the big car moved noiselessly on. "I'll tell you what I do want; I want to come by boat to your cousin's place, I could do that easily; I might do it next vac. and get a little duck shooting at the same time."

"Yes, that could be very easily managed," said Prudence. "I am likely to be there a good deal this winter, for the hunting; you could arrange to come when I am. The house, you know, stands in the middle of acres and acres of marsh, the river which is very wide is less than a quarter of a mile away, but there's a narrow creek comes right up to the house and goes into the cellars. You would anchor out in the river, you couldn't get up the creek."

"Why not? I am blowed if I see why I shouldn't come up the creek; I should love to do it, and get into the cellars. I never heard of anything so alluring."

Prudence laughed. "Yes, that's how they smuggled in old days, but only shallow draught boats can get up, and only at high tide, then the channel can only be found by marks on the shore and I fancy only Ben and one or two of the keepers can do it. It's a remnant of the old days when Wellende was fortified. There was one track over the marshes which has now been made into the drive, and by water it could only be reached at high tide, and then only one or two knew the way, so it was fairly impregnable!"

"By Jove, yes, and now if not impregnable it must be pretty lonely."

"Yes, the marshes have ceased to be swamps. They are now some of the best grazing land in England, but the creek still fills at high tide, and still only one or two can follow its windings through the half-mile of mud, when it's all covered with water," said Prudence dreamily.

"It must feel rather uncanny having that water under the house, and rather damp, I should think," said Thomas.

"Oh," replied Prudence, "the walls are so thick I don't believe it's damp, but uncanny I should just think it can be. The place is haunted, of course, but considering all the queer noises that come whenever there's a wind, and there generally is, it doesn't much matter whether it's haunted or not. You can imagine you can hear anything. I've heard footsteps and doors banging and creaking, and I know it's all the wind really, but it *might* be anything you liked!"

"Now what exactly do you mean, do you believe it's haunted or do you not?"

"Yes," said Prudence slowly, "I do believe it may be haunted, no one but a fool can brush the possibility of all that sort of thing aside, but what I mean is, the sounds heard may be the murdered Temple walking, or may only be the winds."

"What's the actual story of the ghost?"

"Oh, that's clear enough—they've got an account written of it soon after it happened—one of the Temples was suspected of having 'trafficked with witches and magicians,' and one fine morning he was found in the water under the house with his throat 'cutted with a knife.' It's not known whether it was suicide or whether, as I think the paper goes on to state, the witches and magicians did it for him, anyhow he walks along a certain passage downstairs."

They drove on for some way in silence, each engaged with their own thoughts. Then Thomas said, "Isn't Temple a near relation of Lord Wellende?"

"He's a cousin, but their fathers quarrelled and he never goes there. I don't know what it was all about, but they would have nothing in common. Ben is all for sport, and I have heard Professor Temple describe him as a fool," said Miss Pinsent, in extreme displeasure.

"Is he?" said Thomas blandly.

"Not at all," replied Prudence, "he's not what you would call brainy, he's just a simple gentleman with entirely country tastes and pursuits."

"Well, that sounds all right," replied Professor Skipwith. "I like 'em that way myself, especially during the vac., and I am coming to Wellende as soon as possible."

They paused for a moment in Bridge Street, held up by the traffic on the bridge. "Why there," said Prudence, "actually is a small barge—now I wonder if that is on its way to the Wash?"

CHAPTER III

I T WAS SUNDAY EVENING IN THE COMBINATION ROOM OF PRINCE'S College. Most of the Fellows and members of the High Table dined in Hall on Sunday evening, and if the company was good that evening, the setting was even better. Men with brains and ability can be found all over the world, moreover there are always others coming on to fill their places, but such Jacobean rooms as this are not to be found all over the world, nor are they to be reproduced. The ceiling was finely moulded, and the walls panelled with oak, stained and darkened by the passing years. The dominant colour of the room was dark red or red-brown, the carpet was one or the other, the drawn curtains dark red, and two generous fires at each end of the room lit up the ruby tints of the decanters of port on the table and the splash of scarlet of a doctor's hood someone had thrown down on a chair. The Master, with his gaitered legs crossed, was reclining in a comfortable arm-chair discussing a point of doctrine with the Dean. Professor Temple, who had been fidgeting round the room, finally let himself down into another chair with a sigh. His hair was too long, he had whiskers, and one or two front teeth were missing; moreover he was imperfectly shaved; he had, in addition, a generally unwashed appearance which was probably not merited but due to a naturally dark complexion. It was commonly believed outside his own college that he always took snuff in the Combination Room, but if true, he was certainly not doing so to-night.

"The influence of Teutonic thought," said the Master slowly and ponderously, "on the doctrine of the Incarnation—" Professor Temple sighed audibly—"on the doctrine of the Incarnation," continued the Master imperturbably, "is deleterious only so far as—"

Professor Temple sighed again, more audibly. The Master regarded him blandly, "My dear Temple, what is the matter?"

"Look here, Master, how would you like it if I was to discuss the influence of certain poisons on your intestines?"

The Master flinched slightly at the last word, but replied energetically: "Poisonous? No, my dear Temple, the influence of Teutonic thought cannot be described as poisonous at all; indeed, it is only deleterious so far as—" But the end of his sentence was again drowned by the groans of the scientific professor. "Well, well," said the Master, with admirable self-restraint and good temper, "perhaps, Mr. Dean, our friend here is right and we should not discuss our special subjects in the Combination Room."

"I particularly wanted to hear your views on that subject, Master," replied the Dean, giving the Professor an old-fashioned look, "as I have to read a paper on it at the end of term."

"Come back to the Lodge with me later on this evening."

But even though he had gained his point, the Professor still remained surly. Indeed the good temper and manners of Bishop Pinsent seemed to act as an irritant. Presently a young Fellow of a neighbouring college, Brown, who worked with Professor Temple and was present that night partly to create a diversion and partly to get a rise out of the Professor, said: "I've just made an interesting discovery. Sir, I find I have the honour of being related to you."

Professor Temple regarded him with an expression of extreme distaste.

"My mother tells me she is descended from Roger Temple, who was one of Marlborough's generals." The expression of distaste on the Professor's face deepened into positive disgust.

"General Temple," he said, "had only one child, a daughter, and she was a congenital idiot, which lends a certain degree of probability to your statement, but," went on the Professor, raising his voice slightly to drown the expostulations some of his audience looked like making, "since she died before she was of marriageable age—I have the honour to inform you that you are a damned liar," and he replaced the cigar he was smoking.

Brown put his head back and shouted with laughter, and indeed was so whole-heartedly amused at his own discomfiture that even the Professor's ill-humour was not proof against it, and he took his cigar out of his mouth and grinned at the young man he had recently been so rude to. But this was too much for the Bishop. He turned to the Professor in real indignation:

"You go too far, sir, you go too far—the occasion merits no such violent and uncontrolled outburst on your part."

"I apologize unreservedly, Master, for swearing in your presence; the only excuse I can offer is serious provocation. Just as you as a Christian really hate sin—so I as a scientist hate inaccuracy. Brown's inaccurate statement roused my righteous wrath."

"That may somewhat mitigate your offence, but does not altogether excuse it. Your hatred of inaccuracy is right and good, but the personal terms in which you elected to express your hatred I cannot condone."

The Professor, whose good humour seemed to be thoroughly restored by the breeze, again made some sort of apology, and peace was restored. The incident had really disturbed no one so much as the Master; they were all used to Temple's odd ways and temper, though all silently agreed that language of that sort should not have been used in the Master's presence. Presently, as the Master and Dean got up to go, Temple looked up and said hesitatingly to the former: "Er—I hope—er—that Miss Pinsent keeps well."

"That," said the Master to the Dean as they walked across the court from the Combination Room to the Lodge, "is the only consistent effort at good manners that I can call to mind that Temple is guilty of: he regularly and perfunctorily inquires after my daughter, and indeed I would say he seems to listen to the reply."

"He *is* an odd fellow," said the Dean, "and, of course, I know we must make allowances for that type of mind, and a really great intellect. But I thought he went altogether too far tonight."

The Bishop didn't speak for a moment, and then he said: "I have known that man since he was a boy—we are, indeed, as perhaps you are aware, somehow connected—and I can tell you, in spite of what he is now, he commands my sincerest respect for the control he has of his temper."

Meanwhile the Senior Proctor had joined the company in the Combination Room—a tall, dark man, in a rustling silk gown and bands. He threw his gown on a chair and joined the company round the other fire, among whom were Professor Skipwith and Maryon, whose wife we have already met playing bridge. Maryon was a small, clean-shaven man with a nervous face, tanned permanently by hotter suns than ever shone on the British Isles, and he was physically as tough as the bit of leather he resembled. At the approach of the Senior Proctor he looked up eagerly as if to speak, and then seemingly changed his mind and pulled thoughtfully at his pipe. Finally he said: "Find the job of Senior Proctor very worrying?"

"No, I am fairly well used to it by now—it doesn't worry me."

"That means though, I suppose, that there's no serious trouble on," said Maryon equably.

"Yes, I think you may take it it does," laughed the Proctor. "If you think I am worrying about silly letters to *The Times* from irresponsible idiots about the Proctors keeping order in London on Boat Race night, I can ease your mind of that!"

There was a general laugh.

"No," said Maryon, "I hadn't got that in my mind—but tell me now, if a senior member of the University got into trouble with the police, it wouldn't come to you, I suppose?"

"I should think it would come straight to the senior member himself; but what on earth are you driving at?"

"Well, I'll risk your all laughing at me, and I will tell you a story."

"Hold hard a moment," said someone, "while I fetch my drink; I must listen to this."

"You know," went on Maryon, "that I had a small job in the Intelligence during the war. Well…" His company were all listening with real interest now, and certainly no signs of laughing at him; it was generally thought that Maryon's job in the Intelligence had not been quite so small as he liked people to think, largely because he never could be got to talk about it. His lean brown face had a tense look.

"Well, you all are probably rather vaguely aware that our Secret Service was better than anyone else's, and that's come rather from what has not been said than from what has been. But no one who doesn't actually know the facts has any idea of the bravery, ability, and intelligence displayed by that Service. I was only adopted into it temporarily," he added, "not really one of them. But there was one man who was the king of them all; there are fables and legends round him, and I don't even know his name—as far as I was concerned he was No. 4. That man ought to have a row of Victoria Crosses; they wanted to knight him at one time, but they couldn't. He's the most daring and yet the most absolutely level-headed chap imaginable. He's only used on the most serious cases, and he had a diabolical faculty of getting into the mind of his opponent. I lived with him once for two days and nights, believing he was a fool of a boy of twenty-five, and never discovered my mistake at all, and he's a man of fifty or more, and when I once saw him for a few minutes with the face his Maker gave him, I took particular note of it. Yesterday I saw that face again, coming away from the rugger match… there's mischief up, or that man wouldn't be in Cambridge."

No one laughed, then Skipwith, from the depths of his comfortable chair, said: "What is there against his being up here in a private capacity? It seems to me the most reasonable explanation."

"Yes, it would be, except for this. He was looking at me when I first saw him, and I was so surprised I certainly showed in my face that I recognized him. His expression didn't change when he must have first realized that I knew him, he's far too wary a bird for that, but he just looked straight through me; he didn't *want* me to know him."

"Yes," said the Senior Proctor, "it's just that first look that tells so much; I always know if I come suddenly on an undergraduate walking with a girl, by the first look on his face when he sees me, whether she's a girl he ought to be with or not."

"I suppose this No. 4 knows you by sight quite well?" asked Skipwith.

"You bet he does," said Maryon. "I wouldn't like to say what he doesn't know, but, anyhow, if a fellow looked at you with the eager interest I must have done, you wouldn't look through him in that way without a good reason, even if you didn't know him."

"No," said the Proctor, "I am inclined to agree with you, he knew you, and didn't want you to know him, which certainly has the air of his being on business."

"The sight of his face calls up memories that I had hoped were buried, and makes me feel uneasy. The source of the trouble he's hunting may quite likely be in Timbuctoo, and only a tentacle here; but the sight of him makes me somehow uneasy." A coal dropped in the grate, and a spurt of flame lit up the serious faces of the men sitting round. Nearly all of them had grim memories of the War, and their thoughts went back for a time.

"Why didn't you speak to him after all?" asked someone else.

"I had forgotten my old training," laughed Maryon, "and was too surprised by the whole thing, and then the opportunity was gone, and when I came to think of it, I don't even know his name! and it would have been rather like a private insisting on speaking to Haig because he recognized him!" And then, after a pause: "It was hard luck on him that I should recognize him—I happen to have a knack of remembering faces."

"When you lived with him for two days, and he was disguised, were you disguised, too?" asked Skipwith.

"Yes, and I never saw through him, and he saw through me in twenty-four hours—blast him!" with a laugh.

The flickering firelight made the shadows dance about the magnificent old room through a haze of smoke. No one spoke for some time, then the harsh voice of Professor Temple, who had drawn near unnoticed, broke the silence.

"There was some trouble that had its origin in the East, I fancy, that culminated at a certain house in London; had you anything to do with that?"

Maryon thought for a moment. "Grosvenor Square... in the winter?" he said.

"Yes, when the Commander-in-Chief did *not* go."

"How do you know anything about it?" asked Maryon sharply. The Professor gave a grim chuckle.

"I was called in to perform the autopsy on the body of the man that did go."

"And found that he had died of morphine," stated Maryon.

"Yes," said Temple, "and self-injected."

"Then you will be glad to hear that No. 4 shot both Wolf and Stein; I saw him do it."

The Professor grunted. "I should like to meet that man."

"If I have to listen to many more of your stories, I shan't sleep to-night," said Skipwith cheerfully. "Your 'face' is on a holiday, Maryon—that's all."

CHAPTER IV

I T WAS ON A BRIGHT, FINE AUTUMN MORNING THAT MISS PRUDENCE Pinsent prepared to leave Cambridge for a few days' hunting with her cousin in Suffolk. The morning seemed the brighter, and her sense of well-being even greater than usual, in consequence of her father having just told her that he intended to increase her allowance considerably, owing to the legacy just left him by an old cousin. Indeed, it would have been hard for Prudence to have felt more prosperous than she looked. Her leather coat with fur collar covered tweeds, not new, but of unmistakably good cut, and the nickel finish on her Standard saloon twinkled and sparkled in the sunlight. The knowledge that, packed up in her luggage at the back, was a brand new pair of patent leather top-boots, added to the general placidity of her mind. Down Jesus Lane and through Barnwell, Prudence drove slowly and carefully, until with slightly increasing speed she shot out into the grand open rolling country along the Newmarket road. A fine autumn morning, and is there any more perfect time for going through this country? Away to the left the ground rises slightly for the Isle of Ely, and farther still, on the horizon, lies the massive pile of the Cathedral. To the right is the flat country of Fulbourne Fen, and over the ploughed fields the plovers were calling. Just before entering Newmarket the road cuts through that tremendous prehistoric earthwork known as the Devil's Dyke, and then in a few minutes she was slowing down for the little town of Newmarket. Ever since the days of James I Newmarket has been, perhaps, the most famous centre of horse-racing in the world. Surrounded on all sides as it is with heaths, a more suitable spot could hardly be imagined.

Taking the right-hand fork, after passing through the little town, Prudence drove very slowly. Away to the left on the heath were strings of thoroughbreds, some being walked, some cantered. Already the academic feeling of the University was beginning to fade, and the feeling of the country-side, of long furrows made by the plough, of chickens scratching in a stubble field, of tired cart-horses going home o' nights, was beginning to supersede it—the beech woods were all turned to a russet brown, mingling with the soft tints of the ploughed fields and the hedgerows.

She ran into Bury St. Edmunds. But from here on her pace was slower. From straight roads and open country she came to curling lanes and the well-timbered country of mid-Suffolk. In comfortable time for lunch, Prudence was threading her way through the narrow streets of Ipswich to that excellent hostelry known as the "Great White Horse." It is a fact that Charles Dickens visited this inn, and a pleasant fiction that Mr. Pickwick did so. Anyhow, in the jumble of rooms and passages upstairs, and the stone-paved courtyard (now covered in and used as a lounge) downstairs, it requires no great effort of imagination to see gentlemen of a former century moving about. The bar itself must be identical with the one at which Mr. Dickens took his ale after getting off the London coach. And "mottle complexioned, double-chinned, portly men" are still to be seen in plenty. Indeed, there is always a busy and varied company in this old inn.

Miss Pinsent, well accustomed to the ways of the place, drove into the garage at the back, and finding her way into the hotel she proceeded to the grill-room. Here was a white-capped cook, standing in front of his grill, awaiting orders. Prudence chose a careful meal, and then while it was grilling, went upstairs to get a wash. Coming down again ten minutes later, she settled herself down comfortably at a table and looked slowly round the grill-room.

How delightful the prospect of everything was, she thought; the holiday feeling about it all; the hunting she was going to have soon, the good hot meal, after a cold drive, that she was going to have at once, and always the same sort of company to eat it with, in the "Great White Horse." So different from her Cambridge environment. Here was a table of business men, eagerly discussing some project; there was a stout, well-to-do farmer (if there is such a thing nowadays!) and his stout, well-to-do wife, eating in stolid silence; and there again, as sure as fate, over in a quiet corner by himself, a young man who somehow or other managed to have a flavour of salt water about him, though how it was done Prudence could never quite say. She knew, however, from experience that he was certainly living in a small boat on the Orwell, and had probably taken advantage of having to come into Ipswich to get something, to drop in at the "Great White Horse" and enjoy a really good hot meal. This sort is invariably very unobtrusive, and even furtive of expression—due, not as one might suppose, to a criminal past, but merely to the fact that he has not been able to shave! Prudence smiled to herself, as she observed all these familiar types, and then, just as she was beginning on her first mouthful of sizzling hot, juicy sausage, her eye fell on a distinguished-looking, grey-haired man in uniform, who came into the room.

"Why, it can't be—but it is—" And then aloud: "Why, it's Harry Studde," and Captain Studde turning round at that moment, the recognition was mutual.

"Well," said he, "this is delightful and unexpected—I don't believe we've met for something like twenty years, and then to run across you in Ipswich in this way. Here, wait a moment, and I'll get my meal moved and eat it at your table."

"Yes, this is quite delightful," agreed Prudence. "And now I come to think of it, I did hear you had a coast-guard's job somewhere on the East Coast, but I never realized that you came as far south as this."

"Yes, I do, though—worse luck!"

"Why worse luck?"

"Oh, I don't know, and certainly not since it's brought about meeting you. What brings you to these parts?"

"I'm constantly this way," said Prudence. "I have a cousin living hereabouts I have always been very fond of, and I go there for hunting."

"I have always been meaning to come over to Cambridge some time and look you up. How's the Bishop?"

Prudence replied.

"What's that you're drinking?" Studde went on. "Draught Bass? It looks excellent. —I am tired and can just do with a good meal."

Harry Studde was a retired naval officer, a simple, straightforward gentleman, with a deal more shrewdness to him than his bluff, hearty manner might have led one to suppose. His father had been squire of the parish where Bishop Pinsent had once been parson, and he and Prudence had known each other as children. Studde's brother was now squire, and he himself, with a rising family and a younger son's portion, was glad when he retired from the Navy to get an Inspector of Coast Watchers job. After he had eaten a bit, and taken a good pull at his beer, Studde began again:

"Yes, it seems only like the other day that we were all running wild together in the country. Now I'm a family man, and you, I suppose, are a person of some importance at Cambridge. The Bishop holds a big position there, doesn't he, and I suppose you know all the dons and all their little foibles?"

"Father is Head of a College, certainly," admitted Prudence, "but as for the rest of your remark, the generic term 'don' applies, I suppose, to hundreds of men up at Cambridge, and I certainly don't know them all, and still less 'their little foibles.'"

"Oh, well, but you know a good many of them? All the important ones, the professors?" hopefully.

"I suppose I know most of the professors," said Prudence doubtfully, "but certainly not all. But why this sudden interest in my academic friends?"

"As a matter of fact, I am very much interested in your academic friends, but I haven't made up my mind whether I will tell you why."

"You arouse my curiosity," said Miss Pinsent, "and my sense of good manners compels me to inquire after your smuggling friends. I suppose you know them all, and their little foibles?"

"It's odd you should say that," said Studde, suddenly giving her a keen look, "for I would give a good deal at this moment to know one of them, and his little foibles."

"Why, Harry, you don't mean to say there *is* any smuggling done, do you?" said Prudence with surprise. "I was only joking when I referred to your smuggling friends."

"I do mean it, though, but talk of something else while the waiter comes." The meat plates were changed, and the two friends settled down to an excellent Gorgonzola cheese; one could not, as Captain Studde said, eat a sweet with draught beer or after so excellent a grill.

"And who," said he to Prudence, as the waiter handed him the cheese, "is the cousin round about here with whom you so often stay?"

"Round about here is a bit of a phrase, perhaps, since he's about fifty miles off. His name is Ben Wellende, you may have heard of him?"

Studde, who was helping himself to cheese at the moment, clumsily shot the contents of the dish on to the carpet. "Sorry, waiter, very stupid of me," he said, rather breathlessly. "You'll have to fetch us a fresh bit. Do you, by any chance, mean Lord Wellende, in Suffolk—I didn't know you were relations."

"Oh, yes, we are cousins, and I have known him all my life and am very fond of him."

Captain Studde, thought Prudence, seemed more upset by the small accident than need be. He was rather red in the face and, curiously enough, a little breathless. Was it possible that something else had upset him? what were they talking of when it happened? Lord Wellende—that could have been nothing to distress him. They ate for a time in silence until Studde laid down his knife and said in a low voice: "Look here, Prudence, the chance circumstances of our meeting, for one thing, and the lines our conversation have run along, for another, are so odd—they look to me like Providence, and I am going to do a rash thing and take you into my confidence. I don't like talking secrets with a woman, it's d—d risky, they nearly always blab, but there—is there anywhere we can talk in private?"

Prudence's first impulse was to point out to him the unwisdom of belittling the trustworthiness of women in general, to the woman he apparently proposed to trust, but seeing how much in earnest he appeared, she refrained; besides which, she was really curious, and quite at sea as to what she was going to hear. How could possible smuggling be helped or hindered by her? So she contented herself by suggesting that they might find the comfortable lounge upstairs empty and go up there. On going through the downstairs lounge they ordered coffee.

"Am I going to hear something startling, Harry?" said Prudence.

"You are," was the grave reply—"really startling."

"In that case," said Miss Pinsent, "we'll have liqueurs too."

They were in luck, the long lounge was empty, and they established themselves in front of a good fire. Studde shut the door after the waiter, and then came back slowly and stood in front of the fire, stirring his coffee.

"You'll understand better," he said slowly, "when I have finished, why I have ever begun." With a short laugh—"If you talk about what I am going to tell you, you will get me into grave trouble; I think you might help me a lot, but if you don't feel you can, will you just hold your tongue about what I tell you? Can you promise me that, Prudence?"

By now Prudence's curiosity was thoroughly aroused, and she was prepared to promise almost anything to get it satisfied.

"Do you remember," went on Studde, "when we were children, and some of the elder ones took the peaches off the tree in our stable yard? and there was all that fuss, and you knew all the time and never spoke. You can't have been more than ten years old. Well, it's partly because I remember that, that I dare trust you now."

"Yes, I *do* remember, now you mention it," said Prudence slowly. "I thought it rather shabby of them, not much better than outright stealing, but I don't remember that it ever occurred to me as possible to give them away."

"No, that would be the child's, a nice child's point of view, but I hope now your sense of morality has changed."

There was a long pause, while Captain Studde pulled at his pipe, then he began again: "I dare say you know something of the history of smuggling, so much fiction has been written about it, and the fiction, or anyhow what I've read of it, is mainly true. They used to smuggle in gangs, and when the gangs began to get too big and strong for the preventive men to contend with, the coast-guards were started to assist the preventive men. Some families were smugglers generation after generation, and even used to intermarry with their same sort on the French side!—but the worst aspect of it all was that so many highly-placed people were in it, *sub rosa*. Why, there was a case not so very long ago of a hoard of schnapps in bottles being found under the altar of a little West-country church. Obviously the parson had been in the business, and his share of the swag had been hidden under the altar. One supposes the poor chap died and his secret with him. Eventually the gangs got broken up, preventive men and coast-guards together got too many for them. For various reasons smuggling ceased to be so feasible or profitable, and it more or less died out. Now it's begun again—and in somewhat the same way."

"Go on, Harry," said Prudence; "this is perfectly entrancing."

"It's not entrancing, Prudence," returned Studde soberly and sternly; "it's puzzling—degrading—it's worse—it's rotten and bestial… They are landing drugs along this coast; they may be, probably are, bringing in a certain amount of silk, but I fancy, though I may be wrong, they would bring in bulky things at the larger ports. Anyhow, it is not with that I am concerned, it's drugs I am on the track of."

"How do you ever know that drugs are being brought in? have you caught any?"

"I stopped some the other day, but not the stuff I was after. There are various things which make us suspicious, chiefly that the C.I.D. know that there is a perfectly awful stuff, which we will call for short XYZ (I can't even remember its official name, though I've heard it), being circulated, which has no business here at all, and they say it is coming in from the East coast. I can't really tell you, Prudence," said Studde, getting up in his earnestness and standing over her as he spoke, "what an awful thing this drug is; they tell me its power is simply superhuman; taken in one way, it gives the most lovely sensations of peace and well-being, it stimulates the brain to an incredible extent, and then when after a short time he can't give it up, it degrades a man into nothing more than a low, criminal beast. It ought never to exist."

"It sounds awful; I never somehow thought such things really could exist."

"They not only exist, they are among us; and I think, Prudence," said Studde slowly and grimly, "friends of yours are handling that stuff."

"Good heavens, Harry!" exclaimed Miss Pinsent, sitting up in her chair and looking earnestly at him; "it would be idle to ask you to assure me that you are not joking—because I know by your manner that you are not—but do remember I am a respectable spinster, and be careful what you say to me; and my circle of friends are all that's most learned and respectable in the kingdom. Here, you've given me such a shock, I think I'll drink your liqueur brandy, which I see you haven't touched; I've finished my own."

"All right," said Studde grimly; "having drunk two liqueur brandies, I think you are now sufficiently fortified to withstand a further shock."

Prudence sank back into her chair with a weary sigh. "Well—if you *won't* respect my age and infirmities, go on and do your worst."

Studde knocked the ashes out of his pipe, put it back into his mouth and began sucking it as he continued: "It's quite impossible to watch a coast like this; there's miles of seaboard where the marshes come with never a house anywhere in sight, and handy little creeks that a barge or boat can push up at high tide; it would require hundreds of men to patrol it, and we don't really hope to stop the small stuff coming in except by a lucky accident—at least, that's my view; it's the distributing centres you have to get at for the drugs, and that's the work of the C.I.D."

"Then," said Prudence, "I don't quite see where you come in."

"Ah," said Harry Studde, "I come in because I rather hope I may have struck a lucky accident; and you come in, because the C.I.D. is saying the distributing centre is in Cambridge."…

CHAPTER V

THERE WAS A LONG PAUSE. STUDDE SAT FORWARD IN HIS CHAIR, his eyes fixed on the fire, pulling at his empty pipe. Prudence sat up suddenly and gazed at him in speechless astonishment; it was absurd; only a few hours ago she had been breakfasting in the familiar dignified atmosphere of a College Lodge, watching the various members of the University going about on "their lawful occasions." Now she was being asked to believe that among them was a criminal, a criminal of the very worst type, destroying the souls and bodies of men and women for the sake of filthy lucre, and it was no good to try and persuade herself that Studde was "pulling her leg"—he was sincere enough, even if he was mistaken. But what was that he had said? the C.I.D. knew the distributing centre was in Cambridge. At last she found her voice.

"And you really mean me to understand that someone in the University, someone whom I probably know, is doing this dreadful thing?"

"Yes," said Studde solemnly; "someone, too, probably, in a good position; that is why I think it's a hundred to one it's someone you know; not a chemist, I should say, but just the last person in the world you would believe it of—that's the person who is doing it. Has anyone you know lately come in for some money from an unexpected source?" he said after a pause. "Because—" here to his immense consternation he was interrupted by Miss Pinsent beginning to swear. For into her mind had leapt the memory of Thomas's mysterious source of money, which enabled him to buy expensive cars; and the insolent possibility of anyone really daring to suspect him even, made her quite unreasonably and furiously angry; she swore slowly, steadily, and ably for two solid minutes, never pausing for a word, and never, as far as Studde's bewildered senses could tell him, repeating herself once. Then she stopped quite suddenly.

"For the daughter of a bishop," gasped Studde—"for the daughter of a bishop... I say, Prue, where *did* you learn it all—the daughter of a bishop?"

"I feel better now," said Miss Pinsent complacently; "you know I don't care about being completely taken in, especially by an old ass like you, and you really had got me to believe you were in earnest. If you think I was swearing you were mistaken; I was merely quoting the classics to relieve my feelings."

"Oh, you were, were you?" said Studde, giving her a shrewd look; "well, there were parts certainly somewhat reminiscent of the Old Testament, but, by Jove, you've made me regret having missed a 'classical education' as I never did before. For the daughter of a bishop... there are some boatswains and sergeant-majors I know who would give a good deal to have your ability, and—it isn't decent, Prudence!"

"Look here, you've had no consideration for my parentage up to now—so you just leave it alone."

"The daughter of a bishop," still repeated Studde helplessly to himself. "Do you know, if you don't mind I think I will ring for a brandy; I feel I need something."

The bell was rung, the order given, and while the waiter was fetching it the two friends sat silent. When they were alone again, Studde began: "Now tell me something about some of the prominent people in the University. On the face of things, who are the most eminently respectable?"

"I know who your man is," said Prudence nastily; "he's as good as condemned already—my father, a retired bishop and the Master of his College; what could you have more suspicious? He's come in for a little more money, too, lately; it's true he got it from a cousin, whose will can be seen in Somerset House, but don't let that deter you."

"Yes," said Studde without smiling, "if it wasn't that I've known your father all my life, and would stake my all on his integrity, he would be an object of my deepest suspicion. A bishop and Head of his College—why, it's the ideal setting; but," with a sigh, "it's no good; we must look elsewhere. Isn't there a Professor of Greek and Latin?"

"Yes, there are professors of both—and, now I come to think of it, they may both be open to suspicion, for I know nothing on earth against either. They are fathers of large families, and I seem to remember the horrid fact that one of them is a churchwarden and takes the bag round."

"Give me his name," said Studde unsmilingly, as he produced pencil and paper from his pocket. "And isn't there," he went on, "such a thing as a Professor of Ancient History?"

"Yes, but I don't fancy he will be much good to you; his golf handicap is plus two."

"Bless my soul, he must be a likely lad; what age is he?"

"I am sure I don't know; about forty, I suppose."

"Dear me!" said Studde, "I thought all professors were about seventy."

"Really, Harry," said Prudence crossly, "your ignorance is abysmal."

Studde was quite alive to the fact that the beautiful Miss Pinsent had quite ceased to be amused, and possibly even interested, in what he was saying, and that her sarcasm was becoming bitter; but he still pursued his inquiries undisturbed.

"Divinity, now," he said pleasantly; "that should be a likely covert to draw."

"Yes," said Prudence, "and what I can tell you about the Professor of Divinity is as bad as you can want; to begin with, he is a poet of some distinction."

"That's bad," said Studde; "his name?"

Prudence supplied it and then went on: "He has written exhaustively on various doctrines, and was at one time private chaplain to an Archbishop of Canterbury. I should think that pretty well damns him, doesn't it?"

Studde didn't answer; he shut his pocket-book and put it away; for a little while silence reigned. Prudence had forgotten she still had half her journey in front of her, and time was getting on; she could not get over the shock she had felt when the possibility of Thomas's being the distributing centre had occurred to her. For a year or more now, she remembered, Susan had referred to this mysterious little separate account which Thomas kept at another bank and did not allow her to interfere with; but it was a disgusting idea, even to play at suspecting him; she was thankful Harry had said nothing about scientific professors. She might ask him how long this business was supposed to have been going on, without arousing any suspicion, though. She put the question:

"Oh, a year or so for certain—very likely longer," said Studde.

Well, that didn't get her much farther; it just left it where it was, a possibility still. The silence continued for some time, and then Studde spoke again.

"I've another piece of information for you," said he, "but this time I don't think it will be a shock—it will rather entertain you. There's something going on at Wellende that's wrong. I have a pretty shrewd suspicion that Lord Wellende's people are smuggling, and taking advantage of their position as his people to do it, and to do a thing like that is doing the dirty on their master, who has the reputation of being one of the best. I suppose you realize it, Prue, but you know that chap's as near feudal as anyone can be nowadays. It comes, I suppose, from his family having lived in the same spot for so long. Of course I don't mean to suggest for a moment that it has anything to do with this drug—far from it; it's his keeper who is up to something foolish, and that drug doesn't pass through the hands of humble people, you may take your oath on that. It's the keeper and one of the woodmen I've my eye on, but haven't been able to fix anything to them yet."

"This is rather interesting," said Prudence. "There's something about decent smuggling which is extraordinarily attractive. I have smuggled myself and, at the bottom, one's heart is really with the smuggler; besides which I know Woodcock, the keeper, well, and if he is doing a bit on his own he has all my sympathy."

"Yes," said Studde diplomatically, "what you say is very true; one has great sympathy with anyone who can 'do' either the customs or the inland revenue. Why, I've smuggled myself; I once brought in thousands of cigars; hid them between the lining of the funnel and the funnel; told the first engineer that if the customs man so much as looked at the funnel, he was to light the fires at once, so I knew I couldn't be caught; at the worst I could only lose all my cigars, but I didn't—I got away with the lot!"

"And now you want to catch poor Woodcock," said Prudence.

"Yes, I do. Your friend Woodcock isn't doing it once. I'm afraid he's making a practice of it, and that can't be allowed; and anyhow, I am in my present job in order to catch him and his like."

"Well," said Prudence, "I will mention it to Ben, if that is what you want me to do—though really—"

"Not on your life," said Studde, interrupting. "Remember, *all* that we have been talking of is only between ourselves; you promised me that."

"But then, what do you want me to do?"

"Nothing but just keep your eyes open, and if you did see anything you considered of interest, tell me. To tell Lord Wellende would be a great mistake; either he would simply be angry at the idea of his keeper being suspected, or else if he believed it he would unconsciously put the man on his guard. No, nothing must be said, but you just keep your eyes open."

"Really, Harry, you have added quite a new zest to life. I shall go off to Wellende full of interest."

"Yes, but for God's sake remember to say *nothing* about all I have told you; if for no better reason, remember if you talk you will ruin me. I am trusting you very far, Prue."

Prue's face clouded over. "I am not likely to talk about the other. As to Woodcock, he's been in Ben's service over forty years himself, and his father before him."

"Yes," said Studde, "that's what contributes to making your cousin so feudal. Not only have dozens of his people been in service with his family for years themselves, but so many of their fathers were before them, and he owns most of the county. I have never been to the Hall myself, but there are legends that it has enormous cellars, that were used in the good old days for what we have been discussing the whole afternoon, when the Temples were in the business themselves!"

"There are," replied Prudence. "I shall never forget the fearful joy of exploring those cellars when we were children. There's a canal comes right up under the house; it's a fascinating place."

"It's a fascinating old family, too," said Studde. "You know Wellende has very special and peculiar rights all along the foreshore; unlike anyone else that I have ever heard of, for instance, he owns into the sea as far as he can ride his war-horse and throw a spear."

"Yes, I remember hearing that," replied Prudence, "and they still have the deed in which the elder brother gave the younger brother the Manor of Wellende in the reign of William II, and dear old Ben himself is as reactionary at bottom as he can be. It transpired the other day he still wore an old-fashioned night-shirt instead of pyjamas, and when I asked him why, he replied quite seriously, 'Of course I do, my father always did.' And there," said Prudence, laughing, "you have the 27th Lord Wellende in a nutshell."

"Yes," said Studde; "glorious home, a great name, fine traditions, and, as far as I have come up against him, loved by all his people; it would be an awful tragedy if a fellow like that came a cropper..."

"I know no one less likely to come a cropper than he is," said Prudence brightly, "so cheer up."

CHAPTER VI

B Y THE TIME PRUDENCE HAD GOT TO THINKING ABOUT HER journey again, the short November day was so far gone that she decided to send a wire to say she had been delayed on her journey, and to spend the night at Ipswich.

Studde, who was due to hold a night drill at a place on the coast not so very far off, stayed and had tea with her and then went away. As he buttoned up his coat and stepped out into the cold night air, he chuckled to himself, "Well," he thought, "I may be an old fool that hasn't had a classical education, but I'm not quite a lunatic yet. It was fright that made my beautiful Prudence suddenly begin to swear"—the daughter of a bishop, he thought helplessly again, the daughter of a bishop—"because someone she knew at Cambridge could put the cap on, and *not* annoyance at having been deceived, as she would have me believe; and I have left her quite successfully under the impression that the keeper is in the business *without* his lordship's knowledge, whereas—"

It was just as well that there was little traffic in the streets of Ipswich that night, and none at all along the country lanes that Captain Studde pursued, for his thoughts were far from his driving.

For a couple of hours he drove slowly, steadily, and entirely mechanically, along twisting, curling, sandy Suffolk lanes. There wasn't much along the roads, very occasionally a farm-cart, with no lights at all, a little more often a bicycle, sometimes carrying a weak headlight, more often none at all. The few pedestrians kept well to one side, as he came along. His thoughts were far away. The son himself, as has been said, of a landowner, he sympathized thoroughly with that much abused class, and realized how hardly they had been treated by present legislation. He appreciated the fine distinction between the man who inherits property from the father who has bought it, and treats his property like a business in consequence; and the man whose forbears have owned land for generations, to whom tradition is as binding as ownership, and who allows the people on the estate privileges as though they were rights. Before his mind's eye rose the glorious old red-brick pile of Wellende Old Hall, and all it stood for.

The home for seven hundred years of one family in unbroken male descent, who had consistently done their duty by and cared for their own people. Why, it was said the Wellende of the day had been one of the barons who met King John at Bury St. Edmunds in 1214 and forced on him the Charter of Henry I, and, far more remarkable, a Temple had been with Kett in his rebellion. When the poor had been up in arms against the aggression of the rich, a Temple had been on the side of the poor, and justice; and so down to the present peer. Studde remembered a few years ago when he had been putting up in a humble country inn, and the company over their beer were discussing the farming prospects locally—the price of labour, and the prospects of sugar-beet; when one old fellow, who had hitherto inclined to a general pessimism, said ponderously, "There's one thing, his lordship,… his lordship won't never raise the rent, not on any tenant left him by his old dad," and there had been a murmur of assent; and even if Wellende had never made any such statement, which Studde doubted, the fact that it was believed of him spoke volumes. And this, this was the man he was forced against all his instincts to believe was trafficking in this infernal drug. It's true he was said to be hard up, and with a place like that to keep in your family it was a very strong incentive to make money, but no… not like that.

Decent smuggling Studde would have had plenty of sympathy with. If he had really thought the keeper was doing a bit on his own—with spirits or silk, as he had led Prudence to believe—that would have been a very different matter, but he didn't think it for a moment. Whatever the keeper was doing, Wellende knew all about it, though the keeper himself almost certainly would not. Then also—beastly thought—there were more hunters in the stables at Wellende than there had been for years; the hounds had more spent on them, and were doing uncommonly well that season. Non-hunting man as he was himself, Studde yet had good blood in him—and there was something that responded to the music of a hound's first whimper on the line and the wild joy of the sudden discordant screech of "gone away."

At this point his thoughts were abruptly brought back to the business in hand by a gust of strong wind cutting across the car; the road had taken an abrupt bend and for a mile and a half ran across the marshes to the sea. A wide, bare, bleak bank of shingle lay between the marsh and the sea, and on it a single look-out tower and a row of cottages, huddled together, and round them the wind howled. A more desolate spot would be hard to find; the shingle bank was just above the level of the sea on one side, and the marshes on the other, and got no protection anywhere. A little to the north of where the cottages stood a wide tidal river slid quietly and unobtrusively into the sea. Studde drove his car to the back of the cottages, where a little protection was to be got, and was met there by his next in command.

"Everything ready for the drill, Catchpole?"

"Yes, sir; but I just wanted a word with you. There's a barge standing in for the mouth of the river; it's too dark to see who she is, but she hasn't signalled for a pilot, and she is coming in on her own. That means it's a man that knows his way very well, in the dark, and the bar always shifting; if she waited for an hour she could come in with the tide, but she isn't going to, that's evident, sir." Then he added more hesitatingly, with his eye on his superior officer, "It's a risky job coming in against the ebb with the wind the way it is (though I dare say she'll do it), rather than wait an hour and come in on the flow." His eyes searched Captain Studde with a questioning look as he spoke.

"Yes, it will take a good local man to do it," the other replied slowly.

"It will, sir, and it's someone who is in a hurry, and I should say someone who don't want too much notice taken of him."

"Yes," said Studde, "you're right; and mind you, this isn't our usual date for the drill; they might have calculated on there being no one about to-night."

"I was thinking that, too, sir."

After a long pause, in which Captain Studde stood with his hands in his pockets gazing out to sea: "Well, we'll risk it, Catchpole. After all, if she's innocent no harm's done. We're a bit early yet for the drill; tell them to wait till I come back, and you come with me; I don't want anyone else."

The two men walked together across the shingle to the river, and together they shoved a light dinghy down the bank into the water. The tide was racing out, swirling and rippling and gurgling along the banks; a few hundred yards away was the mouth. A bar of shingle showed up in places, and through the one safe channel a huge barge could be seen, slowly making way against the tide. There were a few moments to wait.

"The Collector at Ipswich told me he had had the barges coming up the river all searched, through the summer," said Studde.

"Yes, sir, there was a couple of the water-guards here off and on, but the man who boarded his lordship's barge was a local man; and I am not saying anything against the man, mind you, but he comes of a family which has been here hundreds of years, been smugglers themselves, too, and though I am not saying anything, 'is lordship is 'is lordship to such as 'im, and I'm not saying I shouldn't feel it myself."

Studde laughed outright. "Well, Catchpole, I'll do the searching of the barge, under the circumstances, and not leave it even to you!"

The coast-guard's men waited for the right moment; then, pushing out, were taken by the tide to the barge, which they hailed. Catchpole caught hold of the side, which was only moving slowly against the tide. A nautical face, decorated with grey whiskers, came to the side and asked him in nautical language what he meant by it.

"Coast-guards," said Catchpole.

"You may be coast-guards," said the nautical face, "but you ain't customs, and what the something something 'ave yer to do with me? I don't want a face like yours aboard my boat," and then catching sight, or rather realizing that the second figure in the boat was a superior officer, he suddenly changed his manner. "I beg your pardon, sir, but I don't expect to be boarded by the coast-guards."

"Here," said Captain Studde, "take our painter and make us fast; I am coming to talk to you."

The skipper of the barge, recognizing the peremptory tone of authority, slowly and unwillingly did as he was bid, and Captain Studde got on to the barge.

"What is this barge?" he said to the man.

The skipper did not reply for a moment, than he said, "I didn't know when I spoke to your man as the Inspector was aboard, sir, or I'd have spoken more civil. My owner is on board; might I just go and speak to him?"

Captain Studde, somewhat surprised, nevertheless agreed, and waited while the old man went down to the cabin. After a few moments he came back and invited Captain Studde very civilly to come down. This was indeed an unusual procedure; owners of barges did not generally sail on them—or if they did do so, sailed as skipper; however, even though smuggling might still be going on, the days when Inspectors of coast-guards could be trapped and murdered were certainly over, so he followed the old man down to the cabin in some curiosity; and if he was expecting to get a surprise he was not disappointed, for there, sitting beside an evil-smelling paraffin lamp, was a large, loose-limbed man with a fair moustache—Lord Wellende.

CHAPTER VII

C APTAIN STUDDE STOPPED DEAD WITH SURPRISE; WHATEVER HE had been expecting, it was not this. Why, he thought angrily, did Lord Wellende risk being caught on his barge if she was smuggling? Why, if the barge was innocent, were appearances all against her? And how odious became his duty in circumstances like these. Was this the way, he thought grimly, that the local man in the water-guard had been got round? His thoughts were interrupted by a courteous voice, speaking with a slight drawl.

"Captain Studde, I believe," said Lord Wellende. "I have heard of you, of course, though I don't think I have yet had the pleasure of meeting you," and he held out his hand. Studde took it. There was something about the man—his dignity—a quiet air of self-forgetful-ness—of simplicity; you would have taken his hand if it had been offered you, with all the evidence in the world against him.

"I understand from my skipper you are paying us an official visit. What is it you want?" But if Lord Wellende was a gentleman so was Captain Studde, and he looked him straight in the face and told him the truth.

"I don't mind saying, Lord Wellende, you're the last person in the world I either expected or wanted to see here. There's smuggling going on, and I am searching every barge I can, and I can't let even you go by."

Lord Wellende moved something on the small table and then said quietly:

"You are not customs. Have you the right to search?"

"Yes," said Studde. Putting his hand into his breast pocket, he pro-duced a folded paper. "This is what is called a W.R.6, a search-warrant," and he handed it to Lord Wellende. The latter glanced at it; he saw that the royal arms were on the top, and that the document began with the majestic word "We."

He laughed. "All right, Captain Studde," he said. "I see there is nothing for it but to take you into my confidence, and trust you. It's a confounded nuisance you're being about to-night; this isn't the usual date for your drill."

"No," said Studde, feeling awkward and uncomfortable, and hating his job, "but there's a barge on the sandbank outside, as perhaps you saw, and it's such a good chance to practise having a drill with the real thing, so we changed our date."

"Well, your change of date doesn't leave me much choice, now you've caught me in the act, so listen to me."

The two men talked for about half an hour. Then there was a pause while Studde sat and thought. Finally he said:

"You will get no interference from me, but I cannot speak for the customs. The drug you are using cannot be got by the public. You'll be careful."

"I have it entirely under my own control," replied Wellende.

The two men talked a little more and then Captain Studde went on deck.

"It's better for me not to appear," said Wellende, "if you have a man with you."

"I should think not indeed," said Studde with a laugh. "Good-bye, Lord Wellende."

Studde, with a good night and a remark about the weather to the skipper, got into his own dinghy and dropped down the river with the tide. It was too dark for Catchpole to see Captain Studde's face, and though bursting with curiosity he did not like to speak until his superior officer had done so.

There had certainly not been time for Captain Studde to have searched the barge thoroughly alone, and he had been below all the time, he had not appeared on deck; what had he been doing, wondered Catchpole.

"That was Lord Wellende's barge, as I suppose you know by now all right, Catchpole?"

"Yes, sir."

"And I am quite satisfied that there is nothing contraband on her, and more than that, neither his lordship nor his people are in the business we are after."

"Yes, sir," and then, after a little pause, "I am glad to hear it, sir."

There was a certain awkwardness. It was hardly possible, thought Studde, that his man could suspect him, Studde, of not being straight, and anyhow to defend himself was to court suspicion, so he said nothing. Meanwhile it was perfectly clear in Catchpole's simple mind that there was only one explanation of the business, though discipline, good manners, or tradition—he didn't give it a name in his mind— compelled him to appear to accept Captain Studde's explanation.

"His lordship" had been on the barge and had got round the Captain. Catchpole felt that this wasn't quite right; though he couldn't altogether condemn Captain Studde, "his lordship" was so undoubtedly "his lordship," one had to remember that, and even one who wasn't a local man would have to feel that, if he was a gentleman at all, and though it wasn't right, he felt a certain pride, being a local man himself, that "his lordship's" influence, or personality, reached so far. There was little talk between the two men; each was immersed in his own thoughts. They landed much where they had taken off, and walked back to where the paraphernalia of the drill was laid out. The huge tripod, holding the rocket, was erected and a small flickering light at sea showed the wrecked barge.

Studde ran his eye over the tackle; he saw that the rocket would run clear from its box, and the big hawser on either side was free, too. He then went and inspected the angle at which the rocket was set, inquired the length that the wreck was from the shore, said a word about the strength of the wind to Catchpole, and had the angle slightly altered. Then he gave the word. Bang! rush! went the rocket through the night, out to sea, the cord uncoiling like a live thing after it. There was a slight pause, while all waited; then the thick hawser on either side began to move. Studde gave a grunt of satisfaction. The rocket had been aimed right—it had reached the wreck, and now the men on the wreck were pulling the thick circular rope out to which the cord, carried by the rocket, was attached. Presently, when a signal from the wreck had been given, the men on the shore worked the hawser and sent out a lifebuoy and bag suspended from the buoy.

A huge magnesium flare lit up the proceedings, making the dark figures of the life-saving crew stand up vividly against the light. After an interval a limp, wet figure was pulled back in the buoy, and the practice of artificial respiration was gone through. The life-saving crew were local farm labourers, not very bright specimens, but they had been drilled well, and knew their job.

"When your man comes round," said Captain Studde, "what is it you give him?"

"Very strong coffee, or tea, sir," replied the man.

"And what do you never give him?" said Studde.

"Spirits," was the reply.

"Come to think of it, Catchpole," said Studde, as they walked away, "we practically never get a man in on this flat coast who isn't half drowned by the time he's on shore."

"No, sir, of course not, sir," and they both walked off.

CHAPTER VIII

A FTER PARTING WITH STUDDE, PRUDENCE'S FIRST CONSIDERA-
tion was to secure a room for the night.

"Is the Dickens room empty?" she asked the manageress, "because
I think I should like to have it."

After going up and down what seemed like endless steps and along
twisting passages, they came to a large old-fashioned-looking room.
The two big four-poster beds, with the dressing-table in between in
front of the window, immediately recalled the famous illustration by
Phiz, and an old-fashioned floral designed wallpaper, though new, was
in keeping with the rest of the room. Prudence thought with com-
placency that she could never look like the lady in the illustration as
she sat in front of the glass. She took the room and ordered a fire to
be lighted at once. Then the chambermaid came with the hot water:

"There's many ladies," she said, "as say they can't abide for to
sleep in a room with another empty bed, it makes them fancy things."

"Is that really the case?" replied Miss Pinsent with interest. To
her healthy and well-controlled nerves such fancies seemed wellnigh
incredible. "I don't think it will trouble me at all."

Then she had to consider sending a wire to her cousin to explain
her non-arrival. She thought for a moment; in the circumstances it
might be better not to say it was owing to a meeting with Studde,
so she wired to say she had had engine trouble and would come in
time for tea next day.

Then she dined, and after dinner retired to her room in peace to
think out what she had just been told. She had been considerably
startled by what Studde had told her, though not perhaps for quite

the reasons that he had supposed. A "distributing centre" for drugs was, she fancied, something quite different from being one in a chain of people through whose hands a forbidden drug passed, and she did not believe for a moment that such a centre was in Cambridge. It required the kind of daring and subtlety she felt quite sure no one in the University was capable of. She thought for a moment about some of her own and her father's circle of friends, and smiled at the idea a little pityingly. Harry had a bee in his bonnet, that was what it was. Moreover, he had displayed a most lamentable ignorance of modern university life, he had himself admitted that he thought all professors were old men, and he was probably thinking that the colleges still contained various specimens of bachelor "Fellows" of unknown dark pasts and deplorable present habits, who were seldom seen about in the light of day.

Others, too, who lived double lives. She laughed gently, as she thought of the University as it is to-day. The excellent hard-working fathers of families, the keenness about everything, healthy games as much as work, the desire to get the right sort of men up, undergraduates as well as dons, and she laughed again at the very absurdity of Harry Studde's ideas. It was true, certainly, that Harry had said it was Scotland Yard that suspected Cambridge. It would be exceedingly distasteful, she thought, to have any inquiries made about the sources of one's income; but there, she didn't suppose for a moment it would happen.

She thought of various different men she knew, working hard and quietly at their special jobs, and the strange branches of knowledge that many of them were pursuing. She remembered one had told her, only the other day, that they were touching a force in the universe that was beyond electricity; they didn't know what it was yet, or where it might take them. She thought of the vast knowledge of the University, of the scientific investigations which Thomas was pursuing with such ardour. No, those were not the sort of men who would take the risk of distributing that drug. Except for the mischief the drug could do, which she didn't half believe, the "running" of it meant a good deal of sport. Steady nerves, audacity, and pluck; that was what was required for that sort of work. These were far more likely to be found in people who had a long line of buccaneering ancestors behind them, thought Miss Pinsent complacently and entirely erroneously, as she reflected on her own mother's people, the Temples, than any men of education. Mrs. Gordon had not been so very far out when she told Marcella Maryon that she always felt Prudence had it in her to kick over the traces. She had, and subconsciously aware of it herself, it had the effect of making her sit more firmly on her little pinnacle and draw her skirts round her, away from the moil and toil of common life.

Having settled everything in her mind to her own complete satisfaction, Miss Pinsent took herself to bed, and slept the sleep of an untroubled mind. Next morning she did not hurry her departure, and when she did go, she drove slowly.

Soon after leaving Ipswich she left the main road, and from there on traversed nothing but sandy, curling lanes. There was hardly even a village, only a few cottages collected here, and a lonely farm-house there. Occasionally came a long stretch of heathland and bracken. The screeching cock-pheasants toned to perfection with the russet bracken. Even the clothes of the farm labourers managed to blend with the heaps of sugar-beet that were a frequent sight along the road. All the colouring was soft and brown and russet, except when a flock of gulls made a startling patch of white against the brown earth. Then the road, which had been running through heathland for some miles, took a sudden turn up round a wood, and there displayed before her lay a grand panoramic view. In the far distance lay the grey, cold North Sea; nearer like a curving silver ribbon flowed the wide tidal Wellende river; nearer still, set in the middle of acres and acres of marshland, on a slight eminence, its old red brick glowing like a jewel in the setting sun, stood the stately pile of Wellende Old Hall. Prudence pulled up to gaze. It was high tide, and the river some quarter of a mile away from the house was full. She could even see the thin line of silver of the creek running up to the house. On the other side, on the top of a dyke, with windswept, stunted trees on either side, lay the drive. This had been constructed some four hundred years ago, when labour was a good deal cheaper than it is now, and ran for about a mile over the marsh. The approach to the house itself was under a gateway in a Tudor tower, which led into the courtyard round which the house was built.

Prudence rang the bell, and walked straight in. Almost at once an old man came from the other end of the hall, still getting into his coat.

"You'll excuse me, miss," he said at the sight of her, "but I wasn't going to keep you waiting for a welcome."

"Thank you, Dunning," said Prudence, "and is everyone here going on all right?"

"Yes, miss, things don't change here much, as you know, except his lordship 'as a new shooting-suit," added the old man thoughtfully.

"Well, that is a piece of news, of course; I suppose I may take it his lordship is quite well?"

"He is, miss. I was to tell you he was ratting down in the moat, if you would join him there when you came."

Prudence went under the gateway and turned along a path to the left. The mingled yells of ecstasy and agony of two terriers and a man's voice guided her to the spot. When down the path towards her came scurrying a ball of grey fur, she gave one yell, almost as piercing as the terriers, and flew in the opposite direction. When she had recovered herself and made certain the danger of meeting a rat was passed, she returned.

"Prue," said her cousin, slipping his arm affectionately through hers, "after all the trouble I have taken with your education, I am ashamed of you, to run away from a harmless rat."

"Ben," replied she, rubbing her cheek against the rough tweed of his sleeve, "you know I have always had an inhibition against rats, mice, and ferrets; and I always shall have."

"My dear," he said earnestly, "I hope after a week here you will drop using words of that description and express yourself in simple English."

"After three days," said Prue, laughing, "I won't use a word of more than three syllables—there!"

"Tea is in the gallery," said Ben; "go up, and I will get a wash and join you."

Prudence went up. The gallery was one of the beauties of the Old Hall. She sauntered to the window and looked out. The water of the river had taken all the colour of the setting sun, and was a blaze of glory. A flight of wild duck, like a brown smudge, tailing out, was passing across the red and gold; a couple of herons were flopping slowly along the edge of the marsh; one bird could be heard calling. Prudence listened.

"What gull is it," she asked her cousin, as he came in, "that calls very like a curlew?"

He came up and stood beside her and looked out; one larger white-winged bird was visible. "I think," he said, "it's a herring gull—come and have tea."

They had their tea together cosily by a good fire, the two terriers joining them. Then Prudence went up to her room. Whenever she was at Wellende she always had one room, looking over the creek; indeed it had come to be known as hers. She found a good fire, and a round-cheeked, grey-haired woman, in a neat cap, doing her unpacking.

"Oh, Mary," said she, "how very, very nice it is to be here again." She shook hands.

"Yes, indeed, miss. It's a long time since you've been; why, not all the summer, and his lordship is always so glad when you come."

"Yes, I know, but I can't get away from Cambridge as much as all that. I have duties there," she said, laughing.

"And how is his lordship the Bishop, if I may ask?" said Mary in a prim voice.

Prudence replied suitably, feeling, however, that somehow Mary was implying that Wellende was being neglected for the welfare of her father. Mary was upper housemaid at Wellende, but she was more than that. She had been there as long as Prudence could remember, always keeping herself rigidly in the background. Mary practically ruled the house. It was she actually, and Lord Wellende only nominally, who selected the housekeeper and the occasional new servants that were wanted. The housekeeper was considered new for an upper servant; she had only been there ten years.

At dinner Wellende and Prudence discussed the prospects of hunting and local news, with occasional interruptions from Dunning as he waited.

"I hope my not arriving yesterday wasn't too great a disappointment to you, Ben," said Prudence.

"I bore up; as a matter of fact it was as well, because I was out myself last night."

"You out!" exclaimed Prudence. "You don't mean to tell me you have taken to dining out in your old age!"

Dunning here permitted himself an audible chuckle.

"No, it wasn't quite as bad as that, I was duck-shooting."

"Of course," said Prudence, "how stupid of me, I had forgotten that possibility. I am still unacclimatized to the air of Wellende, and out in the evening suggests dining out to my suburban mind, before I think of duck-shooting."

"We'll soon cure you of that. I had a school managers' meeting this morning. We've got to get a new mistress for the village school, and a golden-haired lady has applied for the post."

"Who are the managers?" said Prudence.

"Well, the ones that attended this morning were Woodcock and Abel Lundy—farms Stanny House Farm, you know—and myself. She got me cornered, the lady did," chuckled Wellende. "Suddenly asked me what my views were about Clause 8 under Schedule B—or something of the sort—but Woodcock came to my assistance by asking her if she ever took a hand at halfpenny nap. And they got off to talking about halfpenny nap, which saved me; hadn't the foggiest notion what Clause B Schedule 8 might be."

"You must be a priceless collection as school managers—you, Lundy, and Woodcock," laughed Prudence.

"It's the best we can raise, anyway; the golden-haired lady evidently agreed with you, for she declined the job; an occasional evening in the big room at the 'Plough and Sail' for halfpenny nap is about the only dissipation there is to offer."

After dinner the cousins repaired to Wellende's own particular den. There were deep window seats, for the walls were very thick at the Old Hall, and a large, old-fashioned fire-place. Sporting prints decorated the walls, and over the fire-place a print, done from a photograph, of the late Lord Wellende as Lord-Lieutenant of the county. A good-sized bookshelf occupied one wall, with a miscellaneous collection—"Handley Cross," Sponge's "Sporting Tour," and "Happy Thoughts," a few books of travel (Ben never left home if he could help it), and some books on veterinary surgery. Ben pulled up a comfortable chair and arranged some cushions in it for Prudence, and then lit his pipe.

"You've seen Mary, I suppose?" he said. "Did she talk to you much?"

"Yes, I've seen her, she was unpacking for me; she wasn't as full of chat as usual. She somehow managed to convey that I had failed in my duty in not coming here this summer. I felt, anyhow, that something was wrong."

Wellende didn't speak for a moment, then he said suddenly: "The ghost has been heard again, with the inevitable trouble with the servants."

"Never!" exclaimed Prudence, looking up with surprise and interest. "The old thing, I suppose—footsteps?"

"Yes," said Wellende, "and the sound of animals scurrying about which have always been heard, you know. I have moved the servants out of that wing; only Mary sleeps there now, she doesn't mind; and I have locked up all the cellars. If it worries you at all, Prue, you can have another room, but Mary was indignant when I suggested it. I suppose it *is* insulting to suppose that you, with your intellect and education, believe in ghosts; but I don't know," he continued with a grin, "you fairly legged it when a rat came along, and you may have a whatever-you-call-it against ghosts."

"But I *do* believe in places being haunted, Ben—with my intellect I'd be a fool if I didn't; but that's not saying I believe a person with armoured feet really walks about this house. Everyone but you believes this place is haunted."

"I'm like you, I don't say ghosts are impossible; I only have to take that line because of the servants. On the other hand, it would be very hard to say in this house what was ghosts and what was not;

the wind here is enough to account for anything, and I have noticed, too, that through all the years when the ghost has been heard or seen it's always been when there's a howling gale. I have come down myself at night, perfectly certain that I heard someone cutting glass in the library below me, only to find it was the wind just beginning to get up and whistling round the buttress outside; there's no sound invented that can't be heard some night or other, when there's a wind."

"It's getting up a bit now," said Prudence. "There's one sound I always connect with Wellende, and that's the extraordinary draught that comes up the wastes of the baths."

"Yes," said Wellende, "I don't think they managed them very well. I don't get it much in my bath-room, but I have noticed it whistling up the others."

"To-night, as I lay in my hot bath," said Prudence, "I could almost hear the cold seawater of the creek flapping against the walls of the house. One gets one's enjoyment so much by contrast, and that sound made my bath seem warmer and more comfortable than ever!"

CHAPTER IX

I N SPITE OF TALK ABOUT GHOSTS, IN SPITE OF A WINDY NIGHT,
Prudence's slumbers were unbroken and untroubled. She awoke
next morning to hear her curtains being drawn and to see the sun
pouring in.

"It's a glorious day for a hunt, Mary," said Prudence.

"It's a fine morning, miss," said Mary, "and Dunning asked me
to say what would you take out in your flask, and he would send it
round to the stables for you."

"A little water and a lot of sherry, tell him," said Prudence, "and
I shall come home early whatever happens."

She dressed, and came down to breakfast to find Lord Wellende
already at it. Dressed in white breeches, slippers, and an old Norfolk
jacket, he was discussing a large helping of kidney and bacon.

"How is it," said Prudence, "that in pictures men are always to
be seen sitting about the house in their pink coats, either before or
after hunting? *I* never met a man yet that kept his coat on a moment
longer than he need."

"How is it," replied Wellende, with his mouth full, "that women
in story-books always come down to breakfast in top-boots and
breeches, dressed like a man? I am so glad, Prue, you don't ride
astride."

"I'm sure you are, old thing," laughed Prudence. "But I don't
believe you ever read a 'story-book,' and the only reason I don't ride
astride is because I can't stick on. However, I may outrage all your
feelings to-day; I've a lovely pair of new top-boots, and if I can manage
it, I am going to take a toss into a ditch, and remain on my head for

a few moments with my legs sticking up in the air, so that everyone can see the glories of my boots."

"If you can do it without breaking your neck," said Wellende, "I have no objection."

All the meets were some way from the Hall, which lay on the edge of the hunting country, and the cousins motored there. Prudence met various old friends, with whom she had to have a few words, but once mounted, her attention was very fully taken up by her mare, who was fresh and fidgety. For the first hour hounds hunted round and round a large covert, the fox declining to break. Then in the far distance came that soul-stirring screech of "Gone away!" Prudence hurried at once to where the cry had come from, to get there in time to see the huntsmen making a cast in a ploughed field. There was a little pause, then one hound whimpered, two spoke to it, and then, encouraged by the huntsman, there was a sudden crash of music, and the whole pack went away at a racing speed on the line.

"My word," thought Prudence, "the scent must be good, at the pace they are going," and she sat down in her saddle to do her best.

A fast ten minutes, to Prudence's infinite relief, ended in a check; she had only just time to get her breath, and off they were again across a grass field. They hunted the same fox backwards and forwards for some time, till at last, when he headed straight away, Prudence, who was not yet in condition, gave up and turned for home. Her mare was tired and steadied down now, so she threw one leg over the saddle astride, and began on the sandwiches. The sound of the hunt soon died down in the distance, and Prudence was left to the peace and quiet of the country-side, the hot smell of her horse mingled with the reek of a chemical manure on the field near by. The clucking of chickens, the occasional barking of a dog, blended with the soughing of the wind in the trees.

Presently she heard the "clop, clop" of a horse behind her, and turned to greet an old friend, Laura Heale, the wife of the local doctor. Mrs. Heale was the essence of the country; she had no children, but she had dogs and horses; she wore thick boots and had a weather-beaten face; she probably got astride a horse six days of the week, all the year round, and if her man was out with the doctor, she thought nothing of grooming her own horse after a day's hunting herself. She liked and admired Prudence, but from the bottom of her heart she believed that life in Cambridge was stagnation, and that Prudence didn't begin to live until she got to Wellende and on a horse again.

"My horse cast a shoe—isn't it infernal luck! and I haven't another one out this mornin'. But what are you doin', goin' home in the middle of a run?"

"My dear Laura," said Prudence, "remember you don't know what it is to be out of condition. This is my first day. I haven't even been out cubbing."

"No," said Mrs. Heale, "it's an unnatural life you have to lead in Cambridge, and no one with any sense or knowledge in the place."

"Oh, I don't know so much about that," demurred Prudence.

"My dear Prudence," said Mrs. Heale, "I met one of your professors the other day, and I give you my word for it, he was mad."

"Yes," said Prudence equably, "heaps of them are, you know. I wonder who it was you met?"

"I thought as I listened to him talkin', if this is a specimen of the men Prudence has to live among, I wonder she has any sense left. I asked him if the Trinity Beagles had moved their kennels, and he said he didn't know. I asked him how many times a week they hunted; he didn't know. I asked him if he knew anythin', and he said 'Very little'; then, though you'd hardly believe me, he said: 'Let me see, what do the beagles do, do they look about till they think they see a hare'!"

"Think they *see* a hare!"—indignation at the very memory of it left Mrs. Heale speechless. Prudence laughed.

"My dear old Laura, he was having you on. He saw you thought him a fool, you aren't very good at concealing your thoughts, you know, and so he pretended to be one. I dare say half was ignorance and the other half pose."

"It was ignorance, all right," replied Mrs. Heale. "Here, Prudence, ride on the other side of me, I want to get my horse on the grass."

Prudence did as she was requested.

"There's a story, you know," she said, "that an American dining at the high table in Trinity, asked how many wives Henry VIII had had. They've a picture after Holbein of Henry VIII hanging there, and though there were several Fellows present, no one knew, and the head waiter supplied the information. Now, I can well believe that story is true. Out of the eight, say, who were there, five probably really didn't know, and the other three were posing. Same with your professor; he pretended to be more ignorant than he was."

"I don't believe that," said Mrs. Heale shrewdly. "He wasn't the sort to be humble about anythin'. Why, he had the beastly cheek to correct somethin' Ben said about injectin' dogs against distemper, and Ben's about the best vet. in England, and so I let him know."

"I wonder who he was. Probably not a professor at all. Where did you meet him, Laura?"

"At Wellende, he was some sort of relation of Ben's, though I've never seen him before."

"You don't mean—it can't have been Professor Temple?" exclaimed Prudence in great surprise.

Mrs. Heale thought for a moment. "I really don't remember ever hearin' for certain what his name was, only that he was a cousin of Ben's, and I think they called him doctor."

"Was he a tall, dark man with whiskers?"

"That's him, and nasty whiskers, somehow," said Mrs. Heale. "He hadn't been groomed for a week, and he looked as if he'd murder you for twopence; fact is, I didn't like that man."

"Well," said Prudence, "I *am* surprised. I can hardly believe it really was him. There was a family quarrel and I have never known him come to Wellende."

"If I was Ben," said Mrs. Heale, "the family quarrel would go on. I didn't like that man!"

The friends parted soon, and Prudence jogged on home alone, thinking over the news she had just heard. As long as she could remember there had been a quarrel between Lord Wellende and his cousin, Professor Temple. She had never known what about, and now she came to think of it, she hadn't the least idea why; she supposed it was something really serious or she would have known. She made a mental resolve to ask her father, it would be better than asking Ben.

She slid stiffly from her saddle in the stable-yard, and crawled slowly up to her room. There she found a good fire and Mary. Her dressing-gown was laid out across a chair, and bedroom slippers, looking so comfortable and soft after top-boots, were warming in the grate.

"Now you get into your bath, miss," said Mary, "and I'll go down and get you a nice cup of hot strong tea, that'll do you good."

The bath done, the tea arrived, and Prudence settled herself with a sigh of comfort and fatigue in her soft chair. Mary, with the privilege of an old friend, sat down too.

"I rode home with Mrs. Heale," said Prudence. "She told me she had met a man here who sounded like Professor Temple. *Has* he stayed here?"

"Yes, miss," said Mary, "and I'll be bound Mrs. Heale didn't take to him."

"No," said Prudence, "she did not; but you know, Mary, appearances are against him. He's not so bad when you really get to know him."

A mulish expression overspread Mary's homely face. She looked almost grim.

To Prudence's surprise, she made no reply; she got up, opened the door, and shut it again firmly, and then did the same by the large cupboard door; then she came and sat down.

"There's something I've 'ad on my mind I must say to you, Miss Prudence. 'As 'is lordship said anything to you about them attacks of sickness 'e's 'ad of late?"

"No," said Prudence in surprise. She also noticed that all Mary's *h*'s were gone, which only occurred when she was frightened or angry.

"'E's never 'ardly 'ad a day's illness in his life, but 'e's 'ad three attacks of sickness lately, and each one 'as been after that there doctor 'as been 'ere."

"What *do* you mean, Mary?" exclaimed Prudence in real consternation. "Do you realize what you are implying?"

"I know what I'm saying, miss, well enough, and that's what's true. That doctor's been here three times, and each time 'is lordship 'as been unwell *afterwards*—though he's mighty put out if anyone says anything to him of it. Says it's nothing, and don't you let on to his lordship I've said a word to you about 'is being unwell, only I had to do it."

This last all came out in one breath. Prudence saw that Mary was genuinely moved, but the inference she was making was so preposterous she hardly knew how to deal with it. "It can only have been chance, his being ill like that each time," she said helplessly.

Then again: "Do you mean you don't want me to mention it to his lordship at all?"

"Not his being ill, miss, but you can mention the professor, or doctor, or whatever he is, being here."

CHAPTER X

THERE WAS A LONG PAUSE. YEARS OF EXPERIENCE OF MARY'S determined character had taught Prudence the uselessness of just pooh-poohing any idea she might have got into her head, and what else was she to say, except that it was utterly ridiculous?

Mary, keeping a vigilant eye on Prudence to see how she was taking it, went on:

"There's more to it than just that, miss. Do you know what it was they quarrelled about years ago?"

"No," said Prudence, and then with a sudden sense of caution: "What makes you think there was a quarrel?"

"You forget I was here at the time, miss. The last time the doctor came he was only Mr. Francis then; it must be nigh on thirty years ago, and something happened. It was 'ushed up, and Mr. Francis, as he was then, left the Hall very sudden."

"I haven't the least idea what they quarrelled about," said Prudence. "I don't think I ever asked, but what was it you were going to tell me—something else you said?" for Prudence suddenly felt there might be things about the family which she did not want to discuss, even with a faithful old friend like Mary. She must ask her father about that quarrel.

"It's this, miss. You know his lordship sometimes gets coal and wood up to the house by water?"

"Yes," said Prudence, "I think I knew it."

"Well, miss, the last barge-load of wood that came up was while the doctor was here; and there was a young chap unloading I ain't seen before. He wasn't one of the woodmen. I was standing at the library window, wondering how a cobweb had got there. The doctor was sitting on that garden-seat smoking, and the young man I see walked along, passed 'im, and without stopping as he walked by I 'eard 'im say to the doctor, 'I landed your lot where you told me without being seen, sir.' If I 'adn't been in the window no one would have suspected 'im of 'aving spoken, and I 'eard it, miss, for certain I 'eard it."

"I must get this straight," said Prudence. "You mean Dr. Temple was sitting smoking on the bench on the terrace and you heard this young man say that sentence as he walked by without stopping?"

"Yes, miss."

"You're quite certain those were the words?"

"I am absolutely certain, miss."

"But what was the man doing on the terrace?"

"There were three men on the barge, and they had come up that way to the bailiff's room to be paid."

Prudence thought deeply. "Did you see the others pass too?"

"I didn't actually see the first, and after the young man passed, the doctor went away. I saw the skipper, as they call him, but the doctor was gone then."

Prudence couldn't make head or tail of it. Mary was a person of no imagination whatever; she simply hadn't the wit to invent such a tale, therefore she probably had heard it. How, then, to account for such words, let alone the manner in which they had been delivered?

"Eh, but it's my lamb I've had since a baby," came the cry, and quite suddenly Mary, the self-contained, precise, undemonstrative Mary, broke down and wept. The bent figure, in her black dress and white apron, the old hands, knobbly from hard work, pressed shaking against her face—the heartfelt cry of love for her baby—made a pathetic appeal indeed. Prudence knelt on the floor by the old woman and put her arms round her.

"My dear, dear old friend," she said, "it's not that—it's not what you think."

She soothed the poor old woman for a bit, and then got up, rinsed out her cup, and made Mary have a drink of her own beloved beverage, hot and strong.

"There," said Prudence soothingly, "there's nothing like a good cup of strong tea if you're upset," quoting the words she had so often heard Mary use.

"There ain't, miss, and that's a fac'," and then she added more shakily: "I am fair ashamed of myself, but I've had no one I could speak to about it; I couldn't go to Mrs. Sims, I couldn't speak about the family like this to no one but you, miss."

"I should think not, indeed," said Prudence; "but I still think the best thing is to go straight to his lordship and tell him everything."

"It wouldn't never do, miss," said Mary earnestly. "I have tried to say something about the doctor, but his lordship is very touchy on the subject. 'E would never, never take it that 'is own cousin was—was—" Here Mary began to sob afresh.

"Mary," said Prudence firmly, "if you are thinking that the doctor is making any attempt on his lordship's life, you are quite wrong. I think I know what it is he is trying to do, and though it's very wrong and must be stopped, it's nothing like that. Now do you realize what I am saying? It wouldn't suit the doctor at all if anything were to happen to his lordship."

"Yes, miss," mopping her eyes and stopping crying, "it's no end of a relief just to have told you."

Prudence thought for a bit, then she asked: "Was Woodcock about that day, when that load of wood came?"

"Yes, miss; at least I didn't actually see him, but he's always there when a load comes up; he has to do with all the wood that comes into the house."

"Did you see the doctor speak to him at all?"

"No, miss; I shouldn't have been in the way to see it even if he had, but Woodcock's all right, miss—he'd do anything for his lordship."

Yes, thought Prudence, but that would not necessarily prevent him from being ready to do a bit more for himself. Was this really, she wondered, the trouble that Captain Studde had warned her of? Was it possible that Doctor Temple and Woodcock were getting drugs through this way, under the cover of Wellende's position? What was to prevent a motor-boat from Holland or Belgium meeting one of Lord Wellende's barges of wood at sea and passing them the drug which they bring up the river? Then Dr. Temple comes to stay and gets it. Prudence thought he would have been as much as eighteen years old when the quarrel took place; he might have remembered the way about the old house. What a diabolical plan! and how hard for an outsider to spot! In the ordinary way one could go out and in at the mouth of the river without any interference; in fact, there was very seldom a soul about, it was all lonely marsh country, except for a few cottages where, Prudence vaguely thought, coast-guards had once lived. Studde had just been telling her that this sort of thing was going on for certain, and that he suspected Woodcock of doing something he shouldn't behind his master's back. *How* she wished she could go straight to Ben and tell him everything; but she had promised Studde, so she could not. On the other hand, she couldn't go to Studde and tell him; if it was true, it was too serious, and she would not care about bringing disgrace on so near a relation of Ben's. If it was all a mare's nest, she would have made a fool of herself, and that was what Miss Pinsent would have disliked most of all.

She looked reflectively at Mary. Now that she had eased her mind of the burden she carried alone, and put it on another's shoulders, Mary seemed to have ceased to worry. Either because she had always been in a dependent position, and Prudence was one "of the family," or else because she was really old, and Prudence was so much younger; now that the responsibility was no longer hers, it didn't even seem to occur to Mary to ask Prudence what she thought the meaning of all this was. For this Prudence was devoutly thankful.

"His lordship was telling me," said Prudence, after a long pause, "that the ghosts have been seen and heard again."

"Yes, miss."

"Is it possible," said Prudence slowly, "that there can be any connection between the ghosts and this business we are talking of?"

"Yes, miss."

Prudence looked at Mary with eager interest. Mary went on: "It was that very night the sounds were 'eard. It was only 'earsay on the part of the girls. I was the only one that saw," grimly, "and I said nothing. Those silly girls sat up all night and then were late down in the morning, but I came down as usual, and the barge of wood was up against the house by six-thirty—that means she came up at night, and that, as you very well know, miss, means that either Woodcock or his lordship was aboard of her, and it wasn't his lordship, so now I come to think of it, Woodcock must ha' bin there, though I never see him."

Mary paused and thought.

"But you said you saw something of the ghost," said Prudence. "What did you see?"

"It was like this," said Mary. "One of those girls had woke up screaming because she heard sloppy footsteps round her bed and some water had been left on her face which hadn't been there before, and well I could believe it of her," bitterly, "as I told 'er—if 'er face was more used to water it would be the better for all of us."

"Yes, yes," said Prudence impatiently, "but what of the ghost?"

"She and the other girl that sleeps with her came screaming in to me, but I soon packed them off back again. There was some scuffling sounds, I thought. Anyhow, I looked out of my window before getting back to bed, and I had Snap in my arms; he'd not been well, and he was sleeping with me; and then I'm bothered if I didn't see what looked like a dog tumble out of one of the cellar windows and go across just that corner of the lawn you can see from my window, and it wasn't no ghost, for Snap saw it too and barked."

"How very odd," said Prudence. "You mean the cellar window that's only half underground?"

"That's it, miss, the one you can see from my bedroom window."

"Was the barge up by then?" said Prudence.

"I'm sure I couldn't say, miss. I can't see the creek from my room."

Prudence thought for a little, then she said, "Did Snap actually bark or growl?"

"Well… perhaps it was half and half… I think," hesitatingly, "he may have begun with a growl and ended barking," replied Mary.

"The reason why I ask," said Prudence, "is that dogs do see the supernatural more, I think, than humans, and if it had been anything of that sort I fancy he would have growled more than barked. Did he seem much frightened?"

"I couldn't really say, miss," said Mary, somewhat vaguely, for she hadn't the least idea what Miss Pinsent meant by the "supernatural," or what she was driving at. "His lordship sleeps so far off that, of course, he 'eard nothing at all. In the morning, when Mrs. Sims told him, 'e was much put about, and angry about it, and he's locked up all the cellars and sent those silly girls to sleep in the attics of the other wing."

CHAPTER XI

I T WAS WITH VERY MIXED FEELINGS THAT PRUDENCE JOINED HER cousin for dinner. She had made up her mind that there was nothing she could do at present but keep her eyes open and her mouth shut. She found Lord Wellende spread in a comfortable arm-chair in front of the huge log fire in the hall. The hall was a large panelled room; a black and white stone floor was covered by fur rugs near the fire, and bits of old armour and pictures of bygone Temples decorated the walls. There was a bank of chrysanthemums in one corner and a bowl of violets scented the whole place. There were one or two electric bulbs burning against the walls, lighting up the pictures, but most of the light came from the log fire. A more comfortable and peaceful scene would have been hard to find.

"Why, Prue, where on earth had you got to this afternoon? I looked for you everywhere."

"Well, I am ashamed to say I turned back. The two hours we hunted round and round those coverts were enough for me, and when the fox headed straight away from home… I, well, I shirked."

"I wouldn't have believed it of you," said her cousin with a smile, stretching his long legs and settling down more comfortably than ever into his chair.

"You and Laura Heale simply don't know what it means to be out of condition. I shall go all the better on Friday for having taken it easily to-day."

"You missed a jolly good run. We ran fast and without a check to Abel Lundy's, there hounds were at fault for a moment or two, then away again over some plough in the direction of Sedgeford."

"How many were up by then?" interrupted Prudence.

"Oh, a dozen or two, I should think. I am glad to say I had young Lundy riding in front of me, and softening my fences for me. I have got to that time of life when I like to have 'em eased a bit. Lundy is a thruster, and a real good 'un to go."

"Yes," said Prudence, "you always say young Lundy is so good across country, and there are few who can hold their own with him—largely because he's the son of one of your own tenants, and you like him; but the Norshires, for instance, I have heard run him down; they say some other young farmer is far the best in the Wellende Hunt; so even among people who really *do* know, it all seems to boil down into a question of personal liking as to who rides straightest. Why, I have even heard one of your grooms maintain that 'there is no one can ride across Suffolk like his lordship, when his lordship wants to go! '"—with a laugh.

Wellende laughed too; he certainly made no pretence now that he was forty of being in the first flight of thrusters.

"It's not as bad as that," said he; "there's no mistaking a really good man on a horse, of the class of Lundy, whether you like him or no; as for the groom, that was a bit of loyalty. He knows as well as I do, really, that I don't go hard now; he isn't going to admit it, that's all."

The discussion about the day's hunt went on through dinner.

"What beats me," said Prudence, "is how you masters of hounds can sit down and allow the fox to be headed so often as he is; that fox to-day would have broken covert long before he did, if he had had a chance; but you allow groups of people to go all round the covert and all talking and laughing, without any effort to stop them."

"We do try to stop it; what do you suppose I have a field-master for, besides myself?"

"I am sure I have often wondered. I've never seen you herd all the field into one corner and keep them there till the fox has gone away; that would be the way to do it."

"My dear girl, this is a subscription hunt, and people would be furious if I did that kind of thing. If they moved about quietly without laughing and talking, they wouldn't head the fox; and, after all, they all want him to break covert; no one wants to head him."

"They may not actually want to head him," said Prudence, "but quite half the people who come out hunting are indifferent and even ignorant as to the real sport. All they think of is so many fences and a gallop; they neither know nor care anything about the real hunting."

"Yes," agreed Wellende, "I suppose there are a large proportion like that; they ought to go out with drag-hounds, of course."

"Do you remember that Mrs. Cox who used to be down here? Came from the shires, I think, and had hunted all her life," said Prudence.

"Face like a hungry tiger, and lived at Rennsholt. Yes, I remember her," said Wellende.

"Well, one day," said Prudence, "when for a wonder the whole field was boxed up in a lane, Mrs. Cox was near me, and she exclaimed: 'Oh, I wish they would do something! how dull this is!' and the hounds were making a cast by themselves in the next ploughed field; she could see it all, and it's one of the prettiest sights in the world, but her eyes were blind through ignorance, and she never even looked at them. I didn't make any comment," said Miss Pinsent, pushing out her chin. "I really didn't think she was worth it."

"That's right, Prue," laughed Wellende; "turn up your aristocratic nose at that sort. Anyhow, when all's said and done, it was a d—d good fox that would take us for two hours round and round those coverts, and then make a six-mile point."

"If you'll excuse me speaking, your lordship," said Dunning, "but I am of opinion that it was a fresh fox you went away on, because Mr. Woodcock and I was standing together, and we saw the hunted fox heading back for the dyke."

"Get out with you, Dunning," said his lordship good-temperedly; "the fox you saw had been routed out along with the other; there were two on the move, but we went away on the right one."

After dinner the cousins moved into the smoking-room.

"What comfort this is!" said Prudence, as she took a sip of her benedictine and a whiff at her cigarette. She looked across at her cousin; his pleasant, well-bred face, burnt by continual exposure to all weathers, with an expression of peaceful satisfaction; his thoughts still obviously running on the good hunt he had enjoyed that day. It was wildly impossible to think anyone wanted to take this man's life!

He was just one of those you would say hadn't an enemy in the world. Other things, however, were possible.

"Ben," she suddenly said, "I rode home with Laura Heale. She told me Professor Temple had been staying here. I *was* surprised."

As she spoke, Wellende's expression changed completely. Prudence didn't feel sure if it was caution, or merely that there was no expression at all on his face as he answered:

"Yes, I am glad to say he has taken to coming here again. It's high time he should, and he seems to like it."

Prudence was longing to ask him what the cause of the quarrel had been, but Lord Wellende was not the sort of person with whom one took liberties, nor, for that matter, was Miss Pinsent the sort of person to take them. The fear that the quarrel might have been something very personal kept her silent.

"Laura Heale fell very foul of him," she said instead; "she really thinks he is mad because he didn't know what the Trinity beagles hunt, and she was very indignant with him for presuming to contradict you about distemper among dogs."

Wellende chuckled. "Yes, they didn't hit it off very well. Francis told me after, he had found old Laura an uninteresting specimen—'her information is limited, her understanding mean; I should diagnose her as neither male nor female.'"

"What a shame!" laughed Prudence.

Here Dunning came in to ask if there were any more orders, and to bring in two old-fashioned bedroom candlesticks, a habit still kept up, in spite of the electric light. When they were alone again she began:

"Ben, I want a long day out in the motor-boat. I thought I would go the day after to-morrow."

"Yes, that would do very well if it's fine, as I happen to be shooting away from home that day."

"I don't mind about the weather," said Prudence, "except fog—I do bar that—but a good blow or rain I simply enjoy."

Wellende looked at her contemplatively. "I believe there's a lot of our buccaneering ancestors left in you, Prue, though I can't imagine anyone who looks less like it. I believe you'd love to 'run' a cargo still, and you'd never be suspected of it."

Prudence coloured, and remarked with some constraint that of course the time for that sort of thing was long over.

Wellende did not reply; he sat back in his chair, crossed his legs, and pulled at his pipe. "You can have Stevens with you, only you must let him know to-morrow."

"Oh, Ben, you know quite well I hate having anyone with me; it would take away all the pleasure. I like a long day quite alone."

"Yes, I know you do, but I don't half like your doing it. Stevens really wouldn't be in your way."

"Yes, he would; he would just spoil everything."

"A wilful woman…" began Lord Wellende.

"Yes, yes, she must have her way, so you'd better give up the contest."

"All right," replied he, "only don't blame me if you're drowned."

"I won't, dear," said Prudence.

CHAPTER XII

N EXT AFTERNOON, AS THE COUSINS WERE WALKING HOME
down the avenue after a visit to the kennels, Wellende informed
Prudence that he would be out that evening duck-shooting. There was
fog hanging about over the marshes, the cattle were standing knee-
deep in it; some sea-gulls came screeching by overhead, hidden by the
mist, and as he spoke there came the sound of a foghorn out to sea.

"There's the Outer Gabbard braying, and the Shipwash has been
bleating all day; it's evidently thick out to sea, and it's getting thick
here; you'll never see enough to shoot, will you?"

"It may lift," replied Wellende, "and if it does there's a good moon,
and there's a flight of widgeon on the river I particularly want a go at."

Prudence thought for a bit. "Do you take Woodcock with you,
duck-shooting?"

"No," said he, "I go alone with my spaniel." And so it came about
that Prudence spent the evening alone. It was one of those rare eve-
nings at Wellende when there was no wind; it had come up thick, as
Prudence had foretold, and the absolute silence and stillness round
the house was only broken by the faint sounds of the foghorns on
the far distant lightships at sea. If ever there was an unsuitable evening for duck-shooting it was to-night, she thought, and wondered at
Ben's considering it worth trying.

Dunning had been in with one candle which he had put down for
her. She was just considering whether she would read or work, when
she heard a scuffle; it seemed so nearly under her chair that she leapt
from it with a stifled scream, and gathering her petticoats tight round
her, she climbed on to the writing-table. From this safe position she

peered anxiously into the dark corners of the room. Another scuffle, from another direction, and a thud, and Miss Pinsent realized with relief that it was rats under the floor. She descended from the table, but it had shaken her nerve, and she decided to take her candle and go and finish her reading by her own bedroom fire. The rats at Wellende seemed to be getting worse.

The heavily engraven "coat" of the Temples on the candlestick she carried set her mind off in another direction. Yes, her forbears on her mother's side must have had some stirring times in this very same house, and she wondered as she went slowly up the stairs how many of the faces that were looking down at her had smuggled. Probably all of them. There had been a secret stairway to the cellars from the house somewhere, but Ben always said it was filled up a hundred years ago when smuggling ceased, and he had never been very ready to talk about it; said he didn't know where it was, and as Prudence undressed she began to wonder if it could possibly have been opened again, and in use; but anyhow, she decided, it couldn't possibly be used by anyone without Ben's knowledge.

At this point of her meditations she got into her bath. The usual sound of the wind was not coming from the bath waste, but she could hear the flap of water against the wall of the house, as she rolled over comfortably at full length in the bath. Then there came another sound; Miss Pinsent suddenly sat upright with a look of intent consternation; she put her ear to the waste—yes, there it was again. It was an unmistakable whistle, very soft and very tuneful. The whistler stopped, and then after a little pause began again, for all the world as if he was waiting for someone. Then the whistling stopped, and though she listened, she could not hear a voice at all, only some muffled sounds.

She sat for a moment considering; to the best of her knowledge the waste from that bath must go down to the water of the creek under the house, therefore… she leapt hastily from her bath, wrapped her huge towel round her, got into her dressing-gown, and crept back into her bedroom without turning on the lights. She felt her way to one of the windows, and very slowly and quietly opened it, and put her head cautiously out. It was quite thick outside, and not possible to see more than five or six yards, and then only dimly, and Prudence drew her dressing-gown closer round her and waited. The window she was looking out of was immediately over the arch where the creek went under the house.

There wasn't a sound to be heard here, not even the sound of flapping water. After a short time, a dark point emerged from underneath her; she dimly discerned that it was the bow of a boat. She drew her head in a bit, only allowing enough to appear just to enable her to see over the sill. A man's figure was standing up in the middle of the boat, pushing it along very quietly by reaching against the sides of the house; and what looked like another figure was in the boat with him. Prudence could only see that it was a man in an overcoat and slouch hat; it was too foggy to see more, and she thought it better to withdraw her head as soon as he appeared. Evidently the sound of flapping water that had come up through the bath waste was the water pushed by the passage of the boat in the tunnel under the house; once outside it had made no sound at all.

Prudence, though all agog with curiosity, didn't venture to look out again, in case the man in the boat should look up.

She went back to the bath-room, dried herself and put on some more clothes, slowly and thoughtfully, and then went along the passage to Mary's bedroom. The opening of the door woke the old servant up, and Prudence sat down and told her all she had seen.

"Fancy that!" said Mary; "just fancy that! I've always noticed how the wind blows up them wastes, blows dirt up, too, sometimes, just when I've cleaned the bath, but I've never thought to *hear* things down 'em."

Then as she got out of bed and put on an old dressing-gown: "Just come with me now, Miss Prudence; there's something I've had in my mind to show you." And she led Prudence back to her own bedroom.

"You wait here a moment, miss. I'll be back."

Prudence sat down by the fire, puzzled and worried. In a short time Mary was back again with a screwdriver in her hand.

"It was some years ago, miss, when this room was repapered. I was giving it a good turn-out, and one of the window seats got loose, and I pulled it right off; and underneath—it fair took my breath away—there's a large hole straight down to the cellars."

As she spoke, she went to one of the window-seats set in the thickness of the wall, threw off the cushion, and started to unscrew the wooden seat beneath.

"I said nothing about it—it was when his lordship was away. I just screwed it down myself, and don't rightly know why I never spoke of it to his lordship; but I never have, and I don't even know whether he knows of it."

By this time she had got the screws out, and lifting the wooden seat, displayed a fairly wide oubliette up which came the damp smell of the vaults.

Prudence was speechless with interest and astonishment. She had a small electric bulb which she switched on, and held down the pipe or funnel.

"It's all stone," she said, "and look, Mary, at those dark places. I believe they are dents in the stone that would enable someone to climb up or down."

Mary shuddered. "Shut it up, miss. I don't like it," she said.

The two women set to and put the screws back and screwed them tight down, and then they sat down to consider the situation.

"Mind you," said Prudence, "we don't know for certain that whoever was in that boat to-night was doing anything wrong."

"Ho, don't we?" said Mary. "Then why does 'e do it at night, and just the night his lordship is out?"

"Yes, of course, it *looks* bad," conceded Prudence.

"It looks bad, and it is bad, miss," said Mary firmly, and then after a pause, "I was wondering when I could be certain of a quiet time to show you that place, miss, without having one of those girls comin' into the room, and now I've done it."

"You get back to bed, and I will think all this over." Prudence put some more coals on the fire, and made a good blaze, which made the room look cheerful and bright, and then settled down in front of the fire to think. She half whistled, half hissed the tune she had heard coming up the bath waste to herself. Yes, there was no doubt about it, it was the *motif* in the G Minor Mozart quintet. There would not be many people who would whistle that so correctly—she had some difficulty in doing it herself. Woodcock would certainly not know it. Ben's ideas of music consisted chiefly in "Old Joe" and "John Peel"; still he could whistle very well, she thought with a sinking heart.

It was quite impossible to be sure who the men in the boat were; it might equally well have been Woodcock or his master. She had Captain Studde's word for it that he believed Woodcock was engaged in some sort of smuggling without his master's knowledge. On the other hand, she had Mary's unshaken belief that Woodcock would do nothing against his master's interests, which she was very much inclined to believe herself. Worst of all was the story Mary had told her about the Professor landing something surreptitiously in the

house, because she now felt quite certain that whatever Professor
Temple was doing in the house must be with Ben's knowledge, and
that brought her to the hitherto unconsidered possibility that it was
Wellende himself in the boat.

Now if she went to him and told him simply what she had seen,
she was, in fact, either making a very serious accusation against an old
and trusted servant, or she was prying into Wellende's own private
affairs, neither of which lines she cared to take. Finally she decided
to say nothing.

Harry Studde, she thought, can do his own dirty work, for I am
quite sure Woodcock is not harming Ben.

CHAPTER XIII

N EXT MORNING WHEN PRUDENCE WOKE, AND FOUND THE FOG gone, the wind sighing gently round the house, and the sun streaming in at her window, she felt as if the past night had all been a dream. Mary came and called her as usual, making no sort of reference to their nocturnal adventures.

At breakfast she found her cousin, clad in hobnailed boots and a sporting check suit, somewhat ripe in years, but still bearing the unmistakable stamp of a good tailor. Evidently the new suit, though bought, was not yet being worn. He seemed cheerful, admitted she had been right about the weather last night, and as he had never had a shot, had come back early.

"Where do you keep your gun-punt?" said Prudence.

"Moored off the jetty," he answered.

"Don't you use the creek up to the house, when you are going duck-shooting?" said Prudence.

"No, never, it's far more trouble to get down than just walking straight to the jetty and getting off from there."

Prudence agreed as they got up from the table, Wellende was lighting his pipe. Prudence said:

"What tune is this, Ben?" and she proceeded to hum to the best of her ability, though rather badly, the air from the quintet. Wellende gave it his serious attention, and then said:

"It isn't a tune at all, old thing; try again."

Prudence did try again, then gave it up and tried to whistle.

"Ah, now I've got it," said Wellende, "this is what you are after," and in a tuneful whistle he rendered "Pop goes the weasel."

"How trying you are," laughed Prudence, "this is what I am whistling," and she made another effort, but finally had to give it up.

He obviously did not or would not know what she was after. If it *was* him in the boat last night, he certainly did not intend her to know it. In that case he was undoubtedly doing something secret, and her common sense obliged her to recognize the fact that it was very unusual for a man in his position to be doing anything secret about his own house at night. Also, it was quite impossible for someone else, like Professor Temple, to be doing anything secret in that house without Ben being aware of it. She didn't like it.

She looked at his quiet face, and her thoughts were interrupted by his asking her her plans.

"Yes, I am off directly after breakfast. Mrs. Sims is getting me lunch, and I shall be home by tea-time."

"You won't take Stevens, I suppose?" said Wellende hopefully.

"No, I won't—'a wilful woman'—yes, I know all about that, and I won't blame you when I am drowned!"

"Well, don't be a fool and go out of the river, Prue; the bar is always shifting."

"Yes, I know it is. I thought I might go down to the mouth and anchor there, and have my lunch, and then come back."

By the time Prudence got down to the old wooden jetty and got off to the motor-boat in a dinghy, the tide had just begun to ebb. It was an ideal moment. She tied the dinghy to the moorings of the motor-boat and went off alone. From Wellende Old Hall to the mouth of the river is about twenty miles, but the tide was with her and she slipped along at a very good rate. A couple of miles away from the Old Hall the village of Wellende lies. Prudence passed its old-fashioned looking wooden quays, and collection of fishing boats, and a few yachts, and after that there was nothing but marshes, marshes everywhere.

As the tide dropped, in places it was impossible to see at all over the river wall. Occasionally a cow stood on the dyke; but more often there was nothing but a gate and posts standing up. Now and then, what appeared to be a grey stake stuck in the mud would move, as the boat came nearer, and finally fly off.

"I could never tell the difference between an old wooden post and a heron," thought Prudence to herself, "if they stayed quite still."

The bright winter sun touched the shingle banks near the mouth and turned them into gold. A flock of very white gulls was circling overhead, and a single curlew was calling. Prudence drove fast.

Arriving at the mouth, she saw a heap of shingle left bare and wet; and in another place a rougher tumble of water. She appeared to have forgotten what she had said to her cousin at breakfast, for without a moment's hesitation she left the shingle heap on the starboard, and headed straight out to sea.

After about two hours Miss Pinsent in her motor-boat again appeared at the mouth of the river, and crept cautiously round the point where she had gone out. The tide had turned for the flow. Once in the river again, she shut down the engine; she had been driving fast all the time, and it was hot. She got out her lunch—it was after two o'clock—and began to eat it. The engine was just turning very gently and the boat was coming up on the tide. The sun was going down a red ball, and the bare mud on the banks was beginning to glow red, like the sky above. It was near the time of dusk as she picked up her moorings, and pulled off in the dinghy for the jetty. She had been out just six hours.

When she joined Lord Wellende at tea he gazed at her in astonishment; her cheeks were bright from the salt air, there was a light in her eyes, and a vigour all about her.

"By Jove, Prue," said he, "you are a good-looking woman."

"Thank you, Ben," said she with a laugh, "but I should value the compliment more if I hadn't heard you use just the same note of admiration in speaking of the coats of your horses."

She collected some letters that had come while she was out, and began to read them.

"Bother," she said. "They are giving some honorary degrees next week, and father has a guest staying at the Lodge, and says I must go home for two or three nights to entertain him."

"Well, next week is only two days' hunting; you ought to manage so as not to miss more than one."

The Wellende hounds hunted five days a fortnight. Prudence had three more good days before leaving for Cambridge, and very good days they were. Twice, on different occasions, they made seven and nine mile points, the foxes running strongly and fast. The other day they had a ringer, but even he took them at a good pace. On one occasion Prudence had managed to get away on very good terms with hounds. Just in front of her to the left was the first whip, and level on the right was her cousin, who was hunting hounds himself that day. After going fast for ten minutes, a huge fence reared itself in front of them. The whip went straight for it, but Prudence observed that Lord Wellende was pulling away; for one moment she hesitated; if Ben wasn't going to face the fence, had she better? Then in thinking, she remembered he had said he was going to ride a mare that wasn't up to his weight, but thought she would carry him all right for a bit. Prudence rode straight for the fence. For a short time there was no one with hounds but herself and the whip; and then out of the corner of her eye she saw a red spot just behind her, and though she was too busy to look round and make sure, she knew well enough who it was.

Oh, she thought, for the knack of being able to ride to hounds like that! To go out of your way and still not lose your place in the run!

There is nothing in the world like sharing a run out hunting for breeding good-fellowship and trust, and Prudence tried to shut her eyes to those puzzles that were worrying her. She decided that at all events she would do her best to shut Captain Studde's eyes; and so she invited him by wire to meet her at lunch at Ipswich on her way up to Cambridge.

CHAPTER XIV

PROFESSOR TEMPLE HAD A SET OF ROOMS ON THE FIRST FLOOR in the Fellows' Building at Prince's College. The bedroom and one sitting-room looked out immediately over the Cam; while the more spacious sitting-room looked over the grass of the front court. They were among the best rooms in College for the Professor was one of the senior Fellows. The front room was lined with books, books from floor to ceiling, a few very comfortable arm-chairs, and a huge writing-table.

It was a morning in November. The Professor sat at his writing-table, frowning at what he had written; then throwing it into the waste-paper basket, he re-wrote it again. But to judge from the expression of his face, this seemed no more satisfactory than the last. He got up with a weary sigh, and stood looking out across the front court.

He was a tall man, and inclining now to a little stoutness, which added a certain dignity to his bearing. His head was fine and his chin powerful; but his complete inattention to the niceties of a daily toilet gave him the appearance of a gorilla.

One or two gowned figures coming across the grass, seemed finally to bring his attention down to earth, and with a muttered exclamation he drew out his watch. He was due at a College Council meeting. Temple got into his gown and went out to the Senior Combination Room, where the meeting was being held, with the Master, courteous and urbane as ever, in the chair.

He sat through its weary length much more patiently than he usually managed to do, largely because his thoughts were evidently far away. After the meeting he walked out with Professor Skipwith.

Skipwith, looking as cheerful and kindly as ever, regarded Temple with a beaming smile. Suddenly the latter seemed to come to a decision; he took Skipwith by the arm.

"Look here, you're a good fellow; I want your help. Come to my rooms with me."

They went off together, but instead of going to Temple's rooms they strolled on the grass, sacred to Fellows of the College, which they had to themselves.

"Look here," began Temple awkwardly, "I want your help."

There was a long pause. Skipwith, thinking Temple wanted assistance in coming to the point, assured him he was ready to give any help he could.

"Yes, yes," said Temple, "but I have difficulty in expressing myself"; this was obviously the case, so Skipwith waited patiently. "It's a delicate matter, in which I would invoke your kind assistance…"

"Look here, old fellow," said Skipwith, thinking he saw a light at last, "if you want a loan of money, I'm your man."

"Money," gasped Temple in astonishment, "money be d—d; come to my rooms with me, I shall get it out better there"; and so up to the Professor's rooms they went.

Temple shut both doors, he then turned to Skipwith and said with a certain dignity:

"The truth is, I admire, have indeed long admired, a certain lady, whom I should like to be nameless. You have no idea who it is?" he said, looking anxiously at Skipwith.

"Not the least in the world," replied the astonished Thomas. "I should never have expected you to waste two thoughts on any girl at all."

"Lady," corrected Temple, "and the trouble is I don't know how to get on with the matter."

There was a silence. Skipwith was trying hard to hide his immense astonishment: after all why shouldn't the man? But he had never somehow seemed quite human enough.

"You are a good fellow, Skipwith, and a married man, I thought you might help me," went on Temple, after having waited in vain for a reply.

"Well," said Skipwith at last, "have you paid her any sort of attentions at all? I rather doubt it, and that is the way to begin."

"I assure you," replied Temple earnestly, "I always pay her very particular court; I invariably see her when I pass her in the street, and take off my hat."

"Yes, my dear fellow," said Thomas Skipwith helplessly, "but don't you do that for every lady you know? There's nothing particular in that."

"Every lady I know!" exclaimed Temple, in undisguised surprise, and not a little indignation; "if I took off my hat to every woman I have met in Cambridge, I should never have done. No," he added firmly, "I simply don't see the others."

No, thought Skipwith, I can well believe it. But what was he to say?

"I even went further than that the other day," Professor Temple went on, nervously trying to help his embarrassment by being busy with his pipe. "I met her struggling against wind and rain in the backs and offered to hold her umbrella for her... I *did* think of offering her my arm," looking anxiously at Skipwith, "but I hardly liked to go as far as that," he added humbly.

"Good God, Temple!" exclaimed Skipwith, suddenly moved to indignation and pity.

This man who had done, and was doing, invaluable work for the human race, who was consulted and sought after by savants from all over the world, to be behaving like a helpless child, and throwing away his attention on some probably quite worthless girl. The thought of it made Skipwith feel really angry, though quite with whom he would have been puzzled to say.

"I am not the man to help you, but if you would only let her, my wife would. You know you need never tell her who the girl—lady," he hastily corrected himself, "is, and I am quite sure she hasn't the least idea," added the guileless man.

Professor Temple pulled at his pipe for some time without speaking; then he finally said: "I could rely in that case on your wife not speaking of it to anyone?"

"Yes," said Skipwith. "If my wife gives you her word, you can rely on it, and I think she really might help you."

"I am due at a wine-tasting lunch at St. Asaph's. Would Mrs. Skipwith be at home about four o'clock?" And so they arranged it.

Skipwith went off with a sigh of relief. Never, never, he thought, had he felt more helpless. Temple, of all men in the world! It was outrageous that a man of his weight and intellect should take so humble a line about a girl. Whoever she was, she would be very lucky to get him; but it was a situation he felt Susan could cope with better than himself. Susan thought so too when he finally broke the news to her, but there their opinions ceased to coincide.

"What are you doing this afternoon?" her husband had said to her at lunch.

"It's my afternoon at the Art School," she replied.

"Well, do you think you could get out of it?"

"Why should I?"

"The fact of the matter is, Temple wants to come and call on you this afternoon. He—"

"Professor Temple!" exclaimed Susan in extreme surprise. "Well, it'll be the first time in his life he ever has called on me, though he's dined here often enough."

"Be reasonable, Susan. You know you can't expect a man like…"

"No, darling, I don't expect, but what *does* he want with me this afternoon?"

And then Skipwith told her.

"Poor, poor old fellow," drawled Susan slowly and very kindly.

"Here, less of that 'old,'" said her husband in some indignation; "he's only two or three years senior to me."

"I know, dear, but it's quite impossible to believe as long as he looks as he does, and… well… as far as age goes, it wouldn't be quite impossible."

"How can you possibly know? It's probably some disgusting little flapper he's proposing to throw himself away on; men of his age generally do."

"It's not a disgusting flapper, Thomas," said Susan, "and she certainly won't look at him!"

"Woman," said her husband, "do you mean to tell me you know who it is?"

"Learned old stupid, I do. I still enjoy the use of my wits, and, to a limited extent, of my eyes, and I don't go about the world with them shut, as you do. You might have seen all I have, if you had chosen to look."

"Susan," reiterated Thomas, "tell me who it is."

His wife would have liked to delay the information a little longer while she expressed her mean opinion of the Professor, but seeing that her husband was really anxious to know, she relented and told him.

"Prudence!" he exclaimed, entirely surprised. "Prudence!… Good God!… Who'd have thought it? I hadn't a notion at all."

"No," said his wife dryly, "I am sure you had not."

"Has she any idea, do you think? Because I gathered from poor Temple his difficulty was that she hadn't."

"No," said Susan, "I am sure the idea has not occurred to her. What with her position and good looks, she is used to a good deal of attention, and has probably never given old Temple a thought. Oh, well, all right, then, *not* old! To tell you the truth," she added, "I have only just noticed it myself."

"Are you sure it's Prudence?"

"Yes. The other night, when we were dining out, I noticed he was watching her the whole time, even when he was talking to other people."

"Well," said Thomas, getting up and standing in front of the fire, while he rattled his money in his pockets, "it wouldn't be such a bad thing—a slight disparity in age certainly, but community of interests, and the Master is getting an old man; he can't live for ever."

"Thomas," exclaimed his wife in real indignation. "That horrid old man; there's not a single advantage in it for Prudence; she's too independent now to marry."

"So she may be, but that's Temple's look-out. If a fine man like him wants her, she ought to be only too thankful."

"If you are going to talk like that, I shall leave the room."

Skipwith laughed. "Seriously, you women go far too much by looks. What does his appearance matter when you think of his intellect? He began with getting the Newcastle from Eton, and he's won every honour that came in his way ever since."

"If I think too much about his appearance, you think far too much about his brains. His hands aren't clean, and I doubt if his heart is pure. That's really the trouble, I am not sure I like his character."

"His character is all right, my dear," said Thomas soberly; "but if you feel you can't help him, let him down gently. He's very much in earnest." And with that Thomas took his departure; and being blest with more native shrewdness than his wife gave him credit for, went off feeling pretty certain that Temple's helplessness would before long win Susan over to his side.

Susan cheerfully abandoned any idea of the Art School for that afternoon, and, having given instructions that she was at home to no one but Professor Temple, sat down to consider the situation. To begin with, she must not let him guess that she knew who it was; that would be awkward, but she must pour cold water very firmly on the whole idea. That was very certain, and it would be the kindest thing from his point of view to do. If he was his usual conceited, didactic self, it should not be difficult. A snub would do the great man no harm, thought Susan. The idea of his lifting his eyes to Prudence! Why... At this moment her meditations were interrupted by the door being opened and "Professor Temple" announced.

CHAPTER XV

I N A VERY SHORT TIME SUSAN DECIDED THAT THE PROFESSOR WAS not showing his usual air of conceited detachment; he even showed signs of nervousness. They talked at some length about the weather; then Temple's eye was caught by some fine embroidery in a frame which Susan was engaged on, and he praised it with real discrimination and interest, so that Susan suddenly found that there was something really likable in the man after all. From this they passed on somehow to the prospects of the 'Varsity Rugger XV, and Susan found her opinions being deferred to with unusual attention. Feeling a good deal softened towards him, she recalled what Thomas had told her about his interview, and thought the time had come when she must bring him firmly to the point.

"Yes, my husband has gone up to the match this afternoon, but he told me you were coming here to call on me about a special matter."

"You and your husband are my very good friends, and I take it as particularly good in you, Mrs. Skipwith, to trouble yourself in this matter. Goodness knows I need your help!" This was not at all the attitude of mind Susan was expecting. "And if I could only make up my mind to confess to you who my lady is, I should have your sympathy even more."

"Good Lord," thought Susan, who was weakening fast. "How am I to pour cold water on this?" Aloud she merely assured the Professor, with perfect truth, that it was quite unnecessary for him to tell her the lady's name.

"Can you tell me something about her?" asked Susan, wishing to appear sympathetic and not knowing quite what line to take.

"I have known her on and off for something like twenty years," said the over-accurate man. "Latterly we have lived in the same place, and I have watched her with pleasure and admiration for a good many years now. Lately I found that the thoughts of her have been getting between me and my work. I think of her as I saw her last," he said after a pause.

Susan's hostility had completely vanished. The only question that worried her now was, how to convey most kindly and without any sort of a snub that she thought it hopeless.

"She is very beautiful," added the poor man, "in face as well as in character."

"Has she any idea of your feelings, do you suppose?"

"None at all; that is my trouble, and I don't know what is the most fitting way of conveying them without being too—er—er—abrupt."

"He means something short of actually proposing by that, I suppose," thought Susan.

And so they skirted round the subject, Temple giving very little away and Susan afraid of saying too much. Her feelings had completely changed. She no longer wished to take him down, or snub him; but what was she to say? She had never seen the great man so human and so diffident before, and it had quite put her out of her stride. After a longer pause than before, Temple said, "I realized how serious a case I was in when I diagnosed two symptoms in myself. The first was a positive desire to murder another man," and he frowned into the fire with his most disagreeable air; "and the second an unaccustomed, but not perhaps misplaced, humility about myself. Do you know, Mrs. Skipwith, the things I have prided myself on most seem of no account, looked at in this new light," and he looked up with a most disarming smile.

Susan was completely won over. "They are the best symptoms in the world!" she exclaimed impulsively, "and I will do anything I can to help you." She looked at the man in front of her and thought she had never seen him appear so pleasant. There was a something about him that had escaped even her observant eye hitherto. She even felt that she might perhaps have been over-critical; had she possibly done as Thomas had accused her, and condemned him too hastily on his appearance, and paid no attention to the man himself? Well, it should be different now.

"If you have your pipe with you, won't you light it?" she said, and the Professor, with a grateful smile, did so.

"Any advice you will be good enough to give me shall have my most earnest consideration, Mrs. Skipwith," he said, and with his beloved pipe in his hand, and a certain feeling of tension gone from between them, the Professor began to feel a good deal less nervous.

But not so poor Susan, who was going to give the sort of advice that needed tact and care, and she felt she didn't know quite the best way to do it. She lit a cigarette herself to make it easier.

"Well, first of all, I must confess I have guessed who is your lady, and she is one of my dearest friends, is it not so?"

Temple bowed.

"And now for the advice," said Susan, pulling at her cigarette, "and though I know exactly what I want to say, it's not so easy to say it…"

"My dear lady," began the Professor.

"You'll bear in mind," interrupted Susan, "I am not taking liberties; I am really wishing to help you by what I say."

"It is I who am taking the liberty in bringing my troubles to you," he said, with a courtly grace of which she had not believed him capable.

"Well, then, Professor, first of all, you must get your hair cut, and then you must shave off your whiskers."

The astonishment with which he regarded her sent Susan off into a hearty peal of laughter, in which after a moment Temple joined.

"I had no notion you were going to say that," said he with a chuckle.

"No, I am sure you hadn't," said Susan, feeling much better after the laugh. "You've simply no idea at all of the value of personal appearance... just think for a moment how you value Prudence's good looks."

"Ah," said Temple, "but that is a very different matter."

"No, it isn't," said Susan, "and you must do the best you can with your appearance. Cut your hair, and always shave every morning," said Susan, gaining in courage. "You've no idea of the trouble I have with Thomas in that direction," added she untruthfully. "There's something else, almost more important than all, that I should like to say... but I don't think I can..." eyeing the Professor speculatively. "I think I'll send Thomas to say it to you."

"Perhaps I can guess," said Temple, with a grim smile at his pipe. "You are sharpening my wits a good deal, Mrs. Skipwith, I think," still looking at his pipe. "You want to tell me what my dentist has been saying for some years..."

"Yes," interrupted Susan with great relief, "I am sure it's the same. How nice of you to guess so soon."

"I will attend to everything you say," he said.

"Do you know first of all I was dead against the thought of a marriage between you and Prudence; but somehow you've made me change my mind completely, and I am going to help you as much as I can."

"Good," said the Professor; and then, looking at Susan with a gleam of humour in his eyes, he added: "But though altering my appearance considerably will, I am sure, be of assistance, yet even my self-esteem is hardly sufficient to make me feel that it's enough!"

Susan laughed. "No, it isn't. I think you might give a dinner-party, rather *for* Prudence, you know."

"Yes," said Temple, "I could manage that very well; but she is away so much this term; in fact, the Master told me she would be away till Christmas. She's staying with my kinsman, Ben Wellende, for hunting," and he drew his eyebrows together with an unpleasant expression.

"He's jealous," thought Susan. "I wonder if that was the man he once felt like murdering!" and added aloud, "Yes, but I've had a letter from her this morning; she's got to come to Cambridge for a few days for the honorary degrees. Write to her and ask her if she and her father will dine with you one night then."

"I will," said Temple, fumbling in his pocket for a small diary he carried, and making a note, "and, of course, I can count on you and Skipwith coming too?"

Susan got up and went to her writing-table and consulted her pad of engagements.

"Yes," she said, "we are disengaged just then, only I shall have a girl staying with me. Might I bring her too?"

"By all means," said Temple. "An extra lady will be particularly welcome."

"And now," said Susan, "I am going to give you some really valuable advice: pay rather particular attention to Miss Boyd, whom I am bringing with me."

Temple looked frankly puzzled. "But it's to Prudence I wish to pay particular attention…"

"Oh, Professor," interrupted Susan, "with all your brains, have you *no* worldly guile?"

Temple relaxed into a smile.

"I will see Beryl Boyd doesn't misunderstand you all right; she is a particularly fascinating person, and for dear Prudence to see you for once paying some attention to a girl like Beryl will do your cause more good than anything; you really must trust me in this."

"I'll think it over," said Temple, getting up. "I have trusted you so far, and met with such kindness, I expect I'll follow your advice right through," and they parted company feeling a warm friendship for each other which neither would have believed possible a couple of hours ago.

CHAPTER XVI

T HAT SAME AFTERNOON, THOMAS SKIPWITH WITH HIS CAR went up to the University Rugger ground, to watch the match against the United Medicos. This was a particularly interesting match, as the 'Varsity were playing what would probably be their full side against Oxford.

Thomas went in, and found a place with some difficulty in the already full pavilion. He sat down next an old Rugger international.

"What sort of side are the United Medicos playing?" he asked.

"Pretty strong," was the reply. "Their pack is said to be very good, fast and active in the open and well together in the scrummage."

Thomas grunted. "It ought to be a good game, then."

As soon as the ball was kicked off, it was apparent to the watching crowd that they were in for something special. The game started fast, and the pace was sustained for a quarter of an hour, then the United Medicos scored a try which they did not convert. After this, Cambridge seemed to play up even harder, and every inch of the ground was fought over. Whenever one of the home side had the ball there rose the low rumbling roar of "'Var-a-arsity! 'Va-a-arsity!" from the crowd, and when finally one small, square-looking, filthy figure, in what had once been white shorts and vest, ran like a snipe's flight through the field, finally breaking into the open with two more dirty figures after him, the roar increased tremendously, "'Var-a-arsity! 'Va-a-arsity!" and then a long-drawn-out howl, as three figures in a tangled mass fell over the touch-line together.

The University converted.

"Five to three," said Skipwith, with a sigh. "Can they keep this pace up?"

"They are all of them in the pink of condition," replied his companion, "fit to play for their lives. It's a magnificent sight."

"I have never seen a better scrum half than ours," said Skipwith. "Look at the way he handles the ball; he seems able to take any kind of a pass."

"You're right," said the international, "he takes his passes in his stride, and yet never runs away from his own centres."

As the Cambridge scrum half was backed up by two useful centres, and had two very fast runners on the wings, and a back with a wonderful faculty for bringing off place kicks, the score of the 'Varsity went up. At half-time it was Cambridge 10 and United Medicos 3. When play was resumed, the visitors, as was expected, made a tremendous effort; a more magnificent effort than even the experienced among the onlookers had believed them capable of. For some time the 'Varsity was on the defensive, and the roar of the crowd rose and fell with the irregularity of the waves of the sea. Finally a Cambridge man intercepted a pass, ran from the half-way line to within a few yards of the goal-posts, then he was smothered by one of the opposing side, but the ball went loose and one of the several backers-up picked it up and scored a try. It was again converted.

"That full-back kicks with the certainty of an angel sent from heaven," said the international in a burst of complete satisfaction.

"If he's an angel sent from heaven, his raiment is somewhat spotted," laughed Skipwith. "Been trying three falls with the devil!"

The visitors now made desperate efforts to alter the course of the game, but every forward rush was beaten back and every passing movement held. The 'Varsity was never long on the defensive, and one of the best matches ever played ended in a victory for Cambridge.

As he moved slowly off the ground with the rest of the immense crowd, Skipwith fell in with Maryon. In tones of satisfaction they commented on the match they had just witnessed, and made some more hopeful and very satisfactory prognostications for the Oxford match.

Then the Professor said: "You're a handy man in a sailing-boat, aren't you, Maryon?"

"I love it," replied the other; "there's nothing like it after a hard term for wiping the cobwebs away."

"Well, look here, I want two fellows to come with me in a ten-tonner at the end of the term. I am going to the East Coast, and shall get some good duck-shooting. Come with me?"

"I really believe I could," said Maryon thoughtfully. "How soon would you be going?"

"Just as soon as ever full term is over. I am going up the coast of Suffolk to the place of a relative of the Pinsents."

"It sounds awfully jolly, and I should love to come."

"If you can think of another kindred spirit who's ready to rough it, let me know," said Skipwith.

As they talked they had moved slowly with the crowd off the ground and down West Road, and Maryon never noticed that moving just behind him and listening to his conversation was the "face" whose fancied presence in Cambridge had made him so uneasy. This time the "face" was trying to look as much like an undergraduate as possible. He had no hat, grey bags, Norfolk jacket, and he was rather more smothered in a large muffler than most. Before the crowd thinned the figure had disappeared.

CHAPTER XVII

NEXT DAY, SUNDAY, MARYON, WHO HAD THOUGHT IT NECESSARY to keep a morning chapel, had lunched in hall and gone up to his rooms in College to get through some arrears of work. He had not been settled to it long when a smallish, clean-shaven man looked in at the porter's lodge, and asked if Mr. Maryon had rooms in College.

"Yes, sir," was the reply, "and I believe you'd find him in if you was to go up now; the opposite building, staircase B, second from the left; you will find his name over the door.

"Not across the grass, sir," said the porter in stern disapproval, having come out of his room to intercept someone else; "you goes round by the path, and well you knows it, I'll be bound."

The gentleman murmured an apology, and with a slight smile pursued his humble course along the path. A few minutes later he was knocking at Maryon's door, and a voice bade him enter. When he did, the sight of him brought the don to his feet with an exclamation.

"By Jove! then it *is* you, after all? I thought it was, last week, but you cut me dead… I am delighted to see you…"

They shook hands warmly.

"Yes, I know I did," said the new-comer. "You took me rather aback by recognizing me."

"Well, if I did, you certainly didn't show it," laughed Maryon.

"I believe I am interrupting you in a lot of work," he said, looking at the paper-strewn table.

"Yes, you are, but the work can wait. I have looked forward for years to making your acquaintance. Here, take this chair and we'll have something to drink and a pipe!"

When they had got settled with their drink, and pipes alight, Maryon again said: "Do you realize how curious it is, though I have no doubt at all you know all about me, I don't even know your name; you are only No. 4 to me. You speak like an Englishman, but there was a report in the Service that your father was a Jew and your mother a Cossack!"

Both men laughed.

"I am what you call over here a Colonial. I was once in the Canadian Mounted Police, and my name is McDonald."

"Is it your name for the moment?" asked Maryon, with a twinkle in his eye, "or was it really your father's name before you?"

McDonald smiled. "It's my name all right, and my father's before me. I've a job at the C.I.D. and am known by that name there, anyhow."

"That's good enough for me, then."

"On the other hand, I know plenty about you. I came across some of your work during the war, and seeing that you were an amateur, I have the greatest admiration for what you did. You were in some very nasty places."

"Thank you," said Maryon soberly.

"You must have a wonderful memory for faces; you saw mine as it is now," he said with a grin, "for three minutes fourteen years ago; you've no business to go recognizing me again like this!"

"I have a good memory for faces," assented Maryon. "But you don't realize what a figure, what a legend, No. 4 was to all us amateurs as you justly call us! and when I got a chance of seeing you I looked at you."

McDonald laughed, but was obviously gratified.

"I feel for you," went on Maryon, "something of what a preparatory schoolboy feels for an All-England cricketer."

McDonald laughed outright.

"Good. I want you to go on feeling that way."

There was a pause while both men pulled at their pipes, then the older man began: "You've settled down to a wonderfully peaceful life here; do you ever regret the excitements of the past?"

"No, I don't. I don't even want to think of a great many of them."

"Well, I don't blame you, and this place must act as a soporific in comparison."

"There's plenty of hard work done up here," interrupted Maryon.

"Yes, I can believe that, but of a totally different kind. There's a wonderful leisure about this place. The streets are crowded, if you like, but College courts are an oasis of peace to-day—it's Sunday, isn't it? There are so many church bells going. Why even the clocks seem to strike slower here than in London! I suppose you mean to finish your days here?"

"I expect so," said Maryon, "and if I am lucky, end up as a Professor or perhaps even Master of a College."

"By gee!" said the Canadian slowly. "By gee! And as I was coming along here this afternoon, I met a gentleman all dressed in black silk, with a white bib, and a funny little flat hat on his head; he had a beautiful expression on his face, rather like God Almighty; and in front of him walked two men as solemn as he was, carrying silver pokers, and after him walked another chap with another poker; and the people all moved off the path for him, and it was all I could do not to make a bow as he passed!"

Maryon laughed, but McDonald went on quite solemnly: "Now, it wasn't King George, because I know him quite well by sight; who the bloody hell was it?"

"The Vice-Chancellor," said Maryon with a grin, "on his way to hear the University sermon."

The C.I.D. man gazed at him in silence. "I don't feel able even to swear," said he helplessly. "What an incredible spot this is! The Vice-Chancellor on his way to hear a sermon! Well—well—well, of course I'd heard of such things, but I never knew quite what it was like; and I'd also heard that grass was sacred, so after asking the gentleman at your gate the way to your rooms, I thought I would cut across the grass."

"I hope you were stopped," said Maryon in mock severity.

"I'd only got as far as *looking* at it when I was stopped, and it wasn't what was said so much as the way it was said. I haven't been spoken to like that since my mother told me to mend my manners at table."

Maryon shouted with laughter. "There's another gentleman in the University, you know, called the Senior Proctor," he said. "He's in something the same line of business as you are; but when he walks abroad on his business he doesn't slink round like a miserable detective; he walks proudly down the middle of the street followed by two men, one carrying a copy of the University Statutes and the other a Bible."

Maryon was laughing unrestrainedly at the limp figure in the chair opposite, who was gazing at him without a shadow of a smile.

"Well—well—well, he's a sort of policeman, you say, and he's followed about by a chap carrying a Bible; do you know it makes me feel all-overish, as mother used to say. Now do you suppose he reads the Bible aloud to the bad man when he's caught him?"

"I don't know," replied Maryon. "I must find out, for one day, I dare say, the job will fall to my lot."

"Well—well—I am sure I don't know whether to laugh or to cry."

"That's how it takes you, is it?" said Maryon, grinning.

"Yes, that's how it takes me," said the detective, without a smile.

There was a complete change in his manner, the limp, bewildered look had gone, he sat up in his chair, and the lines in his face seemed to be intensified; in a moment he looked a much older man, and Maryon, observing all this, realized in a flash how it was this man was able to disguise himself so successfully.

He suddenly felt a chill foreboding.

"I am up here on business, and a darned difficult bit of business, too; I have come to you because I want your help, but first you must give me your word that nothing goes beyond us two."

It was Maryon's turn to look grave now. "I'd be proud to help you if I am able, but wait a moment." He got up, putting a notice outside to say he was not at home; then he sported his oak.

McDonald went on: "It's drug trouble; there's a new and most infernal drug getting into the country. You know how these things first show themselves? A small set in the society of a big city; so far it's only in London and Manchester that we have traced it. There have been one or two deaths we've been very suspicious about, but we had to let them be brought in as suicide; one death we knew was murder, but we had absolutely no proof at all to bring before a British jury."

"I know that sort of case," said Maryon gravely, as he pulled at his pipe. "It's the most maddening sort of all—to *know*, and yet not have proof to convince others."

"Yes, it's heart-breaking to the detective. In this country there's comparatively little drug-taking, and what there is, is in the large cities. Most of our legislation in regard to it has been to help Europe rather than ourselves. The British Dangerous Drugs Act of 1920 was the first one of much consequence; that was amended a year or two later. It has given a good deal of trouble to doctors and chemists, but the trouble has been worth it. For years the drug-takers remained stationary, but now lately there has begun this sudden increase, and in a serious form. We have been working hard on it, and now we have a direct line to Cambridge; there is someone here handling that drug." A long pause followed.

Maryon looked up at McDonald, but did not speak.

"We are of opinion that it is almost certainly a University man," and then, looking directly at Maryon for the first time, "and I want your help."

Maryon pulled at his pipe, then he said: "You'll have to satisfy me that you are justified in suspecting anyone up here, and then I will help you."

"I'm not at liberty to give you direct proof; I am tied. I can only appeal to you on two points."

For the first time McDonald, who had been sitting very still, got up out of his chair, and stood over Maryon and spoke very earnestly. "You were good enough to speak highly of my professional character just now; can't you believe me without proof? Am I likely to go off on a wild-goose chase? Am I easily deceived? Think of my experience! And after that I appeal to you because you know, as so few in England do, the awful havoc wrought by these drugs... think, think, Maryon, of some of those dens out East, those women..."

"Oh, my God!" exclaimed Maryon, "that'll do; let me think a moment."

McDonald sat down again and kept quite still. He looked tired.

"I can't give you a promise to help you blindfold," said Maryon, and he spoke a little hoarsely, "but I will do what I can as far as it is consistent with my ideas of honour."

McDonald gave a short laugh. "I suppose I shall have to be content with that; and as there's honour among thieves I will treat you fairly, and confess that I overheard a conversation between you and Professor Skipwith, and I want you to take me on that boat."

"Do you mean to say you overheard us plan that?"

"Yes; I was in the crowd behind you."

"Well, I'm blowed… and what makes you want to come?"

"We suspect that there's stuff coming in from the East coast. The Inspector of Coast-guards there is an object of some suspicion, and for me to get taken down there by two innocent Cambridge dons would be of invaluable assistance," he said with a smile.

Maryon's tense expression relaxed a little too.

"I don't mind doing that at all," he said; "in fact I should like to have you very much. You are not, I suppose, really suspecting Skipwith or me?"

"No," said McDonald, laughing. "I have promised to be aboveboard with you; but there is another person I *am* suspecting down there, a certain Lord Wellende; do you know anything about him?"

"Nothing. I have heard the name, but for the moment I cannot recall in what connection."

"And there is yet another person, and I am afraid it will get your goat when I tell you who it is—Professor Temple."

"Temple!" exclaimed Maryon angrily. "You're mad!"

"Yes, of course you were bound to say that, but when you are cool again you will remember that I am not mad. I am about the sanest person in Europe."

"And the most modest," said Maryon bitterly.

"Yes, and the most modest," agreed McDonald blandly. They both laughed and felt a little better.

"It's come back to me now," said Maryon. "Lord Wellende is a relation of Temple's; that is how I knew his name."

"Yes, he is; and I wish you could tell me why, after not having been on terms for years, the Professor goes and stays so often with his cousin."

"I know nothing about it," said Maryon shortly; "and as for

Temple—the first sign of a drug-taker is an utter disregard for truth, and a more meticulously accurate man than Temple never walked. Why, the other day—"

"No one suspects the Professor of taking the stuff; we suspect him of handling it."

"I would stake my life on Temple's integrity."

"Good. I am very glad to hear you say it. Then you can have no objection to helping me clear him."

Maryon grunted.

"My great difficulty," McDonald went on, "is that my suspects are such decent people. Take Studde, now, the Coast-guards officer. He has a blameless record in the Navy; he comes of the sort of people that are considered the backbone of the nation; his eldest brother is the squire, another is a dean, and, as far as I can discover, there isn't a rotter or a wrong 'un among them. He has always said Lord Wellende or his people were bringing contraband up their river in barges, and when he gets a chance of searching a barge, he doesn't do it. He comes away, and just says there's nothing wrong, and pooh-poohs all he has said before. And that after lunching and spending the afternoon with Miss Pinsent, whom I suppose you know?"

"Miss Pinsent! are you suspecting her of smuggling too?"—disgustedly.

"No, I am not, only she happens to be a cousin of this Lord Wellende. They might be using her as a cat's paw, which would be an awful shame."

"It's all utter bosh," said Maryon crossly.

"A family that produces Professor Temple," continued McDonald, "who is about the ablest toxicologist we have, and a genius, may very well produce a rotter in the same generation; and I rather expect to find this peer is a decadent. I haven't had time so far to make inquiries."

"I know nothing about him myself, except that I fancy I connect his name with hunting," said Maryon.

"Yes, but isn't there a sort that will go out hunting with scent on their hair, and be met by a car with a good lunch?"

"I dare say; I am sure I don't know."

"I'll tell you one thing, in confidence, mind you, that'll stiffen your back. Do you remember, last year, the death of the Secretary of State for Internal Affairs?"

"Yes; let me see—he died in his club, didn't he, of heart failure?"

"That was the coroner's verdict, given on the medical evidence; but we are morally positive that this drug was administered to him. They were all drinking liqueurs, a lot of them together, and it would have been quite simple to dope his. The man we suspect was one of the company."

"But surely there was an autopsy?"

"There was, but the family had it done by his own doctor, who said he found signs of angina. Now if it was this drug there would be no signs of anything, but it takes a man in a big way to dare to say he can find no traces of anything to account for death."

"I am surprised to hear you say that," said Maryon.

"Oh, no, when you come to think of it, your young doctor says he can find nothing to account for death; another man is called in, and perhaps honestly thinks he can find some trace of something; anyhow, he says he can, and the first man is made to feel like a fool, and the coroner makes sarcastic remarks. But this chap, the Secretary for State, had asked for an interview with the Chief Commissioner, as he wanted to speak to him about this drug: we know that for certain; but he died a few hours before, or was removed just in time." They smoked in silence for some time. "If one of the crowd I have my eyes on here was to die suddenly, then I should be certain."

"I suppose I must help, you devil," said Maryon pleasantly, "but what am I to say to Skipwith? I would like to be above-board with him as much as possible."

"Tell him I am a policeman on a holiday; you must not repeat anything about the drug."

Maryon got up and went to a bookshelf. There he fumbled about till out of a far corner he produced a dirty-looking book in an old-fashioned binding.

"Here, listen to this," he said, and turning over the pages, he found his place and began to read: "'If I understand you rightly, you have formed a surmise of such horror as I have hardly words to... Consider the dreadful nature of the suspicions you have entertained. What have you been judging from? Remember the country and the age in which we live. Remember that we are English, that we are Christians. Consult your own understanding, your own sense of the probable, your own observation of what is passing around you. Does our education prepare us for such atrocities? Do our laws connive at them? Could they be perpetrated without being known, in a country like this, where social and literary intercourse is on such a footing; where every man is surrounded by a neighbourhood of voluntary spies; and where roads and newspapers lay everything open?' There, that's what I say to you, only much better put than I can do it."

"That's good," said McDonald, "very good. Who wrote it?"

"A parson's daughter—more than a hundred years ago."

"Ah—it was about a hundred years ago Warren Hastings in India first described cocaine as a 'pernicious luxury.' It wasn't even known in England, and if you 'consult your own understanding,' old fellow, you'll admit that all I've been saying to you is quite possible nowadays, even though we are English and Christians."

"Well, I'll make it all right with Skipwith and let you know when we start; and, mind you, I am taking you because I *know* Temple is innocent."

After McDonald had taken his departure, Maryon stood for some time gazing out of the window lost in thought. It was a dull day, but the window was open, and through it came the tinkle of a chapel bell. It seemed to claim his attention, and after a moment's thought he put on his gown, picked up his mortar-board, and went down the stairs.

"Yes," he said to himself, "I will go to chapel at King's; it will take the nasty taste out of my mouth, and make me feel clean again." He pursued his way along King's Parade and turned in at the College gate with a stream of other people.

There was a thick, low-lying fog about, and the enormous mass of buildings round him could only be dimly discerned. Then he saw, as he lifted his eyes, that the four tall pinnacles of the Chapel were above the fog and were bathed in rosy sunshine. The sight and realization of it comforted him queerly, and as he stepped over the threshold into that most magnificent of buildings, there fell on his spirit a sudden hush of dignity and peace. He moved slowly up the long length of the dim ante-chapel. There was a soft glow coming from the masses of candles in the chancel, lighting up the two tall figures of the trumpeting angels over the organ.

A verger took charge of him, and seeing he was a senior member of the University, put him into a stall. A Bach fugue was rolling sonorously through the Chapel. The rows of wax candles looked like stars, and behind them were all the mysterious shadows of that stately pile. The old stained-glass windows showed here and there a patch of colour and light, but that soon faded as the time went by. Maryon, in a trance which lifted him far from the moil and toil of life, had not consciously listened to a word of the service, until his attention was caught by the stately words of the College prayer: "For our Founder, King Henry VI, by whose bounty we are here brought up to godliness and the study of all good learning."

"Godliness and the study of all good learning," he murmured to himself, and at the moment his eye fell on the kneeling figure opposite, in surplice and hood, of a Fellow of the College who to his own certain knowledge had risked his life more than once in the cause of humanity.

"I'll stake my life and honour on Temple," he thought to himself.

"Oh, where shall wisdom be found... where... where is the place of understanding?" sang the choir, and the question echoed along the high-vaulted roof and lost itself in the misty shadows. "It cannot be gotten for gold, neither shall silver be weighed in the price thereof," they sang on, in that building which for five hundred years has watched generations of men seeking after learning. Again the clear voices: "No mention shall be made of coral or of pearls, for the price of wisdom is above rubies," and round them sat the men of learning, in their gowns, their surplices and their scarlet hoods. Then with a triumphant crash came the answer: "The fear of the Lord, that is wisdom, and to depart from evil, that is understanding."

Maryon left the place feeling like a different man.

CHAPTER XVIII

C APTAIN STUDDE, FOR HIS OWN REASONS, MADE IT CONVENIENT for himself to accept Miss Pinsent's hastily-sent invitation to lunch with her at Ipswich. This time he took some trouble to make it a pleasanter meal for her. He felt that last time he had probably been rather brutal in his treatment of her. After all, Prudence was well over thirty, now he came to think of it, though, by Jove, she didn't look it. He had seen through her so completely, too, in spite of her efforts in pretending. So he ordered a table to be kept for them, and had cocktails waiting in the stone-paved lounge downstairs against her arrival.

Prudence turned up punctually, and they enjoyed a cigarette with their cocktails. She came determined to beguile away his fears that any smuggling was going on at Wellende, and fully convinced of her ability to do so; and so, each cherishing a slight feeling of superiority, they sat down in the best of humours with each other.

"You do look well, Prudence," began Captain Studde, regarding Miss Pinsent's glowing countenance with real admiration. "You've had a lot of good fresh air lately, I'll be bound."

"I have indeed, and such good sport. Does it convey what it should to you, when I tell you that in five days' hunting the hounds have made one six-mile point—*point,* Harry, and two seven-mile points?"

"Yes, it does a bit; that's pretty good going."

"I should just think it was," said Prudence. "And now I've got to go up to Cambridge to entertain some tiresome people who are coming up for honorary degrees. Why does one know the name Sir Boris Buckthorne so well?"

"Buckthorne?" said Studde with a malicious grin. "Why, he's head of the Criminal Investigation Department. What's he coming up to Cambridge for?"

"How stupid of me," said Prudence, with a heightened colour. "Of course, I knew the Chief Commissioner was a friend of father's, but I had forgotten his name; that is why he wants me home evidently."

"Perhaps Sir Boris is combining business with pleasure. I wouldn't be a bit surprised if he was."

"You don't mean to say you still believe that rot you filled me up with last time, about drugs in Cambridge?"

"I do, every word of it."

"Well, I can tell you one thing: there's nothing wrong going on at Wellende. I have satisfied myself as to that," lied Prudence.

"No," agreed Studde, to her immense but well-concealed surprise. "I have found out since that I was wrong in my suspicions there." He regarded Miss Pinsent's handsome and unconcerned face keenly. Does she, or does she not, know the truth? he wondered.

"Then perhaps very shortly you'll find out you are wrong about Cambridge, too," said she, anxious to get the conversation away from Wellende.

"No," said Studde, "that's the C.I.D., not me. Not much chance of them being proved wrong, I fancy. What a charming fellow your cousin is."

"Who? Ben? I thought you said you didn't know him."

"I met him, as it happened, the evening we met here last time."

"Oh, yes," said Prudence vaguely. "I am glad you liked him." That was the evening, she thought to herself, that Ben had said he was duck-shooting, and Harry had had a drill at the mouth of the river. Very reluctantly she faced the certainty that Ben had been deceiving her. That he should have been shooting duck at the mouth of the river she knew to be an absurdity; since he had met Captain Studde that night, he was not duck-shooting. It made it more likely, then, that the second night when he had said he was shooting was also a blind. Then he may very well have been one of the people in that boat—and what, what could he be doing about his own house with so much secrecy? Prudence found it difficult not to be absent-minded during the rest of that lunch; but she made an effort, and long practice in entertaining came to her aid, and in spite of her worried state of mind she was a very pleasant companion.

Driving home from Ipswich, she was able to think things over, though without any satisfaction to her peace of mind, and it was with some misgiving and much distaste that she faced the problem of entertaining the Chief Commissioner of the Metropolitan Police.

She found the Chief Commissioner, however, a much pleasanter guest than she had anticipated. After listening to Harry Studde's insinuations about "combining business and pleasure," and her own uneasy knowledge of what was going on at Wellende, she had pictured to herself a dour, sharp-faced personality; in this she was very wide of the mark.

Sir Boris Buckthorne had been in the Navy, where he was universally loved and respected. He was an admiral. He had very quiet and unassuming manners, and a perfectly delightful habit after giving some piece of obscure information of adding, "as you know," which invariably had the effect of making those to whom he was talking feel much better about themselves, and created an atmosphere of pleasantness all round. He had a plain face, with a little naval beard and moustache, turning grey, and an absolutely adorable smile, which lit up his face into something beautiful.

Thus it was rather with a sense of pleasure and not duty that Prudence took him out for a walk after the degrees had been conferred. The temptation to confide in this kindly gentleman all that Studde had been telling her, and her fears about Ben, were almost too much for her. She felt certain that Sir Boris would be so nice and kind about it. She didn't even dare to start a vague conversation about drug-trafficking in general, being shrewd enough to realize that while she would certainly learn nothing from Sir Boris, he might learn more than was intended from her.

"No," she thought with a sigh, "I must not let the word pass my lips."

So it came about that they walked out together up Madingley Hill, both thinking, as it happened, of the same subject from different points of view, for Sir Boris did not entertain the smallest desire to open such a subject with Miss Pinsent. When they had reached the top of the hill they instinctively turned to look at the view.

"This is the best aspect of all," he said, "and in this soft, misty light the buildings are made somehow mysterious. See that shaft of light on Clare and King's Chapel?"

"Yes; it is beautiful, beautiful."

Sir Boris turned and regarded his companion with his charming smile; but she was not looking at him, her attention had been attracted elsewhere.

"Look at that bird," she exclaimed. "Is it a rook, or a rocketing pheasant? It looks almost too small."

Sir Boris looked where she indicated. "It's not a pheasant," said he, fumbling for his glasses. "I am sure it's too small; it's a pigeon." As he got his glasses on: "Yes, it's a pigeon. See the colour of its wings?"

"I see now, but it's a curious way for a pigeon to fly, surely."

Sir Boris was regarding it with a good deal of interest. "Observe the light on its wings against the russet-brown of the beech trees. It's worth coming out of London to see a thing like that alone, Miss Pinsent."

"Yes, I entirely agree with you. I wouldn't live in London for anything." As they spoke an elderly and very good-looking man got over the gate from the field; he had a small basket under his arm. As he saw them he lifted his hat to Prudence.

"Who is that?" asked Sir Boris.

"It's our Head Porter, and I am not sure but he's a greater man in the College than my father," she laughed. "He is said to be frequently mistaken for the Master."

Sir Boris looked at him with interest. "What do you suppose he carries in that little basket?"

"His lunch, I should think. I have met him out before like this, and he tells me there is nothing he loves so much as a long day in the country alone, when he can get it."

Sir Boris half turned as if he was going to ask him if he really had got his lunch with him, but evidently thought better of taking such a liberty, and followed Miss Pinsent.

Later on, when nearer Cambridge, they were overtaken by a couple of figures, clad in very short "shorts" and very thin vests, jogging along at a steady pace. They were splashed with mud, and they were hot, but they were not short of breath.

"I think that must be the most healthy form of exercise of all," said Sir Boris as he watched the long, easy strides of the runners.

"If they get into condition gradually and don't overdo it at the outset," agreed Prudence.

"It's a deal less violent than Rugby football."

"Yes, and so much more useful," said she. "One might almost organize a post with those men," musingly, "if you wanted to send something you didn't dare trust to the post. I fancy all the big towns have athletic clubs and a certain number of cross-country runners; they could do it like relay races."

"That's an interesting idea of yours, Miss Pinsent. It had never occurred to my police mind as a possibility."

Prudence looked at him and laughed. "I had completely forgotten you were a policeman." And as Sir Boris smiled at her: "No one could possibly be expected to remember it of you," she added.

CHAPTER XIX

T HE NEXT MORNING AT BREAKFAST THE MASTER OF PRINCE'S consulted his engagement-book.

"My dear," he said to his daughter, "I fear by some oversight I have omitted to inform you that we have engaged ourselves to dine with Francis Temple in his rooms to-night. I trust that you are at liberty to do so."

"With Professor Temple!" exclaimed Prudence in surprise. "What's he giving a dinner in his rooms for? It's very unlike him, and to ask ladies, too!"

"I am unable to satisfy your curiosity on that point. I only know he seemed particularly anxious we should dine with him."

"Temple," said Sir Boris thoughtfully; "that is the great toxicologist, of course?"

"Yes," replied the Master; "he is a Fellow of our College; and that reminds me of a piece of gossip for you, Prue. Temple has recently completely changed his appearance! I couldn't have believed such a difference was possible!"

"Changed his appearance? What do you mean? Has he put on a false beard, or what?"

"Quite the contrary, quite the contrary," said her father, laughing. "He has shaved his face completely, and cut his hair. I think he must have done something else too, though I am sure I don't know what. He manages to look fifteen years younger than he did."

The good man was honestly unaware of the new teeth the Professor now boasted, but he would not have mentioned them in any case.

"Well, I'm—blessed," said Prudence, out of deference to her father; "it's quite certain any change in his appearance will be for the better."

"I think you are a little severe, my dear, but," he said, laughing gently, "I only know of two reasons for a change of appearance. One was suggested to me by your friend Mrs. Skipwith, or I am sure I should never have thought of it, and that is that the Professor has fallen in love." This afforded the good Bishop much amusement, and he even had to produce his pocket-handkerchief and wipe the tears of laughter from his eyes.

Prudence, somehow, didn't find it half so amusing. If the Professor had fallen in love, she thought it was more ridiculous than amusing; interested, however, she certainly was.

"And the other reason, Master?" said Sir Boris, who had been watching both the Pinsents with some interest.

"The only other reason for such a change of appearance is a wish to dissociate yourself from a discreditable past," and the Master laughed again with great enjoyment; the others joined with him.

"Temple's past will take more getting away from than that," said the Chief Commissioner.

"Why?" asked Prudence. "That sounds almost sinister. Have you his dossier at the Yard?"

"I should think we have, Miss Pinsent. We've called him in to help us on more than one occasion; we think a great deal of him," added Sir Boris, with more truth than Prudence or her father guessed.

Sir Boris stood looking out of the window, watching the life in the College court, till his attention was caught, as Prudence's had been before, by the beauty of the pigeons.

"Yes," said the Master in reply to his question. "Our Head Porter looks after them, and feeds them when necessary; but I fancy they are nearly self-supporting. No, I don't suppose the farmers do bless us particularly, but we've always had pigeons."

"I am going up to town for the day," said Prudence, "but I shall be down in time for the dinner; but if I'm to catch the ten o'clock train I must go."

Later on Sir Boris Buckthorne too took his departure. He explained to the Master that he had some calls to make in the place before driving back to London, and went off on foot. He went to the nearest telephone-box, and after shutting himself in as carefully as possible, called up Scotland Yard. Over the wire he gave a careful description of Miss Pinsent's clothes which would have surprised that lady, an accurate and dispassionate description of her appearance, the time of her arrival at Liverpool Street, and instructions that she was to be followed. Then he returned to the College entrance. In the street he paused, and turning round, appeared to admire the old gateway, which was surmounted by a dove-cote, a beautiful bit of work. A junior porter was standing outside.

"Fine old dove-cote that of yours," said Sir Boris to him.

"Yes, sir, it is, sir; the only one of its kind."

"I remember when I was a boy I knew a dove-cote that had a bell inside, that tinkled when a pigeon went in. I wonder if yours is that sort."

"I am sure I don't know, sir, though now you come to mention it I have sometimes thought I 'eard a bell from the dove-cote, but I may have imagined it."

"Yes, yes," said Sir Boris, "you remember that old-fashioned game of croquet where the centre hoop had a bell?"

"Yes, sir, I do mind that. Why, there was a set like that until quite lately in our Fellows' garden."

"I have no doubt of it," said Sir Boris, and after exchanging a few more remarks about the evident superiority of Prince's College to any other in Cambridge, they parted on the best of terms, the porter back to the dim recesses of his lodge and the Chief Commissioner to the market-place.

On the right of the market-place, behind the Corn Exchange, is a "passage" which is often quiet and free from people. Along this Sir Boris walked slowly. He was about to pull out his watch when another figure came in sight from the other end. It was McDonald. The two men met, and talked throughout like equals. They paced up and down, deep in conversation. At last Sir Boris, who had been doing most of the listening, said:

"The fact of the matter is, we simply can't afford to blunder, as far as Temple is concerned. How did this other fellow, Maryon, take it when you told him our suspicions?"

"First of all he said I was mad, and then only consented to take me in his boat because he knew Temple was innocent, and it was so utterly ridiculous."

"Poor fellow, I am sorry for him. Now listen to me, McDonald," and Sir Boris began to talk to him in a low voice. They were perfectly safe, as they knew, from being overheard.

"Yes," said McDonald, "it's all possible, of course. I wish you would leave me here and send another man to Suffolk. I don't like working among people of that sort."

"No, I don't suppose you do; I didn't altogether enjoy my visit to Prince's, I can tell you, but it's you who will go to Suffolk, it's a heaven-sent opportunity. Here," fishing a small object out of his pocket, "what is this?" And he handed McDonald a smallish lump of something a dirty yellow, "Not amber, certainly."

McDonald turned it over, scraped it with a knife, and then said, "I think it's a bit of rock-salt; it does turn this colour, but I am not certain. Why, where did you get it?"

"I picked it up just now, outside the gate of Prince's, and I rather fancy they use that sort of thing, if it is rock-salt. Anyhow, send it to the Yard and have the subject thoroughly looked up."

"If you are right in this new idea of yours," said McDonald, "and heaven send you are, it frees Miss Pinsent from suspicion; she would never have wantonly drawn your attention to it, and she wouldn't ever have forgotten you were a policeman if she was concerned in it."

"No, no, that's true. I cannot bring myself to believe she's in it, but of course I know, alas, that nothing is impossible in this sort of way, nothing at all. I am taking no risks, and I am having her followed to-day in London, to see where she goes, and if she could be passing it on to anyone we know about."

So they parted. Sir Boris paid a visit to the Chief Constable at the "Station," and then was driven back to London.

Late that afternoon Mr. McDonald started out for a good, long country walk, and came home when it was almost dark along the Backs. Unaccustomed to the ways of Cambridge, he had not realized that all the back gates of the Colleges would be locked at dusk. He was lucky enough, however, to find a member of Prince's just coming out of their gate, and was let through. Thus it came about that he was walking through the back court of Prince's at dusk, and chanced to notice what looked like a ball of fur fall from one of the College windows and run away. There had been a slight snowstorm while he was out, and the ground was just whitened. He looked cautiously round to make sure no one was about, and then stepped across the grass to satisfy his professional mind exactly what it was that had fallen. When he came up, there, clear and unmistakable across the snow, lay the track of four padded paws in a straight line. He gazed at it in astonishment.

"By gee!" he said, "by gee!"

He counted the windows, and on inquiry at the College gate learnt that Professor Temple had rooms there.

So it came to pass that as Miss Pinsent emerged from a first-class carriage at Liverpool Street, and walked with comfortable unconcern along the platform, a small, keen-faced, unobtrusive-looking little man followed her, not far behind. He was wearing a cap and was clean-shaven. When Miss Pinsent descended to the Underground and took a ticket to Oxford Circus this same little man was standing next her; he booked for the Marble Arch. They both, however, got out at Oxford Circus, and after a short walk the lady disappeared into a house, whose door was apparently open. The detective allowed a minute or so to elapse, and then strolled by; it seemed to be offices; he stopped to read the name on a brass plate, watched rather super-ciliously by the lift-boy. The choice appeared to lie between a "dental surgeon," a "beauty specialist," and an "insurance agent."

The detective put his hand into his pocket, and withdrew some silver coins which he clinked pleasantly.

"That lady who came in here a little time ago," he said to the boy, "which of these did she go and see now?"

"Garn," replied that gentleman, "which do yer suppose?"

The C.I.D. man, with a smile as from one man of the world to another, put his hand on the name of the beauty specialist.

"Got it in one," replied the boy succinctly, with his eye on the silver coins.

"Does she often come here, regular customer?"

"I don't know so much about *regular*, but she been pretty often in the last two years, so they all 'ave."

"Well, mum's the word," and five shillings changed hands. The detective went off round the corner, from where he continued to watch.

In an hour's time Miss Pinsent came out, looking even handsomer than ever. The two of them, in the same order as before, took another, rather longer walk. This time the gentleman had very suddenly started a small moustache, and was wearing a slouch hat. The walk ended at a well-known ladies' club, where one went in and the other prepared himself for a long and hungry wait. He occupied himself, however, by taking a lively interest in the many women and few men who went in. Especially one tall, dark, handsome woman.

Then, after a long wait, he saw and heard Miss Pinsent take a taxi for Liverpool Street, the number of which he noted and then strolled into the club.

He asked the porter if he could see the secretary, and handed the man his card. A few minutes later a pleasant-faced lady came towards him with his card in her hand.

"You wished to see me?"

"Yes, m'm. Would it be possible to speak to you in private?"

The secretary turned and led him away to her own private room.

"I am quite unused to having anything to do with the police," she said, in a tone of mixed vexation and interest.

"Yes, I am sure you are, m'm, but you must treat what I say to you as confidential. There is a swell lady thief about we are keeping an eye on," lied the C.I.D. man glibly, "and I am not sure I didn't see her come here in company of a lady who would know nothing about her, a Miss Pinsent, from Cambridge."

"Miss Pinsent is certainly one of our members."

"Could you tell me the name of the lady with whom she was lunching to-day?"

"Yes"—the secretary hesitated for a moment—"every member is supposed to write down the name of any guest she may have in a book kept for that purpose; I will go and look."

She remained away for some time. When she came back it was with a worried air.

"I looked at the visitors' book," she said, "and Miss Pinsent made no entry to-day; doubtless she forgot. I am afraid members often do. I asked, however, in the dining-room, and our head-waitress, who has a wonderful memory for faces, tells me Miss Pinsent was giving lunch to a tall, dark, good-looking lady who, she thought, was a stranger to the Club. She was certainly not a member, as she has been put down on Miss Pinsent's bill as a guest."

"Thank you, m'm," said the detective, rising, "and now if I might just ask your porter if he knows where that lady went to, I'll trouble you no further."

He got the information he desired, and apparently followed it up. Late that evening the taxi-man who had driven Miss Pinsent away from the Club was interviewed, to learn only that she had driven straight to Liverpool Street station and gone in there.

It was possible to reach the Fellows' Building from the Master's Lodge by going through a private door into the Library, and so through the Bursary, and it being a wet evening, Prudence and her father availed themselves of this. The Professor's bed-maker, her little black bonnet on the back of her head, full of bustle and importance, was established ready to help the ladies with their cloaks. Prudence knew the woman well, as one of her duties was to organize a yearly treat for all the bedders in the College.

"Yes, 'm," she said to Prudence, "this is an event indeed, 'm. I don't know 'as how I ever remember my gentleman 'aving ladies to dine before, and ten covers laid, so Mr. Robins tells me." Robins was Temple's gyp, who presently announced them.

"The Master of Prince's and Miss Pinsent!"

The large book-lined room seemed full of people, and though Prudence had been warned, she still wasn't quite prepared for the tall dignified man, with a strong look of Ben Wellende about him, who came forward to shake hands with her. It was this last that surprised her most, the unexpected likeness to his cousin. The Professor was a genial and courteous host when he chose to make the effort, and the two things combined made Prudence feel more drawn towards him than she had ever done before.

They moved off to dine in the back room, and as they sat down Prudence observed that though money had been lavishly spent on the table flowers, taste had not: they looked as if they had been arranged, as indeed was the case, by the gyp. The food, however, was above reproach.

The Professor, it is true, was genial, courteous and very, very learned, but as Mrs. Skipwith once exclaimed, he had no worldly guile whatever; and he made the initial mistake, from his point of view, in asking the mother of a former pupil, who chanced to be in Cambridge, a dowager Duchess; and so she was the chief lady, and not Prudence, and moreover, claimed his attention all through dinner.

From Mrs. Skipwith's point of view it was an undoubted success. Her niece, Beryl Boyd, was an exceptionally pretty girl, with a very bright and attractive manner. Through the first part of dinner she had been rather over-awed by the company, but the kind attentions of a young don (the one, by the by, who had claimed relationship with Temple) soon put her at her ease. At the end of dinner she confided to him in a carefully modulated voice, "I have just seen what I thought never happened, that clean-shaven don on the other side of the table has refused the port."

"Yes, it seldom happens, but you didn't see quite enough," said her neighbour, "the College has some very, very famous port, and that don was watching the Master take his first sip, and when he saw him thoughtfully shake his head, he knew it wasn't the best."

"No!" exclaimed Miss Boyd, "you're inventing it."

"Fact, I assure you; I was watching the whole thing, and what is more, I wouldn't be in the least surprised if a bottle of the best wasn't waiting for us after you ladies have gone."

But though the Professor was without guile, he never forgot anything, however small, that he intended to remember; and after dinner, instead of going and sitting by Prudence, as might have been generally expected, and as he himself greatly desired, he singled out Beryl Boyd. He appeared to be talking to her with a surprising knowledge about dancing, but the fact of the matter was, Miss Boyd, delighted at the attentions of the great man, babbled away on the subject (it having been suggested by the Professor), without further assistance from him.

For the first time in his life Temple was enjoying the experience of having a young, modern, and extremely pretty girl making much of him, and he found it very pleasant.

Consequently the time passed much faster than he had anticipated, and the Duchess began a general move to depart before he had time to talk to Prudence.

On their way home the Master said to his daughter: "Who was that unusually pretty girl there to-night?"

Prudence informed him.

"I wonder if it is on account of her 'beaux-yeux' that Temple has shaved off his whiskers; she is over young, I think."

It was a revelation to Prudence the sudden indignation that she felt at the suggestion. As she slipped into her silk night-gown, she realized that she knew perfectly well why she had not enjoyed the dinner as she generally did. Professor Temple had failed in manners; it wasn't that she wanted to talk to him particularly—here she paused for half a moment—no, it wasn't that, but she was sorry he had failed to play the perfect host, and she got into bed.

Meanwhile Temple himself, as he smoked his last pipe, felt that he had spent a pleasant evening, but wasted, as far as his chief object was concerned: she had never given him a thought, and with that *he* got into bed.

Quite otherwise was it with Susan Skipwith. She opened the door between her room and her husband's, and as she disrobed, she discussed it with him.

"Thomas, are you listening?"

"Yes."

"It was a grand success, that dinner, and all owing to me."

"If you ask me," said a voice from the farther room, "it was owing to the College kitchen."

"Professor Temple isn't such a simpleton as you might think," went on Susan, ignoring her husband's last remark, "when guided by a really intelligent—"

"I say," said Thomas, appearing in the doorway half clad, "did you notice how Temple was getting on with Beryl after dinner? It didn't seem to me quite the way to ingratiate himself with Prudence; in fact, I doubt if Prue liked it."

"There is no one," said Susan with vehemence, "who has a lower opinion of the wits of learned men that I have—"

"Oh," said Thomas. "Oh," and then added, as he retreated into his room again, "we had a bottle of the best port after you ladies had gone."

"Disgusting," said Susan.

CHAPTER XX

M ISS PINSENT, IN AN OVERALL, WAS ARRANGING GREAT MASSES of tawny chrysanthemums in the hall of the Lodge when her father and Professor Temple came in. They took off the silk gowns which they were wearing, hung them up by the door, and then strolled towards the fire.

"Yes, it's a very serious problem, one of the most serious that the University is confronted with, in my opinion," the Master was saying, and he held out a gaitered leg towards the fire to warm.

Temple greeted Prudence and then turned to answer her father.

"Everyone admits the problem, and yet we get no nearer to solving it, to making the balance fair between research and teaching. Your opinion, Master, standing outside both as you do, I consider of great importance and value and, for the matter of that, mine is equally so, since I may fairly be said to have a leg in each camp."

"My dear fellow, you're a shining example of a man who does much research and whose lectures are yet crowded!"

Temple grunted. "There's no doubt about it at all that at the present moment a man who does a little, even sometimes a very little original research is rewarded, often gets a Fellowship on it, and a chap who is a genius at teaching is left quite unnoticed."

"He makes money as a coach."

"Yes, he may do that, but he gets no recognition from the University; why, there must be hundreds of men doing good work up here who have no part at all in college life; there certainly are on the scientific side."

"You are perfectly right," said the Master, "and it boils down like most problems now to a financial basis. The Colleges are not in a position to increase their Fellowships."

"And yet those men ought to be digested by them somehow."

"I confess," began the Master slowly, "that... I... should find some of them very hard to digest."

"You're a reactionary Tory; the indigestible ones are as good as any," said Temple in his worst and most abrupt manner.

"Professor Temple," said Prudence in her soft voice, "can you recall to your great mind a simple and elementary work called the Catechism, which I am sure you once learned?"

Temple, who had, as a matter of fact, been watching Prudence all the time he had been talking to her father, replied promptly, "Anyhow, I know what it is."

"Yes, but I *think*—you have forgotten an important part of it."

"My godfathers and godmothers," he murmured to himself thoughtfully, then, turning suddenly to the Bishop, "that revives an old memory of many years ago; I remember as a boy having to repeat something like that to you, in the small library at Wellende it was; Ben was there too, and he could only say the part about his godfathers and godmothers, but I was supposed to know the rest; dear me, dear me, why, I don't suppose you were even born then," he said, turning to Prudence with a smile.

"The part I want to remind you of," said she, busy with her flowers as she spoke, "which you seem to have completely forgotten, is that in one place you undertake to submit yourself to your spiritual pastors and masters, and to call your spiritual pastor *and Master* a reactionary Tory in that tone of voice is deplorable," and Prudence turned and looked at him with a world of derision in her eyes.

Temple was entranced. She had never looked at him like that before, and he was engaged in making the surprised discovery that Prudence's eyes were the most beautiful things in the world! Here his thoughts were rudely interrupted by the Master saying, "and I in my turn would remind you, my dear," turning to his daughter, "of the next sentence in that admirable work, where *you* undertake to order yourself 'lowly and reverently' to all your betters."

"So it does, I *had* forgotten that; 'order myself lowly and reverently to all my betters,'" she repeated; "what a lovely sentiment it is, especially in these democratic days. Why, I've got no betters," she said, looking the Professor full in the face.

"Prudence," said her father, laughing, "at times you go far to make me ashamed of you; there stands Francis infinitely your better morally and intellectually—"

"Yes, and socially too," interrupted the Professor, returning Prudence's look with interest, "a Temple is—" Prudence literally gasped aloud with astonishment.

"You—you—of all men, you."

"That's right, Francis," said the Master, who had observed the twinkle in the Professor's eye, and was perfectly aware of his daughter's weakness, "rub it in well, rub it in well," and he went off chuckling to his study.

"Morally, intellectually, and socially," repeated Temple in a slightly arrogant tone of voice, and drawing up his fine person to its full height, as he stood in front of the fire.

Prudence collapsed into a chair.

"And you call yourself a socialist," she remarked bitterly.

"No," replied the Professor blandly, "I doubt if I ever have, though I have often heard you call me one."

"You say you don't believe in class distinctions; I've heard you."

"You've heard me say I don't *value* them, I have never denied their existence."

"I understand you now to say that you are my social superior?" and Prudence, sitting on the arm of her chair, deliberately looked at him through her eyelashes.

There was a pause; it was an extraordinary thing, thought the Professor, how fascinating a pair of eyes could be; but he wished she would look at him full again and then he would make *quite* sure...

"Yes," he said slowly, "but I am willing to overlook the fact as long as you just bear in mind," and in a moment he got his desire, they were the most beautiful—

"Of all the arrogant, overbearing, conceited and odious—"

"Yes, yes, and I am going to be worse than that; I propose to teach you to order yourself lowly and reverently to one whom your father has pointed out as your better."

"Go on," said Prudence, with a dangerous meekness, "I should like to hear you out to the end."

"I am an able teacher, as your father was good enough to observe; I have taught, and can still teach, those who don't even want to learn." He moved a little nearer her, "To order yourself lowly and reverently to all your betters—come, Prudence—that would be quite a fresh experience for you."

"It would indeed," she agreed fervently, looking at him out of the corners of her eyes; "but fresh experience is the salt of life, and it might end in my teaching the great Professor Temple that there are some things even he can't do!"

"I can spare you a couple of hours this afternoon," said Temple, taking out his engagement-book, "we'll go for a walk."

"Oh, I really don't think I can manage it this afternoon," said Prudence, taken aback by his promptness.

"If you don't come, I shall know that you are afraid you will have to learn from me in spite of yourself."

"Oh, what a mean thing to say, how *very* mean!" laughed Prudence, "that makes me obliged to come."

After the Professor left, Prudence fell into a brown study, and the flowers that morning took long a-doing. She was feeling a little ashamed of herself; she had deliberately made eyes at a man, a thing she hadn't done for years, and at Temple of all people in the world, and what was more degrading, she had to admit that she had enjoyed it. The utterly impossible part of it was that Temple had responded… he had looked at her once or twice in a way—(but of course, it was impossible, coming from him)—in a way that, coming from any other man, would have meant he was flirting with her; and there came in the sting again—she liked it. Here she considered for some time, and finally came to the conclusion that arrogance, if sufficiently colossal, was distinctly attractive.

CHAPTER XXI

WHEN THE AFTERNOON TURNED OUT WET AND COLD, WITH that specially penetrating damp that forms so large a part in the climate of Cambridge in winter, Prudence was distinctly disappointed. To take a walk was out of the question. Soon after lunch, however, when the Master and his daughter were still drinking their after-luncheon coffee, a note was brought in for Miss Pinsent. "Professor Temple's man was waiting for an answer."

"Professor Temple wants me to go to his rooms this afternoon," said Prudence to her father; "he says he has something to show me, and a walk is impossible. I suppose there is no reason why I shouldn't go?"

"None at all," replied her father, and so an acceptance was sent; and when later that afternoon Prudence presented herself at the Professor's open door he was waiting for her inside. Miss Pinsent, for once in her self-satisfied existence, was feeling a little nervous, but she was a good deal reassured by the Professor's ceremonious greeting.

"I take it as very kind in you to have pity on my solitude," he said.

"I think your room is the most delightful of all College rooms, and it's a pleasure to spend an afternoon in it, in weather like this," replied she pleasantly, and as she spoke, her attention was caught by a scuffling noise on the other side of the door.

"What on earth—" exclaimed Prudence, "you don't mean to say you've got a—," and at that moment, as Temple opened the door, a fat, wriggling, twisting bundle of brown fur shot out and began rubbing itself all round his master's legs, amidst snuffing cries and licks.

"This is what I thought you would like to see," said Temple. "I know you are fond of dogs."

"It's a perfect darling; where did you get him? and how do you manage to keep him? Here," as she sat down, "give him to me."

The Professor picked up the wriggling puppy and dropped him on to Prudence's lap. There the dog, with the endearing ways of his kind, so certain that no one could repulse their affection, began licking Prudence's face and literally anything he could get hold of. She did her best to ward him off her face while she exclaimed:

"You terrible little mongrel, but how adorable. Tell me how you got him."

"I have got more real pleasure, apart from satisfaction, out of that piece of goods than anything, I do believe," answered Temple. "Ten days ago he was a shivering skeleton in the streets, half dead of distemper and neglect, and now just look at him!"

Prudence hugged the soft, fat figure to her. "I think it's grand," she said with enthusiasm; "is it a new discovery?"

"Yes, I have been experimenting lately a good deal with a special drug, and to use it in this way for injections against distemper was an experiment which has succeeded beyond my most sanguine hopes."

"I think that sort of thing is simply splendid; you'll tell Ben about it, won't you? He's pretty good in that sort of way himself, isn't he?"

"Yes, Ben is a veterinary surgeon, which of course is unusual in a man of his position. Oh, yes, I shall certainly share my discovery with him first."

Prudence wished so much that she could ask if it was this interest in common which was taking him again to the Old Hall; but she knew too much on the one hand, and too little on the other, to make it possible for her to question him at all.

"Will you show me the drug that you cured this little fellow with?" she asked.

Temple was delighted, and going to a big cupboard he produced all sorts of boxes and glass tubes and bottles; and showed her various things with wonderful powers, explaining their uses in a way that an amateur could follow and understand.

"I never realized before how many different things can be got out of one," she said, "and out of that, which is called ecgouin, you get cocaine? but is anyone allowed such things in their possession?"

"No," replied Temple, "ecgouin in this form is supplied to only two firms in Great Britain, they sell to the chemists, and every grain is supposed to be accounted for, and a history kept of where it goes. People like myself have special concessions for buying."

"Can you always get what you want?"

"I can always get some, but it's difficult or impossible to get it in much quantity."

"Have you any X.Y.X., isn't it called?" asked Prudence nonchalantly.

"What do you know about X.Y.X.?" asked Temple, busy in putting away his things.

"Nothing. I've only heard it mentioned," and Prudence did not fail to note that her question remained unanswered.

"Bless my soul," she exclaimed, looking at her watch, "I had no idea it was so late, I must be going."

"But it's just tea-time," said Temple, as he locked up his cupboard with a key from a bunch in his pocket; "of course you are having tea with me, and here it comes."

His man came in with a bright copper kettle which he put on the fire; it started to sing at once. He then drew the curtains and brought in an ample tea, putting a plate of hot cakes in the fender. Nothing more comfortable could be imagined. The fine old book-lined room, the leaping fire, a kettle singing on the hob and the tea spread out in front of it. The Professor made his own tea with meticulous care, warming the pot before putting the tea in. He then rather formally invited Prudence to pour it out for him. She did so, and as they had it they talked a little of Wellende. Temple told Prudence he was contemplating another visit there shortly.

"Then we ought to meet, as I expect to be there till Christmas for the hunting."

The Professor was sitting in a low chair with his legs crossed, and the puppy had bestowed his fat little person across the foot on the ground, where he was asleep, safe in the knowledge that his master couldn't get away without his waking up.

"When you have done your cup of tea, tell me: don't get up, you can't wake that fat darling, I will get it for you," said Prudence, and when finally she rose to replenish his cup for him, the self-sufficient and conceited Miss Pinsent experienced an odd feeling of pleasure in doing the little service.

"And the hounds are doing uncommon well, too," said Prudence, continuing the conversation. "*What* a dear Ben is! I love that man, even his shortcomings are endearing."

Temple frowned, but as Prudence went on to recite Ben's account of the last school managers' meeting with much humour, his expression cleared. From this the discussion passed on to books, what were the best sort to take to read in bed.

"I like something that leaves a pleasant picture in your mind," announced Prudence, "and for that I don't believe you can beat Somerville and Ross."

"I haven't read any of them," replied Temple. "I find I must have something just interesting enough to hold my attention, but not to make me think. I have one here that I found pleasant, light reading. I will lend it you," and he reached out a long arm and handed Prudence a flat red book. She looked at the title and gave a little gasp.

"I don't hardly think," she said; "you see I have no medical knowledge at all."

"You don't need it, ordinary intelligence is all that's required, you'll enjoy it," said he, thinking of the interest Prudence had been displaying that afternoon. Prudence said no more, but became rather thoughtful. As she rose to go, she said:

"The rule about not keeping dogs in College rooms is not still in force, I suppose?" sarcastically.

"Oh, yes, it is," replied Temple blandly.

"Any law which happens to get into your way, I suppose, you would ignore?"

"No, no," answered Temple gravely, "only laws which impede me in my scientific work, I should ignore them."

Prudence's heart sank, for she felt it was true. She picked up the book she had been lent and, regarding it thoughtfully for a moment, she looked at her host, and said hesitatingly, without her usual assurance of manner: "Professor Temple, you haven't been trying to… to teach me… what you said you would… all this afternoon, have you?"

"What was it I said I would teach you?" he asked, remembering it for the first time since she had been there, and he took her hand as if to say good-bye, and held it. Silence. "Come, Prudence, tell me."

She wasn't looking at him, so she didn't see the ardent expression of his face. "To order myself lowly and reverently," she said reluctantly.

"As a matter of fact, it never occurred to me, till you reminded me just now!"

"That's all right, then," said Prudence, taking her hand away. "I've enjoyed my afternoon enormously."

CHAPTER XXII

O UTSIDE, PRUDENCE COLLIDED WITH MRS. SKIPWITH.
"Oh, Susan!" she exclaimed, "you are just the person I
want. Come along into the Lodge, I have something I simply must
show you. *Who* do you think I have been having tea and spending
the afternoon with?"

Mrs. Skipwith glanced back at the staircase from which Prudence
had just emerged. "Never Professor Temple?" she said.

"Yes; just think of it!"

Thinking of it was what Mrs. Skipwith was very much engaged
in doing. Certainly now that he had once faced facts, the Professor
was not letting the grass grow beneath his feet.

"Do you know, Prue," she said, slipping her arm into that of her
friend, "I am beginning to think that perhaps we have always been
a little hard on old Temple; I almost doubt if he is as inhuman as we
have been inclined to suppose."

"I never did think him altogether inhuman."

"No, but pretty near so. He came to call on me the other day and
was really quite charming."

"Most of to-day he has been like that, and quite as nice as any
other man," said Prudence thoughtfully, "and then, I want to show
you the book he has lent me to take up and read in bed—a soothing
book to go to sleep over was what he said."

They were inside the Lodge by now, and Prudence handed her
friend the volume in question. Mrs. Skipwith took it, looked at the
title, swallowed twice, and looked up at Prudence; then she read out
slowly: "'A Treatise on Anthroposophical Medical Research.'"

"Yes," replied Prudence in a whisper, "nice light reading, was how he described it."

"'Anthroposophical Medical Research,'" chanted Mrs. Skipwith again.

"When I said I didn't think it would be much good my taking it, as I knew nothing about medicine, he said it didn't matter, it only required a little ordinary intelligence."

"'Anthroposophical Medical Research,' and that's his light reading!"

"What do you suppose his deep reading is?"

"God alone knows! Still," said Mrs. Skipwith, after a pause, "you might intone the title over and over again to yourself as you go to sleep."

"I should certainly have a nightmare if I did, if I ever got to sleep, which I should doubt," asserted Prudence firmly. "And do you know, Susan, what galls me most is, I hadn't the courage to tell him that I don't even know what the word means!"

Mrs. Skipwith burst into laughter. "Cheer up, Prue," she said, "after all, it is not your brains he cares tuppence about, it's your face."

"Do you know," said Prudence gently, "I think that is rather a vulgar thing to say; my face has nothing to do with Professor Temple."

"Do you know," replied Susan, imitating her friend, "I think that's a very stupid thing to say; the man is at perfect liberty to admire your face, which he happens to do… He told me so the afternoon he was calling on me."

"Told you he admired my face!" And then, after a short pause: "I'd far rather he admired my intellect."

"There are times," said Mrs. Skipwith, "when I would like to take and shake you. That's not true, as a matter of fact, though I know you genuinely think it is. The truth is, you've always been so sure your face is all right, that you've never given it much of a thought;

but your intellect you are very much less certain of, and so you think more about it in proportion; you've a very average brain, my dear." But Prudence was too much surprised and interested in what Mrs. Skipwith had been saying to feel resentful.

"Tell me what he said about my face."

"Ah, that's better," said Mrs. Skipwith, "but as a punishment to you for adopting that ridiculous superior pose, I shall not tell you any more than that he said he admired you, and he did *not* say it vulgarly, Prudence."

The two friends sat down and pulled their chairs up to the fire, and Prudence took off her hat. They did not speak for some time. Then Mrs. Skipwith said: "Has it really never occurred to you that the man is in love with you?"

"No, never until to-day," said Prudence with perfect sincerity.

"Specialists are apt not to make love like ordinary men, you must remember," said Mrs. Skipwith.

"I am not quite so sure about that." Prudence hesitated, thinking of Temple's conduct that morning.

"They have a confiding way of taking it for granted," went on Mrs. Skipwith, "that you are bound to be interested in their own special line. So great, so wise, they are in some ways, and such simple children in others."

"Yes, to a very great extent I must admit that is true. Do you remember old Dr. Hasgood? I think he was Regius Professor of Divinity?"

"I remember him all right."

"He once came to me, and said in his hesitating way that he felt sure I should 'be able to elucidate a phrase for him which he had long been at a loss to attribute a meaning,' and what on earth do you suppose it was?"

Mrs. Skipwith merely shook her head.

"He wanted to know what a 'glad-eye' was!"

Both ladies laughed.

"Doesn't that just illustrate what I was saying to you about them, Prue? And I suppose old Hasgood was vastly learned on some subject or other?"

"Yes, he had done invaluable work, I believe, on the Pentateuch."

"The what?"

"The Pentateuch—the first five books of the Old Testament."

"I always thought the Pentateuch was something in Euclid."

"In *Euclid*!"

"Now I come to think of it, it is the *pons asinorum* I had in mind."

"Really, Susan, you ought to be ashamed of yourself!"

"Yes," replied she tranquilly, "and yet *how* much wiser I am than you, in other ways."

There was a pause, the fire crackled cosily, and the two friends lit cigarettes.

"Professor Temple was showing me some extraordinarily interesting drugs and poisons this afternoon, and explaining their miraculous powers."

"Yes," assented Susan maliciously, "I remember when the larvae of flies seemed the most absorbing topic on earth."

Miss Pinsent saw the insinuation, for her colour rose slightly, but she took no further notice.

"You know Mr. Edgehill, the engineer?" continued Mrs. Skipwith. "Well, just before he became engaged to his wife, I overheard him say to her: 'The differential equation which represents this state of oscillation…' I can't remember any more, that's mathematics, which you may or may not recognize, and Edgehill is a mathematician."

"What an awful thought," said Prudence solemnly.

"Yes, but I don't know that I wouldn't just as soon struggle with differential equations as with anthroposophy! The next stage will be that he may ask you to go for a walk with him!"

Prudence started to speak, but checked herself. "I really don't think there is much of the simple child about Francis Temple."

"Oh, isn't there... you should just have heard him the other day!"

"What day?" asked Prudence quickly.

"Never mind," said Susan.

"Anyway, he was clever enough to make love to me in this hall under father's very nose."

"Oh, Prue, tell me about it."

"I think he's—somehow or other he's very masterful, don't you think?"

"Yes, that's what makes them so attractive," replied Susan.

But, whatever Miss Pinsent was beginning to think, she was not yet prepared to admit *that*. At night, when she went up to bed she took the "Treatise" with her, and after trying for some time to read it, put it down again. The Professor, though he did not know it, was distinctly up on their bargain.

CHAPTER XXIII

PRUDENCE RETURNED TO SUFFOLK SOON AFTER. THERE SHE found things going on just as usual. Mary had nothing further to report. Ben had had two good days' hunting; a ringing fox both days; but scent very good, and they had hunted one for five hours and killed at the end. There! What did Prudence think of that? Snap had killed three rats, and the last of the sugar-beet had been lifted, and a very good crop, too. Did Ben think there was going to be bad trouble between China and Russia? Ask him another. He had more serious things to think about. A puppy had started what looked uncommonly like distemper, in the kennels, too.

But under all this peaceful, everyday, bucolic atmosphere there lurked something sinister. Ben had lied to her once, if not twice, about what he was doing; and what—what did that extraordinary remark of Professor Temple's mean that Mary reported? It all tended to one explanation, and one only. Prudence had had no opportunity of asking her father what the cause of the old quarrel between the Temple cousins had been. She couldn't suddenly ask without producing a reason, unless the subject had been under discussion, and she had had no opportunity of making it so.

The days passed pleasantly enough, until the time arrived when Thomas Skipwith and his friends were expected. Then something occurred to worry Prudence once again. They were out hunting. Hounds were drawing a large covert, and Prudence, seeing the solitary figure of Dr. Heale watching a distant side, went towards him. He looked up and smiled when she came, but neither spoke. Both their horses were intelligent old hunters, and were listening to the sounds inside the covert as keenly as their riders. In the far distance the huntsman's voice could be heard speaking to his hounds, and an occasional whimper; hounds were some way off, but drawing up wind to where Prudence and Dr. Heale waited. The latter was half whistling, half hissing a tune between his teeth, while his eyes were glued to the long side of the wood. In the distance, a pheasant got up noisily and flew off, another looked out of the undergrowth and then drew back again, a hare broke covert and scuttled away.

"If I swore I saw a fox break, and you didn't, would you 'holloa' to it on my word?" asked Prudence softly.

Dr. Heale shook his head with a smile. "Not if the King of England and the Archbishop of Canterbury swore to me, I wouldn't," said he. Silence again.

A blackbird burst out of the covert, chattering noisily.

"Just whistle that tune very softly," said Prudence, and very softly and very accurately Dr. Heale whistled the air from the G Minor Mozart quintet. Prudence felt quite bewildered. Dr. Heale in it, too... but the next moment, and she had forgotten all about her worries. A slim, brown, four-footed figure slipped quietly out of the covert, and away down a furrow. Heale stood up in his stirrups and gave a rousing "Holloa!" The huntsman responded with a long note on his horn, the crackle of hounds in the undergrowth came nearer, and in a few moments with a crash of music the whole pack was pouring out on the line of the fox.

"Steady, Prudence, steady," said Heale. "Give them a chance."

From the far side of the covert could be heard the thud, thud of the galloping horses of the rest of the "field." It was all Prudence could do to hold her horse—and, oh! she wanted to get off before the others had time to come up. With hounds running hard half a field away, Dr. Heale and Prudence started; and for the next hour and ten minutes they neither of them would have changed places with the angels in heaven.

After a very fast run, the fox had been brought down in the open, and Prudence, with a brush that had been really earned hanging from her saddle, turned for home. Now, for the first time her thoughts went back to what she had just discovered. It was Dr. Heale in that boat she heard whistling. He was very fond of good music, and there were not many who could whistle that intricate air. That made four people in the business—Temple, Ben, Woodcock, and now Dr. Heale. She got back to her room to find everything ready as usual; a tea equipage laid and a burnished copper kettle singing pleasantly on the hob. She rang for Mary.

"You're back early, miss," said she, coming into the room.

"Yes. Shut the door, Mary. I want to talk to you."

Mary did as she was told.

"I mean to go down the *oubliette*, or pipe, or whatever you call it," said Prudence. "It's a good time, we shan't be interrupted. His lordship is still out, so he won't be asking for me, and Woodcock is at the great wood still. I know, as I passed him coming home, so *he* won't be in the cellars."

"Well, let me make you a cup of tea first, miss."

"Yes," said Prudence, "that would be very nice, and then while I am drinking it, you can get the screwdriver and lift the seat."

This was duly done, and a little later Prudence stood ready, dressed in riding-breeches, jumper, and thick stockings. She had stuck her electric torch inside her waist.

"Now, Mary," she said, "when I am down, cover up the seat and stay in the room, and if anyone did happen to come in, it would all look quite natural, but when you hear me come back, lock the door till I am through."

It was with more excitement than misgivings that Prudence let herself down the pipe. It was easier than she had expected. There were notches in the stone on one side, and the pipe was small enough to allow of her leaning against the opposite side for support. When she got to the end of the notches, she got out her light to see where she was. The ground was between three and four feet below her; so she let go and jumped, and then crawled out of what looked for all the world like a fire-place, and as if she had come down the chimney. She found herself in a smallish room, in which she certainly had never been before. There was a door, which from its position she calculated must have led into cellars still farther under the old house.

She looked round by the aid of her torch, but there was nothing, just nothing at all but bare stone walls and bare stone floor. Surely there might be a scrap of paper, or something that would furnish a "clue," but there was just nothing at all. The only suggestion the place did make to her mind was, that it ought perhaps to have been dustier or dirtier; it seemed too empty and too clean. She was considering this point when she heard a scuffle, much the same as the rats she had heard under the smoking-room floor. Miss Pinsent was back in the chimney in two twos, only to find she could not make the first start up without something to hold on to.

"Mary, Mary," she called up the pipe, and was relieved to see Mary's respectful face looking down almost at once.

"Get a sheet and hang it down; I want something to hold on to to make a start."

This was soon done, and Prudence, rather breathless, was back in her room again. She had discovered nothing, just nothing at all, by her adventure. But she was particular in seeing that the window-seat was well screwed down again behind her. Then, upon reflection, she made up her mind to go and see Laura Heale. She must talk to someone if possible, and it would not be hard to discover whether Laura knew anything about this mysterious business or not. She was a simple soul and quite incapable of hiding her feelings. If she had a secret to keep she looked worried and slightly self-important, and it was obvious to the meanest intellect that Mrs. Heale was uneasy about something.

So it came about that next day Prudence borrowed a hack of Ben's, and jogged over to "the Doctor's." There she found her friend busily engaged in bandaging her horse's forelegs. "They always fill up a bit after a hard day," she said to Prudence; "the old mare's getting on now, you know."

"I've come for a gossip. No, I don't want to go for a ride. Come down the garden."

"Right you are. That was a toppin' run yesterday, Prue, and John came home full of your praises and how straight you rode."

"I followed him all through," said Prudence. "You know I can't take a line of my own."

"Yes," said Laura. "I guessed you had."

Prudence laughed.

"Have you heard this last ghastly bit of news?" said Laura, slipping her arm through Prudence's.

"No," said the latter, suddenly startled, her mind jumping from visions of Ben being taken into custody for smuggling to a ghastly paragraph she had seen in the papers about a cinema full of children being burned.

"There's a case of suspected foot-and-mouth reported from the other side of the county, and, if it's true, it'll cut us out of all our Friday country."

"Oh!" said Prudence in relief. "Yes, of course it is bad, but perhaps they are wrong; it may not be foot-and-mouth at all. Look here, Laura, I want to talk to you about something serious."

"Serious?" said Mrs. Heale, "serious? I don't know what can be more serious than foot-and-mouth in the country!"

"Well, perhaps it isn't; but listen to me. There's something mysterious going on in the cellars at the Hall."

Prudence watched her friend's face carefully as she spoke. Mrs. Heale's expression remained pleasantly unchanged. She knows nothing about it, thought Prudence. I had better say no more.

"What do you mean—have the ghosts been heard again?"

"Yes," said Prudence, "and perhaps it's only that. Do you believe in them, Laura?"

Mrs. Heale didn't answer for a moment, then she said: "Have you seen or heard somethin' unusual, Prue?"

"Yes, if you will have it. I saw a boat come out from under the house late at night, and I thought I recognized someone in it that surprised me very much."

"I wondered how long it would take you to discover somethin'," said Mrs. Heale.

"What *do* you mean?" exclaimed Prudence. "What is there to discover, and what do you know about it?"

Mrs. Heale walked on a bit without speaking, then she said: "I know very little about it, if it comes to that; I am not supposed to know anythin'; but they are smugglin', if you want it plain, that's what they are doin'."

"Do you really believe that Ben, *Ben* and Dr. Heale are smuggling?" exclaimed Prudence.

"Yes," said Laura imperturbably, "and why not? Very sportin', I think, I only wish I was in it too. I tumbled on to it by chance, but I think John knows I've guessed all about it, though we still pretend that I don't know anythin'."

"How long do you suppose it's been going on?" asked Prudence.

"I don't know. Two or three years ago John suddenly took the line that it wasn't professional etiquette for me to know too much about his patients, and when he went out at night it wasn't my business to know where he went, so I guess it started about then."

"But, Laura," said Prudence, "I think it's dreadful; it's shocking that men like Ben and John should smuggle!"

"Now don't you be such a prig, my girl; that's the bad influence of a place like Cambridge. If you lived here all the year round, you'd take a healthier point of view."

"But smuggling is swindling," said Prudence.

"Nonsense," replied her friend, "it's sportin' and quite natural... Why, the Temples have smuggled for hundreds of years, and so have several other families that live here; and it's quite right they should go on. Why, Prue, you're half a Temple yourself—"

"That's all very well," interrupted Prudence, "but sentimental reasons won't persuade me into admitting that black is white."

Laura laughed. "And I've been wonderin' all this time if you weren't in it too, and helpin'. I gave you credit for more sense than it seems you've got."

"Look here, Laura, how would you like to see John up at the Assizes for smuggling?"

"He won't be. Do you suppose there's a man, woman, or child for miles around that would give Lord Wellende away, even if they knew? Ben and John, though I says it as shouldn't, haven't an enemy about the place." There was a long pause. "But, you see, no one knows who isn't in it themselves. At the most a fisherman may suspect, or just wonder, but at heart he's all for the smuggler, quite apart from the fact that he'd never do 'his lordship' a bad turn, not if he knew it."

"No," said Prudence slowly, "but it might be found out from outside, so to speak." She was thinking of Harry Studde and what he'd said to her. If the authorities were on the watch— Suddenly she remembered something else.

"Did you hear them say on the wireless the other night that there was smuggling along the East Coast, and how many people had been convicted?"

"Yes," laughed Mrs. Heale. "It was funny. John and I were sittin' together and I looked at him and he looked at me, and we both laughed, but even then he never spoke—I hoped he would."

"Well, I don't like it," said Prudence.

"No one here will give them away. I don't suppose you realize quite how strong Ben's hold on the country-side is. Talk about Socialism and Communism in England, faugh! Why, you know when Mrs. Woodcock was dyin'. I went to see her, and the thing that was worryin' her most was, who was goin' 'to see to his lordship's shootin' lunch? I've got it as he liked it for five-and-fifty years, ma'am.' That was what that woman was thinkin' of, as she lay dyin', not herself! Socialism! Faugh!"

"Yes," said Prudence soberly, "that spirit is wonderful." A pause. "But you know if people like them are smuggling, it's something like drugs, and if they are smuggling drugs, aren't they bound to be doing harm to someone, putting the stuff into the hands of people who oughtn't to have it?"

"No," said Mrs. Heale, "I don't see that in the least. In fact, I am quite certain neither Ben nor John would harm anyone."

"You're an awful good wife, Laura!" exclaimed Prudence. "You let your husband do a thing like this without talking to him about it; when he praises my riding to hounds and you know it's really only a form of praising his own, you see it, and don't comment on it, and you've such unbounded trust in him!"

"Oh, my dear," said Laura, "it's havin' your own man and the right one at that. I only wish you—"

"Yes," interrupted Prudence, "I know what you are going to say, but I'm much better as I am."

"It would be much better for you," said Mrs. Heale firmly, "to have one man whom you had to spoil, instead of being spoiled by many, as you are."

"Thank you for that," laughed Prudence. "Well, if you can, tell your one man whom you spoil outrageously that next time he goes out smuggling he had better not give himself away by whistling... and don't ask me any more about it, as I'm not going to tell you."

Mrs. Heale tucked Prudence's arm a little firmer to her side, then she said: "You know, Prue, you're absolutely made for a smuggler; I've always known it, your beautiful face, your ladylike and refined appearance, my dear; you've a fine position in Cambridge, and you've very wild blood, and no one can keep a secret better than you! And don't ask me any more about it, for I'm not going to tell you."

Miss Pinsent came away with a much higher opinion of Mrs. Heale's intellect than heretofore.

CHAPTER XXIV

B Y THE TIME PRUDENCE GOT BACK TO THE HALL IT WAS tea-time. She went to the library to find the old room flooded by a strong yellow light from the stormy sunset without, the putty-coloured river curving between flats of gleaming yellow, as vivid as the sky itself. The farm buildings and ricks on the opposite shore stood out dark and mysterious against the stormy sky; the reeds and saltings made smudges of brown among the glistening waters, and a flock of wild duck swirled and circled above it all.

Dunning came in with the tea. "It's a stormy sunset, miss, and if I'm not mistaken, it's going to blow hard before morning."

"I see the glass has dropped," replied Prudence.

"Yes, miss, it always goes down for wind here."

"Does it?" said Prudence. "I have sometimes been tempted to wonder if the glass bears any relation whatever to the weather."

Dunning would have liked to pursue the subject and prove Miss Pinsent wrong to his own satisfaction, but the entrance of his master made him abstain and retire.

"Your friends have arrived, Prudence," said Wellende. "I have sent Stevens off with an invitation to them to dine to-night."

"That's very good of you," said Prudence. "I think you will like them, at least Thomas and Mr. Maryon; the third man I don't know."

"Skipwith is an entomologist, isn't he?"

"Well done!" exclaimed Prudence. "You brought that word out fine, you did!"

"Contrary to a very general superstition," remarked Lord Wellende blandly; "they give you an excellent education at Eton, and I haven't forgotten it all yet!"

"I am the last to deny it," laughed Prudence, "but you didn't get a scientific education, not when you were there, anyhow."

"Tell me," said her cousin. "He's a professor, isn't he? And does one address him as Professor? I never know these things."

"Not out of Cambridge, anyhow. In Cambridge it would be correct, of course; some like it, but most are indifferent."

"Oh, I know, some men stand on their dignity and some don't; but, anyhow, you don't use it away from Cambridge?"

"No," said Prudence. "But talking of such things, now that appellation of 'squire.' There's old Mr. Saltlande of Saltlandes, everyone calls him squire, all his people."

"He *is* the Squire of Saltlandes," said Wellende.

"Yes, but what constitutes being a squire?"

"Owning all or most of the parish, I should think," replied Wellende, after a pause.

"It's more than that, you've got to have owned it for a few generations," said Prudence. "Now I know a man who always speaks of himself as the squire, and once spoke to me of his grandson as 'the little squire.' It was on the tip of my tongue to say I had no idea it was an hereditary title, but I forbore," with a reminiscent sigh.

"Cheer up, Prue," said Ben, "you'll always get that sort everywhere. I know people who always speak of their wives as Mrs. So-and-so."

"I wish I was as tolerant of that sort of thing as you, Ben."

"Oh, well, women notice those things more than men do," said Lord Wellende, charitably and untruthfully.

"Well, anyhow, you'll like Thomas; everyone does. I always think he's a specimen of the best sort of University don, keen about everything."

"What, games too?"

"I should rather think so; and a tremendous hard worker who makes other people work. Why, I'll just tell you. I went to stay with him and his wife in Wales, and Thomas is keen on walking, so we walked. Now I don't like walking—I can't do it, and don't like it—but I found myself walking; I reminded myself I wasn't his wife, I was a free, independent woman, but I somehow still went on walking, and I suppose I should be walking still if Thomas hadn't decided to turn back."

"I like the sound of that man."

"He is what is called a 'force,'" said Miss Pinsent, pulling down the corners of her mouth.

The three men from the boat arrived in good time for dinner, all a little ill at ease. Skipwith and Maryon, because there are few things that make an Englishman feel more awkward than knowing he is not dressed right, and it was wrong to eat their dinner in such surroundings as Wellende Old Hall in old flannels rather than dress clothes. No such scruples troubled McDonald. In his case it was the company to which he was unaccustomed. Both he and Maryon were intensely curious to see the man who was suspected of smuggling drugs; the man whose doings and habits were of such interest to far-away Scotland Yard.

Maryon pictured to himself a slightly dissolute, weak-faced degenerate. McDonald imagined a haughty nobleman. They were both confounded when they found themselves shaking hands with a tall man in a shabby smoking-suit, a courteous, kindly gentleman with a certain indescribable and innate dignity, not handsome, perhaps, but an out-of-door face, with singularly beautiful grave, blue-grey eyes, who welcomed them with a quiet voice and unassuming manner. McDonald said "Pleased to meet you" at each introduction. Lord Wellende did not appear to hear. Prudence looked pained.

The talk at dinner was chiefly about their voyage, and Skipwith gave McDonald his meed of praise.

"Did you get a pilot to come up the river without much difficulty?" asked Lord Wellende.

"We had to wait about a bit," said Skipwith. "They told us the bar was always changing."

"The pilot told me," said McDonald, "there was a lady who came from here who constantly took your lordship's motor-boat out without a pilot. Would it be you?" turning to Prudence.

"Yes," said she. "I only go out when it's safe, and a motor-boat is so very much easier than sailing."

McDonald looked at her with added interest, and proceeded to ask a good many questions about the boat, all of which Prudence answered readily enough.

After the servants had set the dessert and left the room, Professor Skipwith turned to his host and said: "This house of yours is a perfect setting for ghosts, of which I hear from Prudence you are the proud possessor."

Lord Wellende pushed the port towards Skipwith. "Help yourself, and pass it on. Oh, yes, we have our ghosts, but if you ask me I think they are chiefly rats."

"Don't spoil it by saying that," said Maryon. "You must own up to ghosts in such a place as this."

"And I expect his lordship's family smuggled, too, in the old days," added McDonald, looking keenly at Wellende and not failing to notice Prudence's slight rise of colour.

"Yes," said Wellende, then turning to Skipwith he said: "Prudence tells me you want to see how the water comes up under the house; we will go down to the cellars later on."

Prudence left the men and took herself off to the library, where not very long after she was joined by Thomas and Maryon.

"What have you done with the others?" she said.

"Your cousin has taken McDonald to show him some early flint instruments he has," replied Thomas. "That chap is about the best informed I ever came across, there doesn't seem to be any subject that he hasn't a bowing acquaintance with; comes of being a sort of policeman, I suppose."

"A what?" exclaimed Prudence, in a startled tone, a colour she was quite unable to control mounting to her face.

"Yes, Prue," laughed Thomas, quite mistaking the real cause of her agitation, "think of it, you've sat down to dinner with just an ordinary policeman, rubbed elbows with him, so to speak. What do you think of that?"

"Do be serious; of course he's not an ordinary policeman," said Prudence, regaining her composure. "It's very interesting; I was wondering during dinner what he was, he has such a keen, intelligent face."

"Yes, that's all very well, but you know his keen, intelligent face doesn't excuse various little things about him, does it?" said Thomas, laughing openly at Prudence. "For instance, his constantly saying 'your lordship' to our host; that's a sin too bad to—"

"Oh, don't be tiresome, you're doing your best to annoy me, and very soon you'll succeed. What is the man really?"

"Never mind, Prue," said Thomas consolingly, "it's not as bad as it might be, he's quite a high-up chap at Scotland Yard having a holiday."

Now Maryon, who had been examining a picture, happened to look up just as Skipwith blurted out the information that McDonald was a policeman, and he caught the first fleeting expression on Miss Pinsent's face. It was not annoyance, as Skipwith thought; Maryon had not served four years in the Secret Service for nothing. It was terror—sheer, unadulterated terror—that had shown for a second in her face. It was very quickly gone, and her mounting colour was the result of shock, not annoyance.

Maryon felt a little stunned at the discovery. In these peaceful, refined surroundings that look had no place. It could only mean one thing, and that was, that Miss Pinsent knew of something that was going on which made her horribly afraid of having a policeman about, and in spite of all appearances, of all probabilities, he knew this must be true.

He left the other two sparring together, and pretended to be absorbed in the pictures while he thought it out. McDonald must be made to go; he, Maryon, was not in the Secret Service now, and whatever was going on, he was not going to be the means of introducing a spy in the guise of a friend. But it would be difficult to get rid of him. He couldn't let him know he thought there was something wrong; how then could he be got rid of? He could do two things, though. Watch McDonald himself, and warn Miss Pinsent.

"Yes," he said, as though it cost him an effort to take his attention off the really fine pictures, "McDonald is a detective all right, and one of the smartest in the world I suppose. He's on a holiday, he came to me and said he wanted one badly, and I asked Skipwith if he might come with us."

"By the by, he's not by any chance that chap you were describing in the Combination Room the other day that was only known as a number?"

"Yes," said Maryon shortly, "that's the fellow."

Skipwith whistled.

"Don't talk to him about his work," went on Maryon, "he hates it"; then turning to Prudence, "he's about the best man Scotland Yard has, and I wonder if that sort can ever take a real holiday. I'll be bound he's noticed far more in this house than either Skipwith or I. Take the dinner, I know the butler's face but I never looked at the footman."

"I didn't even know there was one," said Skipwith, "and I am sure I shouldn't know either again."

"I'll bet you anything McDonald automatically looked at them both, and everything else as well," with a laugh.

The boating party made an early departure. They were to shoot duck at dawn, and Lord Wellende had invited them to lunch. As they walked down to the jetty to their dinghy, Skipwith said:

"There you have the ideal country gentleman, and, by God! what a glorious house!"

The other two agreed.

"What price scented hair and decadence, McDonald?" said Maryon. "McDonald and I," he said to Skipwith, "thought we should find an effete nobleman with scented hair. Why, did you hear him say at dinner one of his under-gardeners always cut his hair?"

"No, I didn't catch that," said Skipwith, "but it would be quite in keeping. I somehow got the idea he was a bit of an ass, I don't know how, but he certainly is not: a charming fellow."

"He's no ass, that man, whatever else he may be," said McDonald feelingly. Maryon looked at him as though to speak, but thought better of it.

Meanwhile the cousins stood over the library fire.

"What do you suppose Mr. McDonald's profession is, Ben?"

"Haven't an idea; I thought him a very pleasant and able fellow."

"He's a very high-up detective at Scotland Yard."

Lord Wellende, who was pushing a log farther on to the fire, did not speak for a moment. When he did, he said:

"Is that a fact, or only a guess?"

"Oh, it's a fact. Mr. Maryon was telling us after dinner; he says he's very great indeed, and wanted a holiday, and that's why he's here, so Mr. Maryon said."

"Well," said Lord Wellende easily, "we must see that he gets plenty of sport."

CHAPTER XXV

NEXT DAY, ACCORDING TO ARRANGEMENT, THE BOAT PARTY turned up for lunch at the Hall. They had had good sport and brought some of their bag along with them. It was a cold day, and the housekeeper had thoughtfully provided hot soup to begin the meal. No servants were kept in the dining-room for lunch; Ben and Dr. Heale, who had looked in on parish business, waited on the party. The talk at lunch was almost entirely on sport of different kinds. McDonald described bear-shooting in the Rockies, much to the interest of his host.

The following day hounds were meeting at a reasonable distance from the Hall, and the duck-shooters all decided that they would go to the meet and get a little exercise.

"In that case," said Dr. Heale, "you had better all finish up with me for a high tea; my house will be on your way home."

This kind invitation was accepted, and it was further settled that the day after that they would lunch at Wellende again.

"By that time," said Heale with a grin, "I should think you would all be ready for a bath. I am not going to offer it you; we've only one bath-room, but Wellende here has half a dozen." They all agreed laughingly that they would be glad of a wash, "though a good layer of dirt on top is a wonderful thing for keeping out the cold."

"Yes," said Skipwith, "if I have a good wash on Friday I shouldn't be at all surprised if I caught cold. I am not sure that I won't let well alone!"

"If you won't wash, Thomas, you shan't come here to lunch any more," said Prudence.

On this they appealed to Lord Wellende, but he laughingly upheld Prudence.

"I saw a most shocking sight, hunting, on Monday," said Heale. "Some girl was powdering her disgusting little nose by the covert side."

"I don't see much in that," said Prudence; "you see them do it everywhere, in the street, in the train."

"Yes, but by the covert side, I ask you; it really quite shocked me!"

Professor Skipwith looked at Dr. Heale with somewhat the same expression of interest with which he would have regarded a new insect. "I know what you mean—much what you would feel if you saw a chap light a cigarette during the sermon."

"Yes, but that, as a churchwarden, I could have stopped."

"The same sort of feeling you would have, Thomas, if you saw a young lady powder her nose while doing a tripos paper," said Prudence, amid a general laugh.

So it came about that Skipwith, Maryon, and McDonald, all unaccustomed to it, spent a day with the hounds, and when they finished up with tea at the Heales' they were still full of the glamour of the sport. They had heard the lady pack in full cry on a burning scent, and for a time it had made them all young and supple again, and taken ten years off their ages.

Skipwith, who had run the mile many years ago at school, found himself going as he didn't know he had it in him to go. McDonald, who had put this sort of thing by with younger days in the force, always in good training, kept pace with him, and a good pace too, and Maryon was not going to be outdone.

At tea-time, after taking a long drink, Professor Skipwith put down his cup and said: "Wasn't there something in some song about 'the sound of his horn would wake me from the dead'?"

"Not quite that," said Dr. Heale; "'the sound of his horn brought me from my bed, and the cry of his hounds which he oft-times led, and Peel's view holloa would waken the dead…'"

"That's it. Do you know, I'm a scientific University don, but I felt that feeling to-day; there's something magnetic in the cry of hounds."

Mrs. Heale turned to him a face of beaming approval. "I knew you were all of you real good sportin' men when I first saw you," she said. "There's the right stuff in you, not like some I've come across," and her face darkened as she thought of Temple; "and you're a Professor, aren't you? Prudence told me so."

"Yes, Mrs. Heale, but don't hold that against me."

"No, no," said Laura in perfect good faith, "I won't. Why, we had a groom once who had done time for manslaughter, and he was the best man with horses I ever met, got their coats—" But here she was interrupted by a shout of laughter from the rest of the company.

"You might have a lower opinion of them, Laura," said her husband, "if you'd been with me outside the Big Wood. The fox went away, and then I am blessed if Skipwith, Maryon, and McDonald didn't go away, at a very good pace too, and after them came the hounds!"

"And great credit it did us," said McDonald. "I am getting on for sixty, which you don't seem to realize."

But even this crime could not lower them in the opinion of Laura Heale.

"No," she said, "they may be ignorant, but they are made of the right stuff."

"One for you, Skipwith," said Maryon, chuckling.

"I'll tell you a curious and very interesting experience I once had," said Dr. Heale. "I was sitting by the bed of an old fellow who was dying; he had already left this world, and was wandering in the space that seems to divide it from the next life; I'd my hand on his pulse, and every moment I was expecting him to go out. He had hunted all his life and he was over eighty. Then I heard the hounds hunting, the sound of them came through the open window; I had heard them a minute or two before I felt the old man's pulse quicken; then the expression of his face changed, and he opened his eyes. 'Gone away,' he said, and believe me, though it was a physical impossibility, he sat up in bed; he'd always had an ugly seat on a horse, you remember, Laura? Rode with toes and elbows stuck out. Well, he stuck out his elbows, he gathered up the sheet as if it was reins, and with the sound of hounds in full cry coming in at the window, and looking ahead, that old warrior rode straight for the last and grimmest fence in life. Then he fell over stone dead."

There was a long pause, and then Thomas Skipwith spoke. "That was a grand way to die."

Laura Heale looked at him, her weatherbeaten face softened by her expression.

"Yes," she said. "I've often wondered what that last fence looked like to him."

"I've seen a good many confronted with that last fence," said the doctor, and turning to McDonald, "I expect you have too, and I'd be glad to feel sure I'd ride straight myself when my turn comes."

McDonald agreed in all sincerity; then he said, "What was he dying of?"

"Old age, practically. He'd been unconscious for hours; I didn't expect consciousness to return, though I wouldn't have said it was impossible, but I *would* have said sitting up without assistance was an absolute impossibility."

"If you can't die in the huntin' field, it's the next best way of doin' it," said Mrs. Heale. "I've often wondered what that last fence looked like."

"It was a curious coincidence that the hounds should have come at that moment," said Skipwith.

"It was no coincidence," replied Mrs. Heale gravely. "Don't you know that hounds always run to dyin' men?"

"What *do* you mean?"

"If a man who has hunted all his life is dyin', and hounds are huntin' anywhere in the neighbourhood, they'll run that way; you may call it superstitious if you like, but I know, I know."

The three sportsmen turned up the following day, as arranged, for baths at the Old Hall. Prudence was sitting in the library when Thomas looked in and asked if she knew where Dr. Heale could be found.

"I believe I heard him in the hall talking to Ben; you'll probably find them both in the smoking-room. Why, what's the matter?"

He didn't answer, but went off in pursuit of the doctor. After a bit Lord Wellende came into the room.

"I hear Mr. McDonald has discovered a rash on himself and has sent for Heale; it is lucky he happened to be in the house."

"By Jove!" said Maryon. "I wonder how long he's had it; he hasn't had his clothes off for days; I noticed he'd a cold this morning."

When Dr. Heale came into the room again, followed by Skipwith, he was looking grave. "Mr. McDonald has a nasty rash, and I am sorry to say it looks like scarlet fever."

There were exclamations all round.

"I feel I ought to apologize to everyone for having brought him," said Maryon, "but you all know how innocent of intending evil I am."

The others laughed.

"Don't worry," said the doctor. "I am not yet sure what it is, and in any case we have found it before the really infectious time begins; and you've been out in the open so much, I don't suppose for a moment you'll take any harm."

"We've had a pretty good fug sometimes in the cabin," said Skipwith.

"Yes, but the peeling stage is the infectious one; I don't think you need worry. Can I talk to you, Wellende, about arrangements?"

Dr. Heale and Lord Wellende left the room together.

"There's no reason why we should wait; let's go in to lunch," said Prudence. They discussed Mr. McDonald's misfortune, and the chances of anyone else coming out with it, till the others returned.

"We've arranged it all very easily, and no one need worry," said Lord Wellende to Maryon's repeated apologies.

"He'll sleep here to-night, and we've sent for an ambulance from the Liverpool Fever Hospital in London, and they'll take him off to-morrow morning first thing."

"None of you is in the least likely to catch it," added Dr. Heale; "it's too early for him to be very infectious. He's got a cold in the head, and he's very stiff after yesterday's efforts, and he tells me he's simply never had a day's illness in his life, so it's quite a new experience for him."

"He's not the only one that's stiff," said Skipwith ruefully. "I could hardly get off my bunk this morning."

Heale laughed. "Poor McDonald will have another new experience to-morrow when the ambulance comes for him, for it's not unlike a prison van; and he'll have a driver and a warder, and he won't be allowed out; very good for a policeman!"

CHAPTER XXVI

THE COMBINED EFFECTS OF A COLD IN THE HEAD, UNIVERSAL stiffness, the sight of a nasty, puffy-looking rash all over him, and sublime ignorance of what it is to feel really ill, made McDonald distinctly sorry for himself. Dr. Heale, who was there at eight o'clock in the morning, was right about the ambulance. McDonald had the choice of sitting or lying inside; he chose the former. He was shown a cord he could pull if in want of anything, then the two men mounted the box and the ambulance set off, for all the world like a prison van.

They made very good running, and by twelve o'clock were in the outskirts of London; an hour later, they stopped in front of some big iron gates; these were unlocked, the ambulance passed through, and McDonald heard them being slammed behind him.

"Well," he thought, "if it *is* like a prison, Heale says it will be a very comfortable one."

At the door of the Hospital itself, as McDonald stepped out of the car, he was met by the doctor in a white linen coat. "Scarlet fever?" said the doctor, looking at him keenly. "Yes"; and he was led off by a nurse up a staircase and a long passage to a room. There was no carpet, and the minimum of furniture, but a bright, cheerful fire burnt in the grate, and the bed looked comfortable.

"I am hungry," said McDonald, who had had an early breakfast, to the youthful-looking nurse.

"Yes, but you must get to bed at once; I'll take your things out of your box; and then after the doctor has seen you, you shall have your dinner."

"What about reversing it, and letting me have dinner first and the doctor afterwards, Nurse; don't you think that would be better?"

But this suggestion shocked the nurse very much; there were the rules of the Hospital, besides which the laws of the Medes and Persians were as nothing.

"Besides," she pointed out, "the doctor will say what you may have."

"Dear, dear," said the detective, awed by his unaccustomed surroundings, and the starched uniform and manner of the nurse, into a most unusual meekness. "You see, Nurse, I have never been ill before, not in any way."

As soon as he was established in bed, the doctor came in to examine him.

"Have you been in scarlet fever infection that you know of?"

"No, as far as I know, I've been in no infection at all."

The doctor examined the rash with great care, then he grunted. "You've a bullet wound, I see," he said.

"Yes, and do you know what that is?" said the patient, turning over.

"Lord, that's a nasty-looking gash; you didn't get that in the war, did you?"

"No," said McDonald, "I didn't get either in the war exactly. I'm a detective from Scotland Yard."

"The deuce you are," said the doctor with interest. "I expect you've been in some nasty scraps, then."

He took his temperature, asked him some more questions, wrote a lot of them down on a card that was hung above his bed, and told him he could have what he liked for dinner.

"I am not satisfied," he said as he went off, "that it is scarlet fever, but we'll know to-morrow; meanwhile you'll remain where you are."

McDonald made a hearty meal, off good plain fare, and then lit his pipe.

"I don't think you're very ill," said the nurse.

"Nonsense, Nurse," said McDonald comfortably; "I'm very ill, I've got scarlet fever."

"Well, we'll see, but it doesn't look like scarlet fever to me."

"When does the post go?"

"The post! You can't send letters from here except twice a week, then they are fumigated before leaving the Hospital."

"Not send letters! but how am I to communicate with my boss?"

"You could send a telegram."

McDonald thought this over. "If I did, how many people would read it?"

"The porter who takes it, and the Post Office clerk."

"Well done, Nurse; most people in answering that question would only have said the porter. I'll think it over," he said; "I suppose I could never have my boss in to see me?"

"Yes," said the nurse, "but he must conform to the Hospital rules."

So it came that McDonald sent a wire asking his "boss" to come and see him next morning. He slept well that night, and knew nothing till another nurse woke him.

"Hallo," said McDonald; "you're another, but I just saw you last night."

"Yes," she said, "I'm the night nurse, and now I am going to wash you, before the day nurse comes on, and you have your breakfast."

It was with a mixture of interest, amusement, and embarrassment, the latter largely predominating, that McDonald submitted to being washed in bed. After making a hearty breakfast which caused the nurse to lift her eyebrows, the doctor arrived. He examined the patient's rash, which was certainly no better, then sat down and looked at him.

"Slept well?"

"Admirably."

"You are generally a good sleeper?"

"I sleep," said McDonald, "with the unfailing regularity of an idiot."

The doctor grinned. "You look healthy enough," he said, "except for this rash. You don't take drugs for any reason, do you?"

"If you knew as much about drug-takers as I do, you wouldn't ask me that."

"No," said the doctor, and then he thought for a bit. "Go out of the room, Nurse, until I call you; I want to be left alone with the patient."

The nurse did as she was bid, though with evident surprise. The doctor turned to McDonald. "Now you tell me you are a detective; were you by any chance on a job when you got this rash?"

McDonald was immensely surprised, but showed nothing at all of it in his face. He thought a moment, then he said "Yes."

"Would it have suited anyone, accustomed to the use of drugs, to have had you out of the way?"

"By gum!" said the detective, "by gum—you don't really mean it... the devils!" he added, with no anger, but in a tone of wondering admiration.

"You've not answered my question," pursued the doctor.

"Yes," said McDonald, "yes, I am sure they wanted me out of the way... but for two innocents like that to trip up an old bird like me—do you mean to say you think this isn't scarlet fever?—only the result of a drug?"

"That's it," said the doctor. "You've a cold in the head, a bit of luck for them, and the rash looks to me like some form of chloral poisoning."

"Hell! who'd have thought it of them!"

"Of course, I can't speak positively till to-morrow, but I am fairly sure. You think you know who it was?" asked the doctor with a good deal of interest.

"Yes, I know who it was all right."

"When could it have been given you?"

McDonald thought.

"Four days ago at lunch I had some thick soup that tasted rather bitter."

"Had the people who wanted to get rid of you access to that soup?"

"Yes; and since then I might have had it each day, but I didn't notice anything."

"Well," said the doctor, "that's what I think it is." A pause followed, while each man was thinking. "The local doctor told you he thought it was scarlet fever?"

"Yes," replied McDonald hastily, immediately on his guard, for he did not intend the Hospital authorities to learn any details. "He did, but said he wasn't sure, it was some time since he had seen it; they don't get infectious diseases in his part of the country."

"No," replied the doctor, "unless a man is in charge of a school, and always seeing rashes, it's often very hard for him to be sure," but he took the hint, and if he had been going to ask any more questions he abstained.

"I suppose now," said McDonald conversationally, "a general practitioner would find it hard to say a rash like mine was nothing infectious."

"That's it; he would have to treat it as infectious, and if he wasn't in the way of constantly seeing rashes, it wouldn't occur to him that it could be chloral poisoning. Well, in the state you are, you must keep in bed for a few days; any chill you got now might turn to pneumonia, and you can't do better than remain where you are."

"That's all very well, but nurse tells me you've smallpox, diphtheria, and measles in the Hospital; I don't want to catch any of them."

"Lord love you, man!" said the doctor, "you won't catch anything here! or at least you're a great deal less likely to do so than in any other house!"

"You really know so well how to deal with your infection?" asked McDonald.

"I should just think so; you're a lot safer here for smallpox than you are in the road outside," and with that the doctor went off.

A short time after, Admiral Sir Boris Buckthorne, dressed in a white linen coat, and a silly little white linen cap covering his head, was let into the room by the nurse.

"Thank you, Nurse," he said, "and I promise you I won't touch the patient, nor eat anything he may offer me... We won't keep you," and Sir Boris, with his charming manner, held the door open, and the nurse, who had not intended going quite so quickly, found herself walking out.

Sir Boris shut the door, and listened a moment to her steps going down the stone passage.

"For a man of your age, and a detective of your standing, to go down with scarlet fever while on a job—I'm ashamed of you!" Sir Boris's face broke into the adorable smile that took the sting out of anything he might say.

"When you've heard what I've got to tell you, you'll be a lot more ashamed of me. Why, I've been plucked!—*me*, and it never even occurred to me as possible till the doctor here told me!"

"What do you mean? Speak low, this bare place echoes so much."

"I haven't got scarlet fever at all! The chap here says it's the result of chloral poisoning; and if it is, it was given me by Lord Wellende and the local doctor down there. Two men twenty-four hours ago I would have said were as innocent as lambs!"

Sir Boris looked grave.

"It isn't that I bear them any resentment for poisoning me, but I am angry at being so done, at my age and with my experience! but hang it all, I don't know what it is to be really ill, and it took me in completely!"

"This makes it look bad for them," said Sir Boris.

"Yes, it does," replied McDonald, "they've just done for themselves. I had come to the conclusion that the drug could not possibly be being handled by them, and now this happens. They've overreached themselves. I suppose the doctor banked on the chance they wouldn't spot it here; the chap here has been smarter than they expected, and so the show has been given away."

Sir Boris got up and walked slowly to the window.

"What else did you find out there? What are your impressions?"

"I found out just nothing at all, and as for my impressions... do you remember how Gaston Bossut of the Prefecture used to accuse me of jumping to conclusions, like a woman, about people?"

"Yes."

"And I say it's not jumping, it's instinct and a lifetime's study of human nature... Well, on these grounds twenty-four hours ago I would have said Lord Wellende was as innocent as you are."

Sir Boris grunted. "He's a charming fellow, what you call the perfect type of English country gentleman. Lives for sport and his own place, but no fool; and the local doctor, who must be hand and glove with him, is just such another."

"And yet he's poisoned you, to get you out of his way?"

"Yes, that's his black mark," said McDonald gravely, "and a chap in his position doesn't do that without serious reason; there must be something wrong."

Sir Boris came and sat down again by the bed. "We have to bear in mind," he said, "that this stuff is coming into the country, and it is coming in so as to blind us to its source. That means it's coming in the last place that we should be expected to look for it. Why, if I could have my way, I'd even have the Archbishop of Canterbury searched! I'd trust no one, no one!" he exclaimed, with some heat, and then went on more quietly, "We know from the coast-guards that Wellende is being secretive about something; we know his cousin in Cambridge is handling the drug; that this same cousin after years of estrangement has lately taken to going fairly often to Wellende. We now know that Lord Wellende is so anxious to get rid of you as to poison you, and run the risk of detection. We made a mistake in not hiding your identity altogether."

"I couldn't; Maryon wouldn't have taken me on those conditions."

"Well, it has had the effect of compelling them to make a mistake. You had better leave them under the impression that you still think it's scarlet fever. Who have you left down there?"

"I've two men," said McDonald; "it's been very difficult to introduce anyone, as everyone knows all about his neighbour there, and his neighbour's concerns, and they all adore Lord Wellende. I have a man reputed to be one of the Harwich Water Guard with the coast-guardsmen at Wellende, and a young fellow living alone on a motor-boat on the river, an ornithologist, and if Miss Pinsent goes out again in her boat, he'll keep her under observation." There was a long pause.

"I arranged that Wickin should meet Professor Temple and get him talking on his own subject, to see if he could find out at all if Temple has got hold of this drug; but he could get nothing out of him, wouldn't talk about his own special work," said Sir Boris.

"If we laid our hand on the table and told the Professor every-thing—it's only if he was innocent that it would help," said McDonald musingly.

"Yes," agreed Sir Boris, "and as things are, I daren't, because if he's guilty we should have given ourselves completely away."

McDonald agreed.

"There was one thing I discovered you may say is a bit more against his lordship," said McDonald; "when my supposed scarlet fever was discovered, they made me up a bed in his smoking-room, and among a lot of sporting literature I found a most surprisingly advanced library on veterinary surgery, and one or two books on toxicology; and what is more, they had been well read."

"That is of importance," said Sir Boris.

"Yes, it establishes the fact that the reader of those books has a good knowledge of drugs, and almost certainly of how to handle them."

"An unusual addition to a country gentleman's education," observed Sir Boris dryly.

"It hurts me," said McDonald, looking at his superior with real pain in his eyes, "it hurts me that a chap like Lord Wellende can be doing such a thing. I've tried to excuse him in that he can't be knowing what he's doing, but he's no fool; he wouldn't have those books if he were," and McDonald fidgeted uneasily in his bed.

"Heredity can play some funny tricks," said Sir Boris gently, "and he comes of a long line of people who have just taken what they wanted—and then he may—I say, may—be led by his cousin, without quite realizing."

McDonald grunted. He wanted to think it of Lord Wellende, but in all honesty he couldn't.

"I'd do a lot to get money to keep such a place as Wellende Old Hall going in my family," said McDonald, "but not that—not that."

"And Temple would do a lot to get money for his work. I hear he applied to the Rockefeller Trust, but got turned down," added Sir Boris.

"It's Lord Wellende's part that hurts me so much," replied McDonald. "All his servants have been with him as long as they can remember, I believe; why, it came out at dinner, he gets his hair cut by an under-gardener—an undergardener, if you please—because seventy years ago the old fellow was in a barber's shop, and he always has cut his lordship's hair for the last forty years, and so he always will! And when he lent me things for the night, he produced an old-fashioned night-shirt, with an apology, as 'he hadn't yet taken to pyjamas,' but offered to get me some from one of the footmen if I preferred it!"

Sir Boris laughed.

"Well, that sort of thing had made me think perhaps he was smuggling game-cocks, and doing a bit of cock-fighting on his own; it's just what would be in keeping with the place; and it's illegal," said McDonald, looking almost hopefully at Sir Boris, somewhat as a child looks who hopes his excuse for ill-behaviour is going to be good enough to pass; but Sir Boris shook his head, and McDonald knew he was right.

"No, it's no good; a man in his position wouldn't poison you on that score. He'd have appealed to your sporting side, if that had been all; for as far as he knew, you weren't there in your professional capacity."

McDonald sighed. He knew that what Sir Boris said was true.

"And when you think of Lord Wellende in his beautiful house, leading his quiet sporting life, beloved by all his people, turn your thoughts away and reflect on the demented, tortured victims of this poison that you have known, the corrupted humanity turning to crime, the ruined lives, the shattered ambitions, the broken families, hiding their shame and haunted by fear—and let that stiffen your back to your job."

McDonald flung himself over in his bed.

"May one smoke here?" said Sir Boris.

"Yes, of course, and it will do us both good," and so one lit a cigar and the other a pipe.

"You are not looking at all well, old fellow," said Sir Boris kindly; "there is something the matter with you, and my visit is doing you no good."

"What luck have you had with your investigations at Cambridge?"

"Not much, so far. I have had someone outside the gate of Prince's most of the daytime. A woman selling flowers, or a man selling matches; the man picked up a bit more rock-salt, *and* some crushed mortar; the woman thinks she heard a bell more than once; but nothing enough yet to justify further steps."

"If there's anything in it," said McDonald with a laugh, "it will let Miss Pinsent out, for she called your attention to it. I don't feel towards her at all as I feel towards Lord Wellende and Dr. Heale; she's much more complicated, but I've never believed her guilty."

"I believe everyone guilty on this, till we prove them innocent," said Sir Boris.

CHAPTER XXVII

THEY HAD BEEN OUT ALL DAY LONG, TRAMPING THE ROOTS and the long soft furrows, then waiting by the brown covert side while the birds were driven towards them. The soft calls of the beaters, the sound of their sticks tap-tap-tapping against the undergrowth as they advanced, the occasional call of "Hi cock," and the soft local sing-song drawl in their voices when they spoke, all blended with the subdued sounds of the country-side. The last rattle of the old game-cart going down the drive had died away, as Ben and Prue tramped home. A vivid autumn sunset was in their eyes, and the massive pile of the old Hall stood up black against it; away over the marshes the curlews were whistling softly to each other. Indoors, they got rid of their heavy boots and outdoor things, and met again over the tea-table.

Said Ben, after taking a long drink, "I've had a wire from Francis; he can come here for to-morrow night, though he has to be off again by the middle of Sunday, but it's better than nothing."

"Oh," breathed Prudence, then was silent, for it had come as a real shock to her that this bit of news was the crown to a perfect day. "Better than nothing!" She laughed to herself. "Why, it's *everything*, just everything." Aloud she said, "What brings him; anything special?"

"Yes, he's just made a great success in an experiment against distemper, and he's bringing the experiment with him to show me."

"Oh, the darling!" exclaimed Prudence.

"Who?" said Ben, looking thoroughly startled, "Francis?"

"No, no," laughed Prudence, "I mean the experiment; I've seen him, and it's the most engaging puppy you ever beheld."

That evening, while dressing for dinner, Prudence said to Mary, "His lordship has just told me that Dr. Temple is coming for a night."

Mary looked grim. "In that case, miss, I am very glad you are here."

"Mary," said Prudence earnestly, "you must believe me when I tell you there is no question of Dr. Temple being after his lordship's life; it is simply unthinkable. Indeed, I know what they are doing together, and the fewer that know about it the better. If any trouble came of it, it would come as much to one as the other."

The next day, Saturday, was a hunting day, and though sport had not been as good as usual, Prudence felt thoroughly happy all day long; it didn't matter what happened, or didn't happen, she was going to see Temple again that evening. She came home in time to change for tea. The old stud-groom helped her out of the saddle, and as he did so he remarked, "His lordship tells me the doctor is coming for the night; he's a fine gentleman, he is, knows near as much about animals as his lordship."

"Does he?" said Prudence in some surprise. "You'll hardly know him this time, Berry; he's shaved off his whiskers and it's made him look extraordinarily like Lord Wellende."

"Has he now, miss? Well, he couldn't do better than look like his lordship," replied that faithful retainer.

Prudence, with Mary's assistance, got into a soft, dark green tea-frock, and with her lovely chestnut-coloured hair and happy face, looked as beautiful as she had ever done in her life. She was feeling a good deal less sure of herself than usual, and extraordinarily happy. Tea was in the library on the first floor, and as she passed along the gallery round the hall, she saw through a window the headlights of an approaching car. She paused. A footman, followed by Dunning, crossed the hall and opened the doors. Prudence heard the scrunch of the tyres on the soft gravel as the big car drew up. A few confused noises—and the sound of the car moving on to the luggage entrance. Dunning's voice hospitably welcoming, and then… and at the sound of it Prudence's well-regulated heart missed a beat for the first time in its life… the deep voice of Temple replying. She was angry with herself, and a little frightened at the strength of her own feelings. It was ridiculous, she told herself; she might be a love-sick girl in her teens, to be feeling like this. Anyhow she must suppress it, and at any cost show nothing of her feelings.

A few minutes later, and Temple, followed by Ben, entered the room. The sight that met their eyes was a charming one. A magnificent old Tudor fire-place with the blazoned coat of the Temples, the shield—"or, a chevron gules, between bears' paws erased proper"; in the middle, a fire of driftwood, with purple, blue, and green flames, and in front of it all a cosy, glittering tea-table with the charming figure of Prudence bending over it.

Temple was looking grim, Prudence thought, as he advanced; and she, to hide her embarrassment, began at once.

"What have you done with the experiment; haven't you brought him?"

"If Prue is as fond of you as she is of your dog, Francis," said Ben, with blissfully unconscious stupidity, "you're a lucky man."

"You shall see him soon," replied the Professor, without looking at her; "at present he has gone round to the back with my man."

"Give me my tea in the slop-basin," said Ben, who, having shed his top-boots and pink coat, was comfortably though inelegantly clad, in socks, breeches, a canary-coloured waistcoat, and an old Norfolk jacket, "and put six lumps of sugar in."

Temple asked with real interest after the hounds and what sport had been shown; Ben, stirring his basin of tea, replied.

"If Ben only knew how to talk to his field, the sport would have been as good to-day as any," remarked Prudence severely. "Why, even I could give him lessons in it."

"I haven't the slightest doubt you could," said Ben, "and you'd have to solace all their outraged feelings after."

"I know a bit now that your father taught me when I was still in the schoolroom; it sounds fine, it does, and it takes me a good two minutes to say it straight through without stopping. There are parts," added Miss Pinsent thoughtfully, "that I don't understand even now."

Ben laughed, but Temple looked black and muttered something. "I am not going to repeat it, because you and Dr. Temple might understand."

"Bless my soul, Prue, you don't call him Dr. Temple, surely? I never knew anything so ridiculous; you're cousins, however distant."

"Yes, Ben, but you don't realize in the least what a respect I have for him," said Prudence maliciously.

"I couldn't dream of addressing him familiarly by his Christian name," she went on, watching Temple's profile, but getting no enlightenment therefrom. "It's only the other day he was pointing out to me how infinitely superior he is to me in every way, and who am I?…"

"Does that mean you are prepared to stand up and say your 'duty' to me?" said Temple, suddenly turning round on her.

"No, it does not," replied Prudence, in a totally different voice.

"Well, if you two know what you are talking about, I'm blessed if I do," said Ben, and whistling for his dog, he left the room.

There was a long silence while neither of the others spoke. Then Prudence got up, and sitting down in an old high-backed chair just opposite Temple, looked derisively up into his dignified face and said, "Francis," softly.

He looked straight over her head and, thrusting his hands a little deeper into his pockets, said, "If you look or speak to me like that again, you must take the consequences."

"And what are the consequences?"

"I shall certainly come and kiss you."

Prudence, though she had asked for it, and deserved it, had got it a great deal straighter than she had expected; but luckily for her at that moment Ben returned. It was only in thinking things over afterwards that she considered Ben's return lucky; it had just saved her from what she was strongly tempted to do—say it again, and take the consequences! Later, when she went to her room to change for dinner, even though she knew her conduct had been deplorable, her heart was dancing for joy. But happiness, especially that ill-gotten happiness which has such a peculiarly enjoyable flavour, generally comes before a fall. Mary came into her room with an expression on her face that is often described as one "to turn the cream sour."

"I thought as I ought to tell you, miss, that that there manservant as Dr. Temple has brought with him is the same feller as was on that barge, and I overheard give that message to him."

Prudence sat down, astonished.

"I don't know if you are still satisfied that things are going as they should, miss?"

"Yes, yes, it's a bit of a surprise," said Prudence slowly, "but it fits in perfectly with what I believe is the case. Mary," she went on vehemently, "you *must* put away all idea of anyone attempting his lordship's life; it's simply outrageous; it's no more a question of his life than it is of yours or mine."

But Prudence's high spirits had gone for the evening, and the old worry as to what was going on returned with redoubled force.

The "experiment" came down to dinner with his master; and Prudence, not feeling much inclined for talk herself, listened to the others discussing various topics. She was intrigued to notice for the first time a strong resemblance between Francis Temple and a Holbein of one of his forbears hanging behind him.

After dinner they all went together to Ben's smoking-room. The wind, which had been getting up all the evening, was moaning round the house, with an occasional scream. The three cousins settled themselves comfortably round the blaze. Temple was looking an absolutely contented man; Ben, after his day in the saddle, was half asleep, but Prudence felt very much on edge. One moment she was transported with joy at the thought of what Temple had said to her in the library (for she knew he was the sort of man to say that to one woman only), and the next, feeling wretched at the thought of what was going on in secret. She realized that Mary had not abandoned her fear that Temple was after his cousin's life. Well, if Mary was going to be such a fool, it was not her fault. She wondered what the two men would say if she poured out all that was in her mind now.

A prolonged scream from the wind. The "experiment" was wandering uneasily round the room.

Between the cousins there was a good deal of real affection and trust; why couldn't she tell them all her anxieties? Her promises to Studde and to Mary were insuperable obstacles. She sighed.

Temple looked up. "Does the wind worry you?" he said kindly.

"Yes, it does rather, I don't know why, quite. Look at that dog."

The Professor regarded his dog, who was uneasily snuffling round the wainscoting. "He's restless in unfamiliar surroundings."

Silence again, while the wind continued to howl. Prudence reconsidered for the hundredth time the chances of Mr. McDonald having been sent there by Scotland Yard; decided, as before, on the improbability of it, and thought with satisfaction that anyhow the measles or whatever it was must have nipped anything he was doing in the bud. Suddenly there came back into her mind something Susan Skipwith had said. She looked at the quiet, sleeping face of Lord Wellende, and then turning her troubled gaze to Temple, said: "Would you ever say that Ben was a person troubled by complexes or unconscious urges?"

Though she had spoken softly, at this outrageous charge Ben opened his indignant eyes—generally the eyes of a peaceful child. Temple looked at him and laughed.

"No," he said, "I never knew a simpler or saner feller in my life."

"Really, Prue, I will not have you call me such names," he said, rousing himself, "it positively woke me up. Here, look at that dog; does he want to go out?"

"No," said Prudence, watching the dog carefully. "I believe he's afraid of something; can't you see his hair standing up down his back?" She rose and picked up the trembling puppy. "Come, my darling, what is it?"

The little creature snuggled up against her, licking her hand. The wind suddenly dropped, and outside in the passage could be distinctly heard a peculiar footstep coming towards the door of the room where they were sitting. Ben sat up abruptly and held up his hand for silence. The footsteps came nearer—the dog was whimpering; then a scuffle just outside the door and a long gurgle. The wind began again.

"Well," said Lord Wellende a little hoarsely; he cleared his throat. "I never heard it plainer than that."

Temple got up and opened the door; there lay the carpeted passage, dimly lighted. He shut it again and came and stood with his back to the fire.

"That our family ghost?" he said in an unconcerned voice.

"Yes," replied the head of the family. "Did you notice that it was not an ordinary footstep walking on carpet?"

"It was not," replied his cousin with a slight smile, "there was a clink or clank about it."

"I experimented once, and it's the exact sound of mailed armour walking on stone."

"Is it? Now that's really rather interesting."

"When the murder was done that passage had no carpet as it has now you may be certain, and the stone is still there. I've always supposed from those sounds he throttled his victim just outside this door, it always sounds like it; does one gurgle like that when throttled, Francis? You're a doctor, you ought to know."

"I didn't know you knew as much about the murder as all that," said Prudence in a shaky voice.

"There's a manuscript in the muniment-room."

But Temple, who had been watching Prudence, saw that she was really frightened. "My dear," he said, "don't let yourself be frightened by a mere coincidence of sound; you know as well as I do that in this old house the wind can play any tricks."

"It's what I never, never have really been quite sure about, whether I do believe in these ghosts or not; I think I shall go off to bed. Are the lights still on, Ben?"

"Yes," replied that obtuse person, "they are always on until I go to bed."

"Come," said Temple, picking up her candle for her, "I am going up to fetch my tobacco pouch, I will see you to your door."

CHAPTER XXVIII

T HOUGH PRUDENCE HAD COME UPSTAIRS, SHE HAD NO SOONER
shut her door than she wished she hadn't. There was something
very comforting in the unbelieving imperturbability of Francis. She
got into bed, however, but made no attempt to sleep for some time.
Though the wind was much quieter on this side of the house, her
mind was no less troubled. She read for a bit, and then, leaving the
lamp by the bed on for company, she dropped off into a restless slum-
ber. It had not lasted long before she woke up with a start. The wind
had dropped completely, and an unearthly silence reigned outside in
comparison. Inside the house, however, there were all sorts of little
noises and sounds to be heard. So many, to which one couldn't put a
satisfactory name. At least when it was really windy, all these sounds
were drowned; now when it wasn't, they could all be heard. There
was a scratching, probably a mouse, the old wardrobe in her room
creaked, that gentle sigh somewhere… of course that was the wind
again. That… what was that? a sound of light paws running down
the passage and a whimper. With a shudder Prudence hid her head
under the bedclothes. Was it one of the animals that ran about the
haunted house at night? Were the ghosts all on the prowl? She thought
she would turn on more light and lock the door. She got slowly out
of bed, controlling with difficulty an old childish fear that as she did
so a hairy claw would come out from under the bed and grab at her
bare ankles. Then the whimper came again, and a snuffle that seemed
more human. Prudence turned on all the lights there were, and with
a real effort to be brave, opened the door. She directed the shaft of
light from her switch down the dark passage; and there, quite alive

and reassuring, was Francis's puppy. He looked, however, frightened and forlorn.

"My poor lamb!" exclaimed Prudence softly, "what are you doing here?"

She crept quietly down the passage, keeping the light on in front. Then she saw that the door of Temple's bedroom was open. She waited just outside, and listened. No sound at all—that meant he wasn't there; it was dark inside, and if he had been asleep, she would have heard his breathing. She looked back down the passage whence she had come. The dog was staring very intently at one of the bare panels on the outside wall. Presently he put his nose down to where the wall-panelling joined the floor-boards and blew violently, as though down a rat-hole. Prudence came up to him and examined it.

"There's nothing there," she said, "not even a mouse-hole."

Then she heard some fresh sounds she could not at all account for, and stopped with her heart in her mouth to listen. A moment later, quite clearly and distinctly, coming from nowhere, and yet apparently quite close to her, came the unmistakable sound of *sloppy footsteps*! With a gasp of sheer terror she seized the dog and fled to her room; she leapt straight on to the bed, dog and all, and then realized that in her haste she had not shut the door! Literally stiff with terror she sat where she was, and waited to hear if the footsteps were going to follow her into the room. The sound, however, seemed to have died away. She thought she heard what might have been a soft click, and then the unmistakable, human sound of a door being shut very quietly; evidently Francis gone back to his room.

Prudence burst into tears, a reaction from her fright. She wished she and the puppy could go along to Francis and tell him how frightened they had been, and could they stay with him till daylight came because they would both feel so much happier and safer in his

presence. She smiled ruefully through her tears at the thought of
his face if she did so. The next moment she was angry with herself
for being such a fool; and almost immediately, as a natural sequence,
became very angry indeed with Francis for being the innocent cause
of making her feel such a fool. Her anger came to her assistance, and
she began to think things over in a more reasonable frame of mind.
If those footsteps had been the ghost, and they were clear enough,
Francis, who had undoubtedly shut his bedroom door a moment
later, must have either seen or heard it. But then, thought Prudence
irritably, he was far too imperturbable ever to see or hear anything
of that sort! But the steps had been quite clear… could they possibly
have been his? And if so, where from? He wasn't in the passage. The
puppy blowing against the crack where the panelling met the floor…
the large buttress that she now remembered came up against the
house! Was it possible the secret staircase came up just there, and
that Temple had been using it?

Her subsequent anger with Temple for having frightened her so
much, quite drowned any further terrors of the supernatural, and
she finally fell asleep.

Next morning Prudence sent down to say she had a headache, and
breakfasted in bed. She sent a message by Mary to Temple's "man"
to say the dog had slept in her room, hoping to make his master feel
uncomfortable. But she felt so restless after a bit that she got up and
decided to go to church. She arrived late, and slipped into a pew at
the back of the building.

The church at Wellende was originally Norman, with later addi-
tions; and across the ages it recorded the history of one family. Stone
and alabaster figures, kneeling and recumbent, filled the chancel; while
on the walls of the building, here was recorded the characteristics of
one Temple, there the deeds of another. In a raised pew stood two tall

figures—the present Lord Wellende with his fair head and tanned face, and beside him the stately form of his cousin. There was no doubt of it, thought Prudence, which of these two was the leader, as she looked at Francis's strong face. Vaguely she thought she had heard that in breeding horses the female strain always disappeared in six generations, but something in the male persisted. What, she thought, had come down to these two living figures across the centuries from all the stone ones surrounding them. Was there any characteristic in that first crusader that had lasted to the present day?

It was an old custom at Wellende, rigidly observed, that no one left the church before his lordship; and so the little congregation kept their seats while the two tall Temples came down the aisle. Prudence joined them outside.

After lunch, Francis, with seeming reluctance, took his departure; he was being sent to catch a train at a distant junction, and Ben and Prudence, after a short nap, began the usual Sunday round of the stables, discussing past sport and the prospects of more with the old coachman. They came in for tea in the library. Prudence did the usual round, with her mind far away and ill at ease. She was trying to face the fact that she must speak out to Ben. Even though he was now safely out of the way, the fact that a detective had been about, in conjunction with what Captain Studde had told her, made it necessary that Ben should be warned. She thought it possible, even probable, that Mr. McDonald had not been on a holiday at all. If there was a thing Prudence, loathed, next to being made a fool of, it was taking a liberty; and speaking to her cousin on the subject she meditated was almost bound to land her in one predicament or the other. She had also to remember that she must not give Captain Studde away.

Ben was standing in front of the fire pulling at his pipe when Prudence began:

"I have something very serious I wish to say to you," she said, her eyes fixed, not on her cousin, but on the shield at his back.

"I hope you will not think I am taking an unpardonable liberty… but I *have* to say it!"

"My dear Prue, why all this? You can say what you like to me!"

She gazed at him, wondering how best to go on. The utter absurdity of it, sitting in that beautiful room, and asking the man who had been placidly reading the lessons in church to stop smuggling! She shifted her gaze to the fire and went on in a hurry, "I know what you are doing, I found out by an accident; I know what you and Dr. Heale are doing on the quiet here… and… and I do ask you to stop it." There was a silence. Prudence looked anxiously at her cousin.

"How did you find out?"

"I can't tell you that. I would if I could, but I just can't; I doubt if it's as secret as you two think, and it's dangerous."

"You've learned nothing from Francis Temple I'll be bound," said Wellende.

"I can't tell you at all, Ben; that doesn't matter. The fact remains that I know, and other outside people may know, and you oughtn't to be doing it, not in your position." Prudence felt half relieved and half shocked that her cousin should take it all so calmly. He continued to smoke, with his eyes fixed on something outside the window.

"It's just my position which has made it possible, even comparatively easy, for me to do it."

"Oh, Ben!" exclaimed Prudence, really shocked—shocked that the man she had always believed her cousin to be should allow himself to take up such a standpoint. What was she to say? It was useless to preach to him about the morality of it, at his age, and if he really thought that…

"I think the greater your position the worse it is in you."

"There I entirely disagree," said Wellende, without any sign of annoyance. "I consider it would be a crime in the smaller people, if they had the opportunity, which they probably wouldn't; but my position all round has made it particularly easy for me, and I know how to handle the whole business better than most."

Prudence was silent, not knowing what to say.

"Take this house alone," he went on, "it's built for smuggling. I have everything to hand, and the results have been more successful than I could have believed possible. Look at the difference in the hunting."

"Of course, I've no right to be saying this to you," said Prudence, in very real distress, "but my point is, the greater your position, the greater the crime is in you. I know you are the last person in the world anyone would suspect of dabbling in such matters, but that makes it worse in my eyes. Why, all your traditions, Ben—"

"I know, my dear," he said kindly, "and, believe me, I didn't go into the business without thinking it over carefully. I didn't like the idea at all at first, but Francis pointed out to me how easily I could do so, and what an immense help to him in his work it would be. Also, of course, what I am afraid weighed even more with me, the help it would be to get better hunting."

"Do you think these advantages really justify you?"

Lord Wellende thought. "To tell you the truth, I am not quite sure; half of me is all against tampering with such things, and the other half tells me it's ridiculous to be so particular."

"Oh! Ben," exclaimed Prudence, "do give it up—and, I am going to use a base argument, I am afraid you will be found out, and you wouldn't like that."

"No, I should not." He paused, and then continued: "I thought we were perfectly safe. I can't think how you—"

"Never mind how; the fact remains that I have found out, and so may others."

"I'll think it over again," said Wellende, "but if I back out, I shall hardly dare to face Francis."

"I feel as if it were a bad dream, my talking to you like this, and in a moment I shall wake up and find it isn't true."

"Don't take it to heart like that, my dear," he said, and he deliberately changed the topic of conversation.

CHAPTER XXIX

I T WAS A FINE, WINDY MORNING IN CAMBRIDGE. DOWN KING'S
Parade the wind came swirling along, sweeping the insecurely-
propped bicycles on to the road and pavement, picking up sheaves of
loose white papers and sending them dancing along. Those who had
hats were holding them on, and those who wore gowns were holding
them down. Young women with bundles of books under their arms
and preoccupied expressions, hurrying tradesfolk, and gowned figures
of all ages and sizes, filled the street.

Among all this busy, familiar crowd one alien figure, watching it all with obvious interest, was making his leisurely way. He
was a tall person, dressed in a lounge suit of sober check which
somehow yet managed to suggest sport; his trousers were of "an
almost godly fullness," his billycock hat was placed straight and
decorously on his head; the pin which held his sombre-coloured
tie in place was a large horseshoe; he carried a very neatly folded
umbrella, and yet... and yet... the whole figure was reminiscent
of the stables.

Outside Prince's College he paused, and after having declined to
buy a bunch of violets, he asked the porter the way to Dr. Temple's
rooms. Having got the information, he walked slowly round by the
path. Temple himself opened the door.

"I am very glad to see you, Ben," said he, "though I can't think
what should bring you up to Cambridge."

"My dear fellow," replied Wellende, shaking hands, "how the place
has changed! I haven't been up for I don't know how many years, and
the crowds about!"

"Ah, well, you must remember the University is twice the size it was in our day as undergraduates."

"Yes, crowds everywhere now, I suppose, and all the dear, familiar sights gone!"

"I don't know so much about that. Here, take this chair, it's more comfortable, and sit by the fire. We still have Trinity Gate and King's Chapel standing."

"King's Chapel!" exclaimed Lord Wellende with some disgust. "King's Chapel! Why, God bless my soul, I remember Green Street so full of polo ponies you couldn't walk down it!"

"Oh!" said Professor Temple, readjusting his point of view; "yes, yes, that's true, you don't see so many horses about now, though the fact had not occurred to me till you pointed it out."

"It's these d—d motors and bicycles have done the mischief; why, we feel it even in the country. Most of the farmers now are beginning to keep a car instead of a hunter, and it's that will be the ruin of hunting in the end. I don't know what we are coming to, and that's a fact; I don't indeed," and Lord Wellende laid his neat umbrella and pair of dogskin gloves on the table.

The Professor regarded his cousin with interest, but without sympathy.

"You seem to bring a musty odour from departed centuries along with you, Ben; that and a strong suggestion of the stables; I don't know how you manage it," he observed sourly.

"Talking of stables, I remember I used to keep my horses at a livery stables opposite that museum place—I don't remember its name."

"The 'Fitzwilliam.'"

"That's it. I ought to have remembered that. I have had one or two very good days with the 'Fitzwilliam.' Are those stables still going?"

"I believe so."

"And there was a chap sold rats," continued Lord Wellende reminiscently; "he lived down by the river, I wonder if that goes on?"

"I haven't the least idea in the world; but get to business. What brings you up?"

Lord Wellende sat back in his chair and crossed his legs. He took his hat off and put it carefully on his knee.

"I am afraid I am going to disappoint you a good deal by what I am going to say. I have decided to give up the business we are engaged in."

Temple, with an angry exclamation, stood up. His face darkened and a little pulse began to beat on the side of his forehead; for a few moments he looked most unpleasant, and then with an obvious effort he regained control of himself and spoke comparatively quietly. "What has made you come to this sudden conclusion?"

"It isn't sudden. I have been thinking it over for some time, and one or two things have happened lately to decide me."

The Professor snorted.

"I didn't at all like having to get rid of that detective as we did; but doing a business in secret like ours will always lay us open to that sort of necessity, and I don't like it."

"It was as stupid a bit of work as ever I heard of," said Temple angrily. "I gave Heale credit for more sense than that. The man could have done you no harm once you were on your guard."

"There you are wrong. I couldn't have him about the place at all when I was moving a cargo."

"Did the Fever Hospital accept the case as scarlet fever? It was taking a great risk."

"Oh, yes, I think so; he wrote to me some days after from the place, saying he was very comfortable and not at all bad."

Temple was pacing restlessly up and down the room.

"I suppose it's no good my appealing to you in the interests of science?"

"Not the least use saying any more at all. I have not come to the conclusion without careful thought, and, having made up my mind, you know me well enough to realize I shall not change."

The two cousins, though alike to a certain extent, were at the moment looking very different. The Professor's strong, nervous face was black with anger, while Wellende's kept tranquil and composed.

"You—you—" the Professor burst out angrily again. "The life of a fox is of more value to you than all the science in the world."

"No," said Lord Wellende good-temperedly, "there you do me an injustice."

"And you're safe enough," went on the other. "It's not as if you ran any danger of being shown up."

"Then tell me how it is that Prudence Pinsent has found out about the whole business?"

The Professor stopped dead. "Prudence!" he exclaimed.

"Yes," said Wellende tranquilly. "She didn't find out through us, and she won't tell me how she did. It distresses her so much, I couldn't press her more to tell me."

"Prudence," murmured Temple to himself. "So that's at the bottom of it!"

He went and stood looking out of the window for some time. The pulse was beating fast in his forehead, and his face looked positively murderous with temper. After remaining in silence for some time, which Lord Wellende made no effort to break, he turned and said, in a more controlled but somewhat shaky tone of voice:

"I've got an appointment that won't keep me long; I'll give you something to drink before I go."

He opened a cupboard, and having taken some time about it, he came back with a tumbler, which he put down at his cousin's elbow, his usually steady hand shaking as he did so.

"Thanks," said Wellende pleasantly. "I'll wait here till you come back."

But he did not.

Scarcely had the last sounds of the Professor's footsteps on the wooden stairs died away, when quite suddenly, without a sound and with scarcely a movement, Benedict Compton Temple, 27th Lord Wellende, who seldom left home, and never left England, set out on his last long journey. His head was fallen back on the cushion of the chair, and there was a look of contented peace on his face; and who shall wonder, for he had gone to a land where the pure in heart find a warmer welcome than the rich or the famous.

CHAPTER XXX

I N THE AFTERNOON OF THE FOLLOWING DAY TWO MEN WERE sitting in a room above the police station at Cambridge. Colonel Marton, the Chief Constable, had a bloated, purple face, an ugly nose, and little pig's eyes; but the face was a most horrid libel on the sober, shrewd gentleman behind it. When moved by deep emotion, especially anger, his face would turn a rich crimson, and at the present moment it was glowing like the setting sun. The other man with him was Mr. McDonald from Scotland Yard, an older-looking McDonald than was at Wellende, with the lines in his face sunk deeper in.

"I can't feel professional about this," Colonel Marton was saying, as he pushed back his chair and got up. "It hurts me, it really hurts me."

"I know just what you are feeling," replied McDonald. "If people like the Temples are not to be trusted to run straight, there's no one you can put your faith in. Why, I'd—"

"I know, I know; a business like this shakes all your faith in humanity. I've known these people for years, I've stayed more than once at the Old Hall for a day's hunting; why I'd—" He finished with a sigh, and ran his fingers through his grey hair with a weary gesture. "I'm no detective, God knows, but I've had a bit of experience, and I had an uneasy feeling when Sir Boris came to me about having the gate at Prince's watched that there was more behind it, but I'd no idea it was as bad as this... For all his pleasant manner, he doesn't give much away."

"Who? Sir Boris?"

"Yes."

"I should think he didn't, indeed; that pleasant manner and smile are worth no end to him!"

They both remained silent, each deep in his own thoughts. Then McDonald suddenly thumped the table with his fists so that the ink jumped out of the pot, and the pens rattled in their dish. "It's murder—murder under our very noses. And I can do nothing, and that devil Temple knows it."

The Chief Constable was a tidy man, and with a preoccupied air he slid a bit of blotting-paper into the spilled ink.

"No," he said, pulling down the corners of his mouth; "if we had Tom Temple in here now and told him all we know, even if he believed us he would sooner leave his brother's death unavenged than have him proved to be a drug trafficker."

"And the Professor knows it, of course."

"Yes, he knows it all right, that's the strength of his position."

"Tom Temple is the new Lord Wellende, I suppose," said McDonald.

"That's it. It occurs to me," went on Colonel Marton, speaking slowly, "that if Tom's in this drug business too, he will know his brother's death is murder, and if I know Tom, he will get back on the Professor somehow or other; but if, on the other hand, he is absolutely innocent, he will accept the verdict of the inquest without question."

"Yes," said McDonald, "but as long as he accepts the inquest, there's no way I can get it upset and have another without bringing very serious charges which I am not in a position to prove, and that devil the Professor knows it."

"You've one consolation out of the business, McDonald; you are saved from catching Ben Wellende at it, which you would have hated. I am not sure," he said with a sigh, "I wouldn't sooner have him dead as he is than caught out as a trafficker in drugs."

"Yes; it's a thin consolation but it's something; and at any rate no more drugs will get into the country from that source."

There was a long pause. The noise of the traffic of the street outside came up to them, but they heeded it not.

"You've known the Temples some time," said McDonald. "Have you ever heard of there being insanity in the family?"

Colonel Marton thought. "No," he said, "I haven't. It certainly has never been admitted to be so, but I was just trying to remember if there was any who might have been mad."

"Have you ever heard of any of them being in homes for drink, insomnia, or dyspepsia? That is the form in which it is generally served out for publication."

"No, I really don't think I ever have. I fancy there was something a little mysterious about the death of Mrs. Pinsent, the wife of the Master of Prince's; she was a cousin of sorts, a Temple, anyhow. But I could make inquiries."

"No, no, it's quite immaterial. The verdict of the inquest was death from heart disease, and nothing but evidence of foul play can upset that. I was merely trying to account for the Professor. The line between genius and insanity is a very fine one. Say the Professor gets this drug through his cousin, who is peculiarly well placed for smuggling. His lordship, for some reason or other, wants to give it up, and shews signs of splitting on the business, and the Professor does him in, as he is well able, and what's one life in the cause of science? Temple himself would probably give his own life, if it was necessary; he has often risked it, as it is; that is how he would argue, and that is just where you have insanity creeping in."

"I have heard him say we place too high a value on life."

"I have no doubt of it, and it does make it less bad to take life in the cause of science when you're willing to give your own in the same cause."

"I suppose that is the way in which he would argue," said Colonel Marton; "but you know Creasey, who performed the autopsy, is a very reliable man."

"Look here," said McDonald, "just put yourself for a moment in his place. A well-known man has died suddenly in his chair; there's not a breath or a thought of foul play anywhere; he died in the rooms of his own friend and relative. That doctor hasn't a doubt that it's some form of heart disease; it can be nothing else. Is it therefore surprising that, going to work with this preconceived idea, he really thinks he does find disease? On the other hand, if he couldn't find anything he'd be in such a d—d awkward position that it would take a very strong man to say so. To go to the coroner and say he can find no cause of death would raise a most awful shindy. The coroner would certainly be rude; and another doctor would be called in, and ten to one he would say he *had* found traces of disease, and a nice fool the first would look... No, he isn't going to risk all that."

At this moment there was a knock on the door, and a constable came in, shutting the door behind him.

"What is it?" said Colonel Marton shortly.

"I thought I had better interrupt you, sir. There's a person downstairs asking for you, sir; she is determined to see you about this death of Lord Wellende."

Colonel Marton's whole expression changed, while McDonald, who was certainly no less interested, didn't turn a hair.

"What sort of person?" asked Colonel Marton.

"It's very hard to say, sir," replied the constable hesitatingly.

"Would you say she was one of the family, for instance?"

"No, sir, a nurse, perhaps; she's a very respectable-looking person, and says she has lived at Wellende in Suffolk all her life."

"Bring her up."

Colonel Marton and McDonald waited with interest, when a few moments later "Mary" from Wellende walked in. Mary looked respectability incarnate. Her grey-black clothes, her small hat, her neat umbrella, her black bag, and her grey cotton gloves, they all spelled sober respectability. She hesitated on seeing two men, both in mufti.

"It was the Head Policeman I was wanting to speak to," she said, looking hard at Colonel Marton.

"I am he, and this gentleman here is in the force, too, so you can speak freely before him."

Mary looked suspiciously at McDonald.

"Him a policeman too?"

"Yes."

She sat down in the chair given her, folded her hands in her lap, and said very quietly: "I have come all the way here to tell you that his lordship was murdered—murdered by his cousin, the doctor; he's been trying to do it for some time, and there's others of the family could have told you the same, but they won't speak, for the sake of the family."

There were a few moments of tense silence in the room, broken only by the ticking of a clock, and sounds from the street below.

"This is a very serious allegation that you are making," said Colonel Marton hoarsely. "Do you quite realize what you are saying, I wonder?"

It was quite obvious that Mary did. "I don't know about no alligators," she said cautiously, "but I know what I am saying all right. It's years ago. Mr. Ben, as he was then, had only just left school, and Mr. Francis was a few years older. They quarrelled about something, and Mr. Francis tried to murder him then, and very nearly did, too, and the old lord said he should never come near the place again, and if it wasn't for the disgrace to the family, that had always been decent, he'd proceed against him for attempted murder—I heard him myself, shouting it out. He never came to the Old Hall, not until the last few years, and then he and his lordship became friends again." Here Mary paused, then she said firmly: "He has been to the Hall several times, and each time after he has gone his lordship has been took sick—he that's never had a day's illness."

"What was Dr. Heale doing then? Didn't he know of it?" said McDonald suddenly.

Mary looked surprised, evidently wondering at the "other policeman's" knowledge.

"I doubt if he knew of it; his lordship didn't like it mentioned."

"What are you at the Hall?"

"I am head housemaid, sir. I began in the nursery, when his lordship was a baby, and then went into the house."

"See here," said Colonel Marton, "what is your name?"

"Mary Woodcock, sir."

"Can you give us any proof of what you say? Can you tell us something which would make us believe you, supposing we were not inclined to?"

Mary thought. "If you was to go to Bishop Pinsent, sir, he knows it all. He knows Mr. Francis has tried once already to murder his lordship, only being one of the family he won't speak!"

Colonel Marton looked thoughtful.

"I knew the Professor had quarrelled with Lord Wellende, but I had no idea of the cause, and I had no idea he ever went there now."

"I think I've seen you there, sir, haven't I?" said Mary.

"Yes, you have," he said. "I was waiting for you to recognize me. Now, if you'll wait here, this gentleman and I won't be long."

They went into another room. "She's genuine," said Colonel Marton, looking apprehensively at McDonald. "I remembered a grey-haired housemaid, but I wanted her to recognize me." He was looking worried and anxious; McDonald was not.

"Oh, yes, she's genuine enough. She wouldn't come here with such an outrageous story and offer to face the Master of Prince's with it, if she were not. Look here, Marton, you must come with me and that gallant old woman, and introduce me to the Master, and I'll relieve you of all further responsibility in the case. This is just the handle I wanted."

"Are you going to ask for another post-mortem on the strength of this?"

"I don't know what I am going to ask yet," said McDonald; "but you and I and the old woman are going together to confront the Master of Prince's."

They rang up and found that the Master would be at home, and so it came about that Colonel Marton was seen taking his inflamed countenance and his two companions into the Lodge at Prince's. The promptness with which the door was answered after their ring made McDonald wonder if the butler had been waiting in the hall. They were ushered straight into the Master's study. There, to Colonel Marton's added distress, they found Miss Pinsent as well as her father. But the poor man agitated himself needlessly, for after shaking hands with him and bowing somewhat frigidly to McDonald, Prudence slipped her arm through Mary's and took her out of the room.

The three men were left. There was a long pause. McDonald had told Colonel Marton to leave it entirely to him to conduct the interview, so the Colonel was left to clear his throat anew and to say nothing. The Master said nothing either, but looked inquiringly from one to the other. After a pronounced pause, McDonald said slowly:

"I dare say your lordship is not altogether surprised at our visit?"

"I was warned by your telephone message to expect you."

"I meant, rather, surprised at the reason for our visit."

"I shall be glad," replied the Master imperturbably, "to hear exactly what your reason is."

McDonald, who had been trying to get the Master to give away some information first, saw now that he would not succeed. The Bishop was an able man, and there was nothing for it but to come down with the story. He therefore related shortly Mary's accusation.

"I asked her," he said, "what she could bring to support such a charge, and she told us that you knew all the story, but that you wouldn't speak for the sake of the family credit."

"There," said the Master quietly, "she did me an injustice, but she is a brave woman, and a faithful servant."

There was a pause, while the Master seemed lost in thought. Then he looked up and said: "I am afraid there is nothing for it but to tell you the whole story."

He got up and, putting his hands behind him, walked up and down the room as he spoke.

"My brother-in-law, the father of the present Lord Wellende, was a man of violent and uncontrolled temper; he was also a man of irregular life. He was as different from his son Ben, whom you knew," looking at McDonald, "as two men can be. Professor Temple, Francis, has something of the same temper, and in early life he entertained leanings towards socialism. Accidentally he came across a natural son of his kinsman, Lord Wellende, whom he thought was not being fairly treated. Hot with indignation, Francis went down to the Old Hall, and

there he encountered Ben. Ben, as a matter of fact, knew absolutely
nothing of his father's wrongdoing, and the two cousins quarrelled.
Ben thought Francis was wrong in accusing his father, and for once
in his life lost his temper. Francis thought Ben was supporting his
father, and he lost his temper so completely that he did, in fact, very
nearly kill his cousin. It was not till long after that they realized how
they had both been talking at cross-purposes… Old Lord Wellende,"
said the Bishop slowly, "was the man to blame for that quarrel, and
neither of the lads. I have watched Francis since, and I can tell you
that man deserves unstinted admiration for the way in which he has
mastered his evil spirits."

"Thank God," said Colonel Marton in undisguised relief. "I am
d—d glad to hear your account of it," and he looked at McDonald
to see what he thought, but McDonald was looking curiously at the
Master.

"And the natural son of your late brother-in-law is now your
Head Porter?"

The Master started violently and the colour poured into his face;
it was unnecessary for him to reply.

"How—how did you find out that?" he stammered.

"Oh, just routine work and putting two and two together."

But the truth was McDonald had taken a long shot in the dark,
and no one knew it better than he did.

"Good God!" said Colonel Marton helplessly. "Good God! who'd
have thought it? Drask!… Good God!…"

"It's a secret which has been very well kept for many years," said
the Master. "I hope that it may remain a secret."

"I see no reason why it shouldn't," said McDonald.

A silence fell on them, while each man was busy with his thoughts.
Then the Master said, looking at McDonald: "I should like you to tell

me, when you were staying at Wellende lately I suppose you were really there in an official capacity?"

It was not a question McDonald wished to answer, but he didn't much care about lying deliberately to an old bishop, so he grunted an affirmative, wondering what was coming.

"I thought as much, and when I got your telephone message I sent for Francis Temple. I can't make out quite who is suspected of what, but I think he should tell you his tale."

CHAPTER XXXI

NEXT MORNING RUMOURS WERE FLYING ABOUT CAMBRIDGE, and tongues wagged fast and furious. Those who knew nothing talked most: those who knew little, a very little, said little; but the half-dozen who could really have provided some information were hardly seen and never heard.

One tale was that Professor Temple had murdered the Master. This, though repeated freely, did not gain much credence. What had really happened was, Temple had committed suicide, and Drask, the magnificent College porter, had died of a broken heart at the scandal that had come upon the College, and that if the Master would tell all he knew, some very horrid stuff would come out. Certain it was, however, that the police were in charge of Prince's College.

"In charge" in this case meant that the great gate was shut and a uniformed policeman was standing in front of it. Temple had not been seen for several days, and nor, for the matter of that, had the Master. Those who were bold enough to go to the Lodge and ask for Miss Pinsent, were told that she was "not at home." No information could be extracted from the large blue policeman at the gate; and those members of the College who were thought to be likely to have information and were asked for it severally and individually, replied that they had none to give. This, as it happened, was the simple truth, but it was not believed.

It was through an atmosphere of this kind that McDonald slipped quietly into the College and up to his friend's rooms. He found Maryon making no pretence even at work; he looked as if he hadn't slept. McDonald looked whimsically at his tired, anxious face, and said solemnly:

"If I understand you rightly, you have formed a surmise of such horror as I have hardly words to— Dear Maryon, consider the dreadful nature of the suspicions you have entertained."

"Blast you," said Maryon, his face relaxing somewhat.

"What have you been judging from?" went on McDonald. "Remember the country and the age in which we live. Remember that we are English, that we are Christians, consult your own understanding, your own sense—"

"If you don't stop that blether and tell me the truth, I'll—I'll…"

"If you think Temple killed his cousin, you're wrong," said McDonald, in a different tone of voice; "though I give you my word, twelve hours ago I thought it myself."

"Thank God!" said Maryon, sitting down rather suddenly. "Thank God! Then what is wrong?"

"There's much that is wrong, but not as bad as might well be. I say, old chap, put 'Not at Home,' or 'Out,' or whatever it is on your door; we don't want to be interrupted."

Maryon complied with the request, and then, like McDonald, began filling his pipe.

"There is one thing I would like to say first of all," continued the detective. "I would like to express my sincere admiration of your unfaltering faith in Temple's integrity. I felt a beast making you take me in that boat."

"But, you see, I never believed he was drug-trafficking."

"I know you didn't, and you proved it by taking me."

"I've had an awful time since," said Maryon, leaning back in his chair. "When news came of Lord Wellende's death, it came back to me what you said about a sudden death, and how you would know they were in the drug business if such a thing occurred, and then I had noticed something else at Wellende which worried me."

"What was that?"

"It can't matter telling you, and I should like it explained. Why, when Skipwith blurted out that you were a C.I.D. man, should Miss Pinsent have looked horrified for a moment, and then concealed it?"

"Oh, she did, did she?" said McDonald; "then she must have been in it too."

"In what?" asked Maryon sharply.

"I'll explain all if you have patience. I always found it hard to believe the Professor was a wrong 'un, but I was being forced by facts and circumstantial evidence into that belief, though always against my better judgment. We knew the drug was coming into Cambridge. We knew the Professor was handling more of it than he could buy legitimately. There had been one or two curious Dutch barges hanging about the coast of Suffolk, and the conduct of the Inspector of Coast-guards there was not above suspicion. When I met Lord Wellende, I knew he was straight. Indeed, so firmly did I believe in him, that even when I discovered that he and Dr. Heale between them had poisoned me, to get me out of the way, and sent me off with reputed scarlet fever—"

"They didn't... I'll never believe it!" interrupted Maryon.

"They did, though," laughed McDonald. "Those two innocents did in an old hand like me! But something I happened to have seen up here in Prince's College, put together with something I chanced to observe in Lord Wellende's smoking-room the night I slept there, gave me a new line of conjecture... After all, if you think it was outrageous of me to suspect Temple, what do you think of Sir Boris Buckthorne, who was suspecting the aristocratic Miss Pinsent?"

"God bless my soul! Do you really mean that seriously?"

"I do indeed. It was always quite possible, though I didn't think it myself. It isn't that I would put it past her altogether," added McDonald, who did not like Miss Pinsent, "but I just didn't think it was her. Sir Boris angled for an Honorary Degree, then asked his old school friend to put him up, mentioning at the same time what a pleasure it would be to make his daughter's acquaintance. So the good Master, all unsuspicious, tells his daughter she must come home and do the entertaining! When Lord Wellende died in his cousin's rooms (from natural causes, as I haven't a doubt now), I really did believe Temple had done him in. Then, just when I was wanting it most, a fresh tool came to hand, and I was able to go to your Master and tell him I was dissatisfied as to the cause of Lord Wellende's death, and he—he's a wise old bird—he saw the only course to take, and he used his influence with Temple and made him come down with the whole tale."

"Look here, McDonald, are you trying to tell me that you have actually found the drug distributor in Cambridge?"

"Yes, I am, and it's going to be a bit of a shock to you, I'm afraid." A pause, then Maryon said in a curious little voice: "Are you trying to tell me it's the Master?"

"Good God, man, no! It's not quite as bad as that. It's Drask, your Head Porter."

There was a few minutes' silence, then Maryon said quietly: "I suppose you've proved it beyond doubt?"

"Yes," replied McDonald, soberly enough, "and the poor fellow has acknowledged it. He took his own life early this morning; hence the police in the Gateway."

There was a long silence, then Maryon said: "Tell me, when you came to me first of all and said you suspected Temple, did you really?"

"Yes, in conjunction with Lord Wellende, and then, as I was saying before, after meeting and talking to his lordship, I discarded all idea of his being a drug-trafficker; but against that you must bear in mind that I was sure Lord Wellende was getting something secretly up to his house. That first night we dined there, do you remember? He took me into his own den, and I noticed he had an unusually good library on veterinary surgery."

"Yes, I remember you went off with him. It was then that Skipwith let out to Miss Pinsent that you were a C.I.D. man."

"Then, later on, you'll remember they put up a bed for me in the study, when I was supposed to have scarlet fever?"

"Yes, I remember."

"Well, that night I spent some time in examining his lordship's library. One or two of the books were very advanced, not the sort of thing an average Master of Hounds would be reading at all, and they all had been read. All the pages were cut and one or two were marked. That gave me to think. Then I heard what the household were pleased to call rats, under the floor. Lord Wellende said to me himself that he hoped I shouldn't be disturbed by them, but they sounded rather heavy for rats, I thought. I looked round, and found one or two loose boards, and I pulled them up, and I punched a little plaster, and then I put out the lights and waited. I heard them but I could see nothing, so after a bit I put my head down and *smelt*; and then—as I'm a living sinner—it was *foxes* I smelt, not rats!… I put back the boards, and covered up any traces of what I had done, and thought. Curiously enough, one dark evening when I was walking through your College, I saw something fall out of a window. I concluded it was an animal of some kind, and went to see. There'd been a light fall of snow, and there, quite plain and unmistakable, was the line of a four-footed animal across the snow, the four pads all going in one straight line, and a fox is the only animal in England that runs like that."

"I don't understand," interrupted Maryon.

"If you take a horse or a dog, you can see where its hind feet have come together, and its forefeet; but with a fox, 'he tracks the line,' don't they call it, in sport?"

"I see."

"Well, I asked at the gate whose window it was, and was told it was Professor Temple's. Now here we have one cousin keeping foxes in his College rooms, and the other in his cellars—surely an unusual proceeding in either case! and a common interest between them— one being, as you may remember Mrs. Heale saying, the 'best vet. in England,' and the other the greatest toxicologist. With this in mind, I began to think Lord Wellende had a secret of his own with foxes, though why a secret at all, I could not make out. Then when Lord Wellende died in Temple's rooms, I thought again it *must* be murder."

McDonald knocked out his pipe, and while refilling it told Maryon about Mary's interview at the police station, and their further interview with the Master of Prince's.

"I don't know but for the Master Temple would have spoken at all. He is very loyal to his cousin. It seems Temple has discovered a drug himself for which he claims all the power of X.Y.X. He is working on one special line—injections—and he is anxious to increase human strength with injections of this drug. He wanted to experiment first of all with one of the cat tribe, though for some obscure reason a cat itself would not do, and with extraordinary difficulty he persuaded Lord Wellende to let him have a fox. Then they went on and found that it not only made the foxes much stronger but increased their scent, and the two combined made hunting ten times better. Temple says all the time he had difficulty with Lord Wellende, who, he said, had old-fashioned ideas about foxes, and thought that if one was killed in any way except hunting it was little better than murder. I just can't understand that."

"I can," said Maryon; "a fox is sacrosanct to plenty of people still."

"However it was, Temple was glad of secrecy for his work, and Wellende was more so. They did their injecting in the cellars at Wellende, and when they moved the animals, did so in the wood barges. It was a load of this sort that Studde lighted on, and not the drug! No wonder the poor chap turned round and said nothing; it was no business of his. They were going to move a load of foxes just when we were there, and Wellende said I must be got rid of. He must have rather lost his head, for of course I shouldn't have interfered; and then he came up to Cambridge to tell Temple he was fed up with the whole thing and was going to chuck it. Temple was furious, left him in an awful temper, and came back to find him dead. He's terribly cut up about it."

"And you say Temple has never had X.Y.X. at all?"

"No. He tells us he meant to get some, but has not had it yet. When Sir Boris was staying here, Miss Pinsent took him for a walk, and during it she called his attention to what she thought was a rocketing pheasant. Sir Boris saw that it was a pigeon, and a moment later they met Drask with a pigeon-basket under his arm. It was very evident Miss Pinsent knew nothing about it. Do you know anything of training carriers?"

"No, I don't think I do."

"They take them certain distances from their cote, increasing the distances, in specially made baskets, and as the bird is let out it goes up in a spiral, taking its bearings before making off. Sir Boris knew all this, and there before him lay a possible means of getting that stuff into Cambridge. Then, next day, he stepped on a piece of rock-salt in the street, just outside the gate of Prince's; and that and crushed mortar is what they always keep on the floor of pigeon-cotes."

"He had some luck," said Maryon; "still, he had the knowledge to turn his luck to good account."

"Yes," agreed McDonald, "he had great luck. Well, since then we've had someone outside your gate watching. We've also had a keen ornithologist on a boat off the coast of Suffolk, and yesterday afternoon he wired to say he had seen a bird leave a barge he had been watching. Our watcher here thought she had seen a pigeon go into the cote above the gate, and heard a bell ring. We redoubled our watchers, and an hour later we had seen two go in. Then we searched the Head Porter's lodge, and found the stuff."

"You mean to say," said Maryon slowly, "that Drask—Drask has been training and keeping carrier pigeons among the College pigeons?"

"That's it; right under everyone's nose"; and then McDonald told Maryon the story of Drask's birth. "He may always have had a grudge against society as it is at present constituted, or, which I am more inclined to believe, it was in his blood to smuggle, and heredity is a very strong factor."

After Colonel Marton and the detective had taken their departure from Prince's Lodge, the Master went to look for his daughter. "Francis wishes to speak to you," he said. "You will find him in my study. He is terribly cut up at having lost his temper with Ben. Be kind to him, my dear."

When Prudence entered the room, Temple, who had been striding up and down, stopped; he pulled out a chair for her, and in his most awkward and abrupt manner said:

"I want you to hear the story of these doings from myself, if you will be so good as to listen."

Prudence murmured something and sat down.

"You know that for some time past, the C.I.D. have been on the track of a certain venomous drug, which they had reason to believe was being brought in illicitly from the East Coast, and distributed here in Cambridge?"

"Yes," said Prudence, "I know all about that."

"And that they have been proved perfectly correct in their deductions," went on the Professor; "and you know the nature of the private business that Ben and I were engaged in?"

Prudence nodded.

"The police got track of that, and thought, not unnaturally, that we were in the drug business."

Prudence made as though to interrupt.

"No," said Temple; "they were justified in their suspicions in the circumstances. What I want you to realize is, that I assume all responsibility for that concern. It was I who persuaded Ben into it; he was always rather dubious, but it made the hunting so much better that he consented to go on. For me," said Temple, turning and looking out of the window, "for me it was a means to a much greater end."

He seemed lost in thought for a moment; and Prudence experienced the novel and not unwholesome sensation of feeling very small. Then he turned.

"Is there anything about it all that you don't understand, and would like to ask me?"

"Yes—yes, there is," said Prudence thoughtfully. "Have they found the distributing centre in Cambridge?"

"Ah," replied Temple without a pause, "that you must ask Mr. McDonald; I can tell you nothing there."

"Another thing I want to know which you can tell me: Is there a secret stair in that buttress which comes up past the library to the floor above? And were you using it that last night we were at Wellende?"

"Yes," replied Temple, "it is there, and I was using it. We had some animals in the cellars that required attention."

"You frightened me horribly that night," said Prudence.

"I was afraid I had… dear."

Then after a little pause Prudence said:

"What was it that made Ben sick after each visit of yours? It made Mary very anxious; she told me about it."

"He was helping me with a certain injection, and until you get used to it, it always has that effect." Temple smiled grimly as he went on. "It was that, I understand, combined with the knowledge of our old quarrel, that made the faithful Mary really think I was trying to do Ben in."

"Yes," said Prudence, "it was."

Temple turned quickly.

"Did she come to you with her suspicions?" he asked sharply.

"Yes, she did."

"When?"

"When I first went there in the autumn; and I had found out then that something queer was going on."

"Did you believe her?" asked Temple carelessly.

"Not for a moment," answered Prudence quietly, without looking at him.

A slow colour rose in the Professor's face, and then after a pause, with a short laugh, he said:

"McDonald believed it all right… and upon my word, when I look at it through his eyes, I cannot altogether blame him."

"Can't you?" said Prudence, still quietly, and avoiding his eyes. "Well, I can; I blame him; he had no sort of right to think it of you."

There was a little silence, and then Temple began:

"You know Ben came up here to see me, to tell me he wouldn't go on with the experiment any longer?"

Prudence nodded her head. "I guessed as much," she said.

"And I," said Temple, in a voice of real pain, "I lost my cursèd temper with him... He said something about giving it up because you wanted him to... and... and I have always been jealous of the affection between you two!... But no one, not even you, Prudence, can blame me more severely than I blame myself."

Prudence opened her large and beautiful eyes, genuinely shocked.

"Blame you!" she said, "who am I that I should blame you?" with a clarity of insight seldom vouchsafed to her. "All my blame is for myself, how could I for a moment believe, as I did, that you and Ben were smuggling drugs... it was all very well for the police to suspect you... but in me it was abominable," and without a shade of coquetry in mind or manner she exclaimed:

"Why, I'll order myself lowly and reverently towards you all my life... you *are* my bet—" Here her sentence came to an abrupt conclusion. Silence reigned for some time. Then Temple said in a voice of deep satisfaction:

"I had no idea there was anything so good in all the world."

Prudence's reply was inaudible.

A little later they were sitting on a sofa together, and Temple regarded with infinite content the bronze head against his shoulder.

"I have always held that if you go for a thing with sufficient determination, you can get it... eventually," he said.

"There is such a thing," said Prudence gently, after a short silence, "as a broken engagement. Especially when people are too cocksure... too self-satisfied."

"Darling!..." said Temple, "darling!... Now are you going to talk more of broken engagements?"

"No," said Prudence, sitting up and looking a little ruffled and bewildered.

"I think I'm not used to you yet," she said hesitatingly, "you sort of take away all my feelings of independence; but you wait till I am used to you—you just wait!"

"I am writing for a special licence to-night; we'll be married by the end of the week, and then there'll be no more talk of independence."

It was a source of great satisfaction to Thomas Skipwith that events should turn out as they did; and when on one occasion he went out of his way to inform Prudence that she ought to be grateful to so great an intellect as Temple's for sparing her a single thought, her meek acceptance of the statement quite frightened him; but marriages, however suitable, seldom afford universal satisfaction, and Laura Heale was never quite reconciled to Prudence's. It is true that her attitude towards professors in general had been considerably softened by her acquaintance with Skipwith; and after strong representations from her husband, she admitted freely that Temple was justified in having, and even retaining, his own opinions on the injections of dogs; but when she once heard Prudence maintain in public, and that without a blush of shame, that a good seat on a horse was not a necessity to a good man, there was no getting round that. Prudence with all the makings of a fine woman had been ruined; and that by the pernicious influences of Cambridge.